# SONS A

No family celebr
of Texas. Every
celebration and gifts (always homemade) from the rest of
the family. But the twentieth birthday of a Daltry child
is a special event. When a Daltry turns twenty years old,
Grandmother Minerva (a great fan of classical mythology)
assigns the young one a "labor," in the tradition of the
twelve labors of Hercules. Only three aspects of Minerva's
challenges are predictable: the labor will last one year, it
will help to build her grandchild's character, and it will not
be easy . . .

**The Ladies' Man** by Lorraine Heath
Oldest son Hercules must quit ranching and be the town
schoolmarm for a year . . .

**The Wallflower** by Linda Francis Lee
Shy daughter Persephone must spend a year as a New
York debutante . . .

**The Matchmaker** by Debra S. Cowan
Lovesick Cupid has one year to find a husband for a
comely girl . . .

**The Flirt** by Rachelle Nelson
Flirtatious Venus must spend a year in the company of a
blind man . . .

**The Tomboy** by Mary Lou Rich
Atalanta has to learn to cook, dance, and be a lady . . .

**The Perfect Gentleman** by Elaine Crawford
Atlas must put away his lists and take out a popular
widow . . .

# The Perfect Gentleman

## Elaine Crawford

**J**
JOVE BOOKS, NEW YORK

THE PERFECT GENTLEMAN

A Jove Book / published by arrangement with
the author

PRINTING HISTORY
Jove edition / April 1996

All rights reserved.
Copyright © 1996 by Jove Publications, Inc.
This book may not be reproduced in whole or in part,
by mimeograph or any other means, without permission.
For information address: The Berkley Publishing Group,
200 Madison Avenue, New York, New York 10016.

The Putnam Berkley World Wide Web site address is
http://www.berkley.com

ISBN: 0-515-11845-1

A JOVE BOOK®
Jove Books are published by The Berkley Publishing Group,
200 Madison Avenue, New York, New York 10016.
JOVE and the "J" design are trademarks
belonging to Jove Publications, Inc.

PRINTED IN THE UNITED STATES OF AMERICA

10  9  8  7  6  5  4  3  2  1

To Carola,

Another young gypsy
who never quite lived up
to the wild and woolly legends.

My special thanks to Sue Rich, Rachel Druten,
and Lynda Carpenter for being there and doing it.

And to Judith Stern Palais for having to go above and
beyond.

# The Perfect Gentleman

## ≈ 1 ≈

*Abilene, Texas, 1887*

Atlas Daltry leaned out the train window in the midst of screeching brakes, flying embers, and the pungent aroma of stockyards. Few steers waited to be shipped, however. Precious few. He'd heard last winter's blizzards had decimated the herds across the plains, but he hadn't expected to see the evidence this far south.

Why hadn't his father written? Or his mother?

He shook his head. Even though he was six feet two and weighed one hundred eighty-five pounds, his family still thought of him as "the baby."

Okay, so he was the youngest. That didn't make him any less a man—and it was high time he brought that fact home to his family. Because if they ever needed him, it was now. He hadn't spent three grueling years in Chicago getting a business degree for nothing.

The train slowed to a crawl as it slid alongside the station's loading dock, and Atlas eagerly scanned the small group waiting, wondering who had come to pick him up. He'd not been home since last fall, and until this very second hadn't realized how very much he'd missed his rambunctious family.

An explosion of color burst from the crowd. A young woman. Dressed like one of those carnival fortune-tellers, she was all bells and beads and tiers of multicolored skirts. Was there a circus in town?

She headed his way, and he looked past the costume to her equally flamboyant hair. Strawberry blond, it curled in wild disarray, kept at bay by a bright blue scarf.

She was utterly outrageous. And utterly gorgeous. Atlas couldn't tear his eyes away.

In long, leggy strides, she came abreast of his window. At first he thought she didn't notice him; then, as if he'd called her name, she swung her attention to him. Her steps faltered. . . . Her lips, full and lush, parted. . . .

His pulse picked up speed.

A cloud of steam snorted from the bowels of the engine, tossing the beauty's skirts into a crazy kaleidoscope while treating Atlas to a flash of trim ankles before the fog completely enveloped her.

When the vapor cleared, she was no longer there.

Dazed and a little startled by his own reaction, Atlas leaned out the window. He had to be sure he wasn't hallucinating.

He wasn't. Walking toward the trailing boxcars, she glanced over her shoulder with wide green eyes that were as seductive as the rest of her.

"Atlas! Over here!"

Dragging his attention from the vision, he discovered his cuddly, plump grandmother, Minerva Daltry. Standing on the tips of her toes, an exuberant smile dimpling her cheeks, his eccentric but lovable grandmother waved a snow-white hanky.

Atlas laughed out loud as he sprang to his feet and grabbed his valise. Damn, it was good to be home.

Reaching the outside steps, he couldn't resist one last look at the gypsy whose jaunty strides kept her hair and skirts in a constant dance. Music in motion.

Warmth danced through his own midsection.

"Come down here and give your old grandmother a big hug." Minerva, stopping directly below the train steps, shifted her gaze from him to the retreating woman with eyes that were far too knowing, far too wise.

Heat crawled up his neck till he burned hotter than the June sun directly overhead. To cover his embarrassment, he quickly trotted down and hauled his grandmother into a hearty embrace, lifting her off the ground.

"Put me down!" she demanded with a choked laugh.

Returning her to her feet, he noticed she seemed smaller than he remembered, more fragile, despite her plumpness. Older.

She stepped back and held him at arm's length. "Let me get a look at you." Then she became the fussy Grandmother Minerva he remembered, straightening the lapels of his gray suit, tightening the cravat he'd loosened in the heat. "Chicago must have been real good to you. You're all filled out. Grown into quite the strapping young man. And handsome. That head of sunny brown hair, those searching gray eyes," she added with a devilish tilt of her chin. "Small wonder heads are turning your way."

No doubt remained. She had noticed him ogling the

gypsy. "If anyone is looking handsome, it's you, Grams. You're a sight for these homesick eyes."

"Oh, pshaw." Though she disputed his words, her smile widened.

"And that hat. It makes you look at least a foot taller."

"Do you think so?" She stretched to her full if diminutive height while fanning a hand across enough feathers to ensure her bonnet's flight in the next gust of wind.

Recalling what a sudden gust of steam could do, Atlas looked over his grandmother's head to see the gypsy now standing two boxcars down. The huffs and groans of the train engine prevented him from hearing her as she spoke to a crewman lounging against the open doorway. But Atlas was sure her words were as lively as the expression on her face.

The man, too, was all smiles as he reached out and snagged her, pulling her to him.

Loud laughter blared above the roar of the engine— the gypsy's loud, raucous laughter as she disappeared with the man into the dark recesses of the boxcar.

Atlas's fists knotted. Catching himself, he shook them loose. What had he expected? Had he really thought the woman would be a lady? Pure as first snow?

"We'd better see about getting your trunk unloaded." Minerva took his arm and accompanied him in the direction of the unbridled laughter.

Luckily the baggage car was directly behind the passenger car, and he wouldn't have to escort his grandmother past the sort of goings-on that were supposed to be kept in the back rooms of a saloon.

A barbed-wire salesman who'd sat behind Atlas on the

train was ahead of them, collecting his carpetbag and sample case.

"How's business, Roy?" Minerva said to the slim, stoop-shouldered man as he turned from the opening, a piece of luggage in each hand.

"Could be better." He accompanied his words with a sad smile Atlas suspected he used on customers for effect, considering Atlas had overheard him tell another salesman earlier that he'd quadrupled his sales this year.

"We haven't received the rolls of wire we ordered from you two months ago," Atlas's grandmother remarked icily.

"The factory got a little behind." Obviously not liking the conversation's direction, the man started backing away. "They should be coming anytime now. Good day to you now." Tipping his hat, he made a hasty retreat.

Atlas stepped up to the porter and pointed out his oversized trunk, then helped him load it onto a baggage cart before turning to his grandmother. "Well, Grams, where's your buggy?"

"I didn't bring the . . ." Her words trailed off as she looked back toward the station. "There she is."

Waving wildly and coming at a dead run was his sister Atalanta. "Bub!" she shouted loud enough for that miserable nickname to be heard clear down to Austin, then flung herself at him, all arms and trousered legs.

As Atlas fought to keep his balance, he saw that marriage to Hal hadn't changed Allie one smidgen. She was still a tomboy through and through. He unpeeled her arms from around his neck. "If I ever hear the word Bub pass your lips again I'll—"

"You'll what?" She snaked out a hand and tousled his

hair, knocking his brand-new Stetson onto the dusty boardwalk. "Oops." She laughed and leaped out of reach.

"Atalanta," Minerva scolded. "Quit teasing your little brother. At least wait until we get him home," she added, breaking into a grin.

With a smile playing across his own lips, Atlas shook his head and snatched up his hat. "I see nothing changed while I was away." A splash of color again caught the corner of his eye as he brushed a smudge from the tan felt.

The gypsy had emerged from the next boxcar and was staring at him. He could swear she looked at him *as if he'd disappointed her* . . . her eyes wide, brows drawn, lips slightly parted. So beautiful . . .

His heart kicked.

An instant later, she disappeared inside again.

". . . and pick up a new saddle for Hal," Allie was saying as he turned back to find his grandmother eyeing him again. "It's for his birthday. Hal's pops up not long after yours. Your *twentieth*, you know," Allie said in a singsong tone.

Her teasing words reminded him of the day he, like all his brothers and sisters before him, would learn of his "labor"—that assignment his grandmother dreamed up for each of her grandchildren when they turned twenty— something she insisted would improve their character. And, as with Hercules of Greek fables, their success would be rewarded with an extravagant prize . . . a prize she kept secret to tease them on to success.

". . . but the train whistle blew before I ever got to the saddlery," Allie continued to rattle on. "We'll have to stop by there on the way out of town."

Taking the handle of the baggage cart, Atlas was almost afraid to wonder what labor his grandmother had dreamed up—or more aptly, schemed up—this time.

Atlas drove the buckboard onto the main street of Abilene, maneuvering between all manner of other vehicles as well as dodging pedestrians. Astounded and thrilled by the bustling sight, he noted that not even the worst winter of the century had slowed the new town's growth.

Pounding hammers and the aroma of new lumber attested to the fact that enthusiasm was still as high as it had been when the railroad first came through.

"The businessmen around here certainly are on the scent of prosperity now that Abilene is linked to Fort Worth and New Orleans, and from there the world," Atlas remarked, feeling the fullness of promise himself.

"Yep," Minerva said, looking around with a disgusted expression. "About as quick as the rest of us would smell the stockyard on a hot summer day."

Atlas sloughed off her sarcasm, knowing how older folks hated change. Judging by what he saw, prospects here looked as good as the man dreaming them. And he himself had some pretty ambitious dreams.

But, Atlas noted with dismay, saloons were as big an idea as a good many of the entrepreneurs had managed. Each block had no fewer than two. Nearby, out-of-tune piano clanking spilled out of Whiskey Jack's batwing doors, along with a stumbling cowboy who sported jangling dress spurs.

A brassy-haired woman stepped through the swinging doors behind him. Her skimpy red dress, trimmed with ostrich feathers, left little doubt as to her profession. Smiling at her customer, she ran fingers across the hills of her thrusting bosom. "See you next payday, Jude."

Then the saloon girl's sultry glance slithered its way to Atlas, while her tongue traced a come-hither smile in a blatant invitation.

At a rush of his male urges, Atlas felt a need to loosen his collar; then he got the terrible feeling his grandmother had caught him at it. *Again.* Grandmother would surely think he'd returned home nothing but a rutting young bull. And she was probably right. He slanted a guilty glance her way.

To his relief, both Grandmother and Allie were staring straight ahead, their backs board-stiff.

"*In broad daylight,*" Allie railed through stiff lips. "What's this town coming to?"

Minerva patted Allie's denim-covered leg. "Progress, my dear. We're seeing some of that progress the railroad men promised."

"Pull up over there, Bub." Allie pointed to a tack and harness shop, new since last summer. "I shouldn't be more than a few minutes. The saddle is supposed to be ready."

Before the wagon rolled to a complete stop, Allie vaulted off and ran into the store. She was about as ladylike as a twelve-year-old boy.

Atlas chuckled. "Lucky for her, Hal likes a diamond in the rough."

"Yes," his grandmother drawled as her mouth slid into the smug smile of a satisfied matchmaker. "They're like two sides of the same coin."

"How are they doing, anyway? Were they hit hard by the blizzards?"

"Not too bad. They haven't stocked their spread with cattle yet, and you know how they dote on their horses. They kept the herd close to the house and fed them extra rations of oats."

"What about our place? How did we fare?"

"Oh, look. Here comes Parson Baxter, our new minister."

The middle-aged man guided his team and buggy along on a cross street ahead of them. Like most men of the cloth, he wore somber black and drove a black buggy to match. Even its spokes were painted that color.

"Wonder what brings him all the way into Abilene," the ever-curious Minerva mused with lifted brows.

"Probably a funeral, from the looks of him. Why do ministers always have to wear black?"

"For the same reason a trail hand sings to his herd. It instills confidence."

It didn't really make sense to Atlas, but he filed the information away and returned his thoughts to home. "Getting back to cowpokes, how *did* the ranch weather the winter?"

"The ranch?" His grandmother fanned her hand at an imaginary fly. "I leave those bothersome details to your father."

"Since when?" Things must be worse than he'd thought if she was sidestepping the issue. "You've always been as interested in the Circle D as you are in your incessant matchmaking."

"I don't make matches."

"And cows don't eat grass. Every one of your so-called

labors has resulted in a marriage. I can hardly wait to find
out who you've picked for me."

His grandmother swiveled away, obviously avoiding
his probings. "Why, here comes Charlotte."

Above all the other clomps and creaks of traffic, Atlas
heard the tinkling of scores of harness bells. Turning, he
sighted two white draft horses decked out with more top
feathers than those decorating his grandmother's bonnet.
The brightest yellow and blue ribbons streamed from
their manes and tails. They pulled a colorful wagon
sporting gay flags that fluttered from poles sticking up
from each corner.

Driving this carnival-like wagon was the alluring redhead from the train station. He caught a slight flare of
surprise in those green eyes as they met his . . . eyes
the same green as the first touch of spring. Eyes, he
reminded himself, that should be downcast in shame.

"Howdy, there, missy," Minerva called as the wagon
pulled by. "How's business?"

"Just wonderful! Couldn't be better." She had the gall
to treat his grandmother to a dazzling smile. "See you
Saturday in Paradise Plains."

As the wagon passed, Atlas read on its side, PROFESSOR
PUFFINWICK'S POWDER. The words were printed in bold
letters and framed by flowers painted in every hue.
Gaudy . . . just like the woman herself.

"Sweet girl," his grandmother stated, her gaze following the wagon.

Had Grams gone dotty while he was away at school?
He took a hard look at the old gal, from her silly hat to
her modest summer print in muted browns, down to her

sturdy button shoes. She looked perfectly normal. "Grams, you don't really think that woman's—"

"Got it!" Atalanta came bursting out the shop door, hoisting a new saddle with more fancy scrollwork than wrought iron in New Orleans.

He wrapped the reins around the brake and hopped down. "Let me." Taking the saddle from her, he examined it more closely. "There's some fine workmanship here."

"And see?" she said, pointing to her husband's name emblazoned along the front rigging strap. Her fingers then traced the words so tenderly, only the blind wouldn't see how much she loved Hal.

Touched by this rare glimpse of his sister's feminine side, he tossed the saddle onto the wagon bed while looking up at his grandmother with more charity. Perhaps her matchmaking in Allie and Hal's case was warranted. Most likely they'd been buddies too many years to see beyond their friendship without a little grandmotherly push.

Atlas strode around to the front of the buckboard. Mounting it, he caught a last glimpse of the big carnival wagon as it turned onto the road to Buffalo Gap. He was headed east, and the beautiful flimflammer was going south.

Shaking off his nonsensical disappointment, he collected the set of reins. He had important plans for his life that included neither whores nor snake oil salesmen, and she was probably both.

# ❦ 2 ❧

"Has that boy been out counting cattle again?"

Atlas couldn't help overhearing his mother through the open kitchen window as he strode up to the back door, which was banked on either side by her prize flower beds.

"He's only been home three days. You'd think he'd take a week or so off first."

He stepped inside to find her and his father sitting at the breakfast table having a midmorning cup of coffee.

Minerva stood at the work counter, rolling out dough for what he hoped would be a pie filled with the rosy peaches he'd picked for her the day before. Their cook, Bo Jack, had gone back East to his brother's funeral, leaving the chore to the women. Seeing Atlas, Minerva's cheeks puffed with a cheery smile. "You sure were out early this morning. Sit down. I'll pour you a cup, too."

"No, I'm too hot for coffee. I'd rather have some of that lemonade you made last night." Wiping perspiration from his forehead, he dropped down in the seat between his parents and offered his mother a forced smile. "And yes, Mother, I've been out on the north range, hoping to find a few more stragglers."

"Son, I know it looks pretty bad after two killing winters." His father's beefy face had a weary look that didn't come from lack of sleep. "But we're in better shape than a lot of the other spreads in the county. Barnett sold his place last month. Said he wanted to get out while he could still get a decent price."

"He always was a pessimist, dear," his mother, Jane, said, absently stuffing a strand of her fading blond hair into her bun. "Two bad years, and according to him the world was coming to an end."

"Isn't that the truth," Minerva added with a playful lilt as she set down Atlas's glass of lemonade. "If Jason Barnett knew anything about Greek mythology, he'd know the gods are absolutely capricious. They simply love to give us a good spin now and again."

Atlas opened his mouth, then clamped it shut. Nothing he could say would ever get her head out of those fanciful clouds of Mount Olympus.

"I think most of us'll make it, even if we don't ship much beef," Odysseus, Atlas's father, said. "We've all done pretty well since the railroad came in. I know I've managed to put a tidy sum away."

Atlas pulled his notebook from his pocket. "According to my tally, you've lost so many of your breeding cows that you're going to have to keep all your fall heifers to replenish the herd. You'll do well to ship a couple hundred steers."

"I know." His father settled back in his chair and took a sip of coffee. "But don't worry, we'll get by."

"I'm glad to see you've started fencing, even though it's an extra expense. Luckily, you won't have my college tuition to pay anymore. And this winter, if we get enough wire strung, we'll be able to keep the stock from wandering off, miles from home, freezing in snowdrifts. And we'll need to fence off more pasture for alfalfa. Store a lot more hay for winter."

His father grimaced. "That sounds an awful lot like farming to me. But you're right. After the third bad blizzard, I ran out of hay, and by then there wasn't a bale to be had. At any price."

Jane placed a hand on Odysseus's burly arm. "Odie, dear, these last two winters were a fluke of nature. It won't happen again."

"Don't count on it, Mother." Atlas took a cool drink of the tart, quenching ade. "Professor Harding said weather runs in cycles. There's a better chance of having another bad winter than not."

"How interesting, dear." His mother used that same tone she had when he was a child. Jane wasn't treating this crisis with any more seriousness than Minerva had.

He turned back to his father. "We need to diversify. Expand our profit base."

"What do you mean?" Odie looked confused.

"Build a meatpacking plant in Abilene."

"A stinking slaughterhouse? That doesn't interest me in the least."

"If you'd let me quote you some figures, you might change your mind."

"I doubt it." Odie picked up his cup and settled back in his chair. "I'm in the business of raising cattle—not killing them."

Thwarted for the moment, Atlas didn't let his disappointment show. "I'd at least like to take a look at the books this evening. And, Grandmother, while I'm at it, I should probably look at your records, too."

Wiping her flour-dusted hands on her apron, she turned to him. "My, but we have gotten our money's worth, sending you to college. But you needn't worry about me, my little Atlas-Who-Carries-the-World-on-His-Shoulders. Your grandfather left me quite nicely provided for."

Would he always be just a baby to her? "Grams, no matter how much money Grandfather set aside for you, it will eventually run out if you're not prudent. Take those extravagant twenty-first birthday prizes you've been lavishing on us. Libraries, for instance, don't come cheap."

She clapped her pudgy little hands together. "Oh, yes! And your twentieth birthday, your *labor birthday,* is just a few days away."

His father and mother bubbled into laughter, but the idea of being at the mercy of that twinkle in her lively gray eyes unnerved Atlas.

"Grams, I realize these labors of yours have become traditional, but—"

"Oh, yes, traditional. And one should never break with tradition."

She was hopeless, and so were Mother and Father . . . they kept right on laughing.

Atlas took another slaking—and hopefully calming—swallow of lemonade.

Jane stood up as she brought her sputtering laughter under control. "I'm so glad you reminded me. I need to get into town. There's so much to be done before the children come home for Atlas's party. And a bonnet . . .

I want Miss Lavender to make me a straw one to go with that white lawn frock I bought when we were visiting Atlas in Chicago at Easter. What do you think of lace and powder-blue ribbons?"

"It sounds delightful," Minerva said. "What do you think, Odie?"

"The blue will go beautifully with her eyes."

After the talk they'd just had about the losses the ranch would take this year, Atlas couldn't believe his ears. He slanted his father a frustrated scowl, but the man was looking up at his wife with nothing but a syrupy smile. The intimate overture stole the harsh words from Atlas's mouth as he saw his father through adult eyes for the first time and realized how much the man loved his wife.

"I think I'll go with you into Paradise Plains." Minerva removed her apron. "This old pie can wait. I'd like to have a bonnet made of navy and white and just a touch of red—to be patriotic, of course. And maybe a parasol to match."

Spinning away like a pair of whirlwinds, the women rushed from the room.

As Atlas listened to the rapid patter of their feet ascending the stairs, he slumped back in defeat. They all seemed beyond redemption, but somehow he'd have to get through to them that money earned from a generation of hard work could be tossed out the window as quickly and easily as dirty dishwater.

"Son," his father said, drawing Atlas back. "I'd like you to take the women into town. I'd do it myself, but Frank Spears is coming by with his prize bull."

"Why can't they drive themselves? I really feel it's important to check the books."

"Don't mention this to the women, but I always see to it that they don't go out on the road alone anymore. What with the end of the long trail drives and these last two winters, there are a lot of cowhands roaming around, falling in with bad company. And, well, your mother never did learn to shoot."

Atlas rose to his feet. "I see." Every time his father opened his mouth, the picture got grimmer.

"So that they don't worry, tell your ma you're going in to pick up barbed wire. And let's hope it's finally there. We ran out yesterday. And while you're at it, ask Hank at the mercantile if the fireworks I ordered came in. I want this Fourth of July to have the most spectacular display ever. After all, we are celebrating your twentieth birthday, too. Your *labor* birthday."

Atlas threw up his hands and walked out the door. It was useless to talk about anything sensible until this birthday business was over.

The big clock standing against the side wall of the Buccaneer Restaurant struck the half hour. One-thirty.

Aggravated, Atlas shifted in his seat and looked out the window. He'd taken care of his mother's grocery list and the loading of the barbed wire, then had been waiting since twelve-fifteen for her and Minerva to meet him for lunch. But they had yet to come out of the millinery shop.

He shook his head. *Women.*

Ginger, the youngest Tittle daughter, was at his elbow again with her pitcher. "Did you want more cider?" Her smile was as eager as it had been two minutes ago. At that awkward not-quite-a-woman age, she hadn't once allowed his glass to fall below half-full before rushing over to refill it.

"Thank you—just a little."

Tittering softly, she poured the cider, then sauntered a scant few feet away, swinging what little hips she had.

Not that he wasn't flattered, but the towhead was simply too young. He picked up his newspaper from the red-checkered tablecloth to hide behind, but soon realized he'd already read it front to back. Not to mention, he reminded himself, he'd also chatted with every customer in the Buc he knew, catching up on the local gossip.

Where *were* those women?

The yip of an animal gave Atlas an excuse to look outside again.

A big orange cat dashed across the road from the direction of Lucky's Saloon.

Two noisy little boys and their flop-eared pup chased after it, kicking up a cloud of dust as they ran.

Atlas smiled, knowing that chaos would ensue if they actually caught that tom. All three put together were no match for a cornered barn cat.

The orange ball of fur flew up the trunk of a big sycamore that shaded the street in front of the mercantile. The cat settled down into the crook of two limbs to gloat at its hapless pursuers. Sunlight speckled through the leaves onto the feline's bright coat, and an instant picture spilled into Atlas's mind . . . one of wildly curling hair afloat around a beautiful gypsy's face.

He quickly looked away. If he was going to have thoughts about the opposite sex, they should be centered on the sophisticated young ladies who strolled down Chicago's tree-lined avenues, young misses whose fathers were bankers or brokers. Young ladies who would be an asset to an up-and-coming businessman.

At the tap of footsteps on the veranda, Atlas saw his mother and grandmother at long last, their bustles bobbing.

Along with them came Miss Lavender. Dressed in ruffles and frills, the only thing plain about the rail-thin spinster was her gray hair. It was pulled into a severe bun.

He groaned. He'd be surrounded by their female chatter of ribbons and bows and buttons and lace.

Then, to his relief, he saw Lee, his oldest brother, walking just behind the ladies. Atlas would have a male ally. He came to his feet.

Lee, a burly horse of a man, banged through the screen door and rushed up. Looking more like Father than ever, he grabbed Atlas's hand in a hearty welcome. "Good to see you, Bub. Sorry I haven't gotten out to the ranch, but I reckon Father told you I'm adding a room onto the schoolhouse. I want to be finished before your birthday."

"*Gracious me.*" Miss Lavender wedged between them, her hands going to her face. She looked from Atlas to Minerva. "Minerva, the boy's even better looking than you said. Look at that slash of gray eyes, and his skin . . . it's tanned so smooth, and—" She must have read Atlas's embarrassment, because her birdlike glance suddenly darted back and forth. "I mean, rugged. No, strong. There's real strength of purpose there. I can see it. Can't you, Lee?"

"Absolutely." A mocking grin came through Lee's innocent expression. "And his hair. Don't you think the gals will just keel over when they get a gander at those golden brown waves?"

"That's enough, *Hercules*." Atlas pointed to a chair. "*Sit*! Let's get this meal over with."

Laughter erupted. Atlas had thought Ginger Tittle a giggle-box, but she couldn't hold a candle to this bunch, or the folks sitting at the next table.

With swift dispatch, he seated the ladies, then called for Ginger. Before she had time to reach them, he ordered five lunch plates. "And please bring them as quick as you can."

"What's the hurry, Bub?" Lee lounged back in his chair, looking as if he were about to take up residence.

"Young gentlemen are always in a hurry," Miss Lavender said, taking an inordinate amount of time arranging herself to prim, ruffle-bedecked perfection.

"But I'll wager he'll slow down when he catches sight of the Blakely sisters." Jane turned to Atlas. "They're the daughters of the man who bought the Barnett place. They're quite comely and well-mannered. Wouldn't you say so, Minerva?"

"Oh, yes," Miss Lavender interjected swiftly, an expert at gossiping. "They've been in with that gracious mother of theirs, ordering bonnets to go with absolutely *precious* dresses for the Fourth of July celebration." She leaned closer. "Maybelle over at the store said Mrs. Blakely comes from a *very* prominent St. Louis mercantile family. Walker, Wilder, or something like that, and both girls have been to a fancy finishing school back East. Can you imagine—all that *and* they're pretty as cameo pictures, and—"

Atlas took in a breath for the prattling woman as Minerva broke in. "Let's hope they're not too all-fired pretty. There's already too many young bucks hanging around with nothing better to do this summer than get into mischief."

"Well," Atlas said, hoping to change the subject to something other than their matchmaking, "I've come home with a plan that will take care of that."

"Which?" His mother raised one light brow. "The young ladies or the cowhands?"

"Yeah, Bub, I'd like the answer to that one myself." Lee sure was enjoying himself.

Atlas slanted his brother a narrowed gaze, but Lee showed not an inkling of remorse. Atlas turned to his mother. "While I was in Chicago, I checked out all the meatpacking houses. And I've drawn up some plans for what I think would be a very efficient operation for Abilene. It would provide employment for thirty or forty men. And there's no reason why we couldn't expand later. A tannery for the hides would be the next logical step." He eyed each of them. "Who's to say, maybe Abilene will one day become the shoe-manufacturing center of the West."

"No more business talk, dear, until after the Fourth," Jane said, then looked over Atlas's shoulder. "Good. Here comes our food."

"Good," Lee parroted with a grin. "I'm hungry enough to eat one of Bub's entire steers. Hooves, hide, and all."

Obviously Lee wasn't taking Atlas any more seriously than his parents had.

During the meal, talk switched back and forth between the latest Paris fashions and the size and weight of the new bull Frank Spears had recently purchased. No one seemed to notice that Atlas no longer had anything to say.

As they finished their meals, Ginger returned. "*I* made

the dessert today. Pies with crusts that'll melt in your mouth." She looked directly at Atlas, then ducked her chin and giggled.

"What kind?" he asked.

"Peach. Fresh peach."

Atlas's mouth watered. If nothing else, he was going to get some peach pie, even if Grams had abandoned hers.

Abruptly, Jane swung toward the window. "That sounds like . . ."

The clomp of big horses and the roll of heavy wheels were almost drowned out by the jangle of harness bells, slamming doors, and excited voices as folks spilled out onto the street.

"It is!" Minerva bounded to her feet.

Jane and the others did the same, practically tripping over each other as they made a beeline for the entrance.

Atlas stared after them as they slammed out the screen door. *What in the world*?

His mother poked her head back in just long enough to say, "Atlas, be a dear and sign for our meals."

Then he saw what had sent his family outside as if the Buc were on fire. Driving past in a gaudy flash of color was the gypsy, sitting high up on her wagon, waving at everyone she passed. And bursting from those lush lips came that loud, boisterous laughter.

No less enthusiastically, folks returned her greetings as if she'd arrived with a three-ring circus instead of a mere medicine wagon. Echoing from porch to porch came, "Howdy, Miss Charlotte. Howdy."

## ❦ 3 ❧

Ginger handed Atlas the bill for lunch and the stub of a pencil.

"Sorry about the pie," he said, glancing down and checking the addition. "I reckon I'll have to wait for another time to try some."

"Uh-hum," the young girl murmured absently, her attention on the commotion in the street. Glancing back, she bounced up and down on her toes. "Would you please hurry? I want to go, too."

No sooner had he signed the tab than she snatched it up and, stuffing it into her apron pocket, raced out.

The screen door banged several times in her wake.

He shook his head. What would the other customers think of her desertion? As he stood, he looked around and discovered they, too, had vanished, leaving half-finished meals.

This snake oil saleswoman seemed to have bewitched the entire town. He fully understood the effect she might have on the male population . . . but the women, too?

By the time Atlas walked out onto the veranda, the medicine-show wagon had come to a stop in the pecan- and elm-shaded area between the church and the school, and only a few stragglers hurrying down the street had yet to reach it. His family, along with everyone else who'd come to town on this Saturday afternoon, crowded up to a platform that jutted out from the rear of the wagon.

Atlas kept his pace deliberately slow as he strode to join the others. This backwoods charlatan couldn't possibly have any tricks up her sleeve that he hadn't already seen in Chicago.

The sheriff, Tom Sampson, strode past, his barrel of a belly leading the way as he stepped so quickly that dust billowed up behind him.

Atlas matched his own stride to Tom's. "From all the excitement, you'd think the President of the United States just drove into town."

"Bub Daltry." Tom slowed and extended his hand, his snow-white mustache a stark contrast to his flushed face. "Well, howdy there. It's been awhile."

Atlas returned the rangy man's firm grip. "Yes, but I'm back for good now."

"Are you getting those long legs of yours all stretched out for the Independence Day footrace? I'll be putting my money on you."

Atlas grinned. "You know I'll be ready." He nodded toward the wagon. "What's this all about?"

"Why, boy, you *have* been gone a spell. It's Charlotte Saturday. Everyone makes a point of coming into town on her Saturday."

"There's that much excitement over medicine powders? What's the woman got mixed in them?"

"Nothing out of the ordinary." The sheriff's round face

puckered into a frown. "It's Charlotte. Everybody loves Charlotte. And she always brings a surprise."

The sheriff hurried on ahead as if it were Christmas morning . . . rushed off before Atlas could ask any more questions—pertinent questions like where did this woman come from, and had Tom bothered to check her out, find out if she'd ever been arrested for larceny or fraud or . . . prostitution?

At a sudden swell of oohs and ahs, Atlas saw the back door of the wagon swing open onto the platform, and out stepped the woman with a loud laugh. A top hat of red, white, and blue stripes sat on her head at a rakish tilt, warring with the crazy mix of her bangles and clothes.

Atlas started walking toward the wagon again.

An excited child cried from atop his father's shoulders, *"What's the surprise?"*

"Yeah, Charlotte, what is it today?" called another voice that sounded very much like Lee's.

The charlatan tipped the Fourth of July hat in as grand a flourish as any politician. Then, resettling it among her strawberry curls, she strutted, all smiles, the few steps across her "stage."

Everyone laughed at her and applauded and cheered.

Atlas heaved a disgusted sigh. Gullible country folk, the whole lot of them.

In that instant another blaze of color pranced out the back door—a miniature duplicate of the woman. This three- or four-year-old, complete with the woman's wild mop of unruly hair, twirled a red-striped parasol while attempting to cool herself with a fan equally as patriotic.

As the throng wildly applauded the small child, her mother disappeared into the wagon, returning a moment later. Her expression as gay as ever, she carried a stack of top hats, along with more parasols and fans.

"Charlotte, how much for the hat?" yelled Gus Dolby, the local blacksmith. A tall, broad-chested man, he stood at the back of the crowd near where Atlas had come to a stop.

The woman's gaze lifted in Gus's direction—but halted at Atlas. Her expression stilled. She remembered him. The gorgeous hussy remembered him.

Atlas took a step forward.

"How much for the hat?" Dolby repeated.

She jerked her attention from Atlas and inhaled deeply, her lovely breasts straining against the turquoise fabric of her peasant blouse. Then she flashed that smile again. "Twenty-five cents, Mr. Dolby. Just two bits. And the same for the parasol. And only one thin dime for the fan. But, Gus," she said, waving the hats, "you can't buy just one. You've got three boys at home."

Everybody started calling out their orders at once, waving dollar bills, crowding closer. And she was a sight to watch as she flitted back and forth, her skirts swinging around her hips—obviously enjoying herself.

In the middle of the clamor, the woman glanced up, and her eyes connected with Atlas's again, enticing . . . beckoning. . . . And as much as he intended to, he couldn't drag his gaze away from hers.

Then abruptly she returned to business, and Atlas felt his heart leapfrogging inside his chest. The woman wasn't simply a flimflammer, she was a temptress, a siren—her lure stronger than any of the sea nymphs he'd heard about in his grandmother's Greek tales.

Well, she wasn't getting this sailor.

Atlas wheeled around . . . and spotted Lucky's Saloon at the far end of town. No sideshow charlatan would lure him into the depths of her eyes. His future was planned. Right down to the last detail.

A dull pain behind his eyes greeted Atlas the next morning when he awakened. From the slant of sunlight in his upstairs bedroom, he knew it was well past the break of day. He squeezed his eyes shut a couple of times, trying to dispel the gnawing ache as he rolled out of bed. Grabbing the bedpost for a moment to make sure of his footing, he decided maybe it hadn't been such a good idea to down four quick shots of whiskey yesterday. And on the way home, the sun's rays had been child's play compared to the searing glances he'd received from his mother and grandmother.

But he refused to feel guilty over a few measly drinks—he was a man now, full grown, and it was time everyone understood that.

He reached for his Levi's, then remembered it was Sunday. Groaning at the thought of getting dressed up for church, he splashed water on his face, then walked to the big oak closet in the corner. Wouldn't do to beg off. Not this morning. His pounding head couldn't take all the harping that would surely follow.

The starched collar seemed to scratch his skin more than usual, and he felt the direst need for fresh air. He opened the window wider and stuck his head out, taking in a deep breath of cool, fresh air.

His mother's husky soprano drifted up from the kitchen as she prepared breakfast. He closed his raw eyes and let her sweet melody soothe them.

"Blindly we stumble when we walk alone," she sang.

Stumble when we walk? Obviously she was sending him a message.

As he reached her sunny kitchen, his mother gave him a stiff smile. "Good morning, dear." Suddenly her expression brightened. "I'm so pleased to see you dressed for church. How many eggs do you want?"

His stomach rebelled at the thought, but he had no intention of letting her know. "Two." A nauseating picture of oozing yellows and whites came to mind, and he quickly added, "Scrambled."

Her fair brows lifted slightly, but she didn't mention his sudden change of preference.

Atlas plucked a cup out of the oak cabinet above the drain board, then moved to the woodstove beside her and poured himself some coffee. Catching a whiff of his mother's perfume, he took note of her attractive attire beneath her bibbed apron and decided now would definitely be a good time to mention it, to get on her good side. "That's a very pretty dress you have on. That soft yellow brings out the color of your hair, and—"

Spurs scraped on the stone walk outside, followed by quick raps on the door. Opening it, Roper, the ranch's wrangler, stopped at the threshold and doffed his beat-up hat. "Sorry to bother you, ma'am." Roper was in his mid-forties, and his face looked even more weathered than his hat. He turned to Atlas, a sadness in his deep-set eyes. "Thought you'd want to know, Bub. Old Zeus is down. Looks like a bad case of colic. Real bad."

Atlas came to his feet. "You say he's down?"

"Yeah. And it looks like he's already been thrashing around for quite a spell."

Ripping loose his tie, Atlas started for the hall. "Give me a minute to change. Where is he?"

Roper, already out the door, called over his shoulder, "Out yonder, behind the barn."

"But what about your breakfast? Church?" his mother called, walking after him, spatula in hand.

Atlas paused at the stairs. "I can't, Ma. It's Zeus. You know he's been my horse since I was seven."

"And he was no spring chicken then. You can't expect him to live forever."

"I know. But he never let me down when I was just a green kid. I have to be there for him now. And, who knows," he said with a shrug, "maybe we can save him."

His mother sighed on a sad smile. "Don't count on it, sweetheart."

Jamming his shovel into the sun-baked earth, Atlas was grateful for the task. Nothing he and Roper had tried eased the suffering of his aged roan, nothing except the bullet in Zeus's head. It had been the hardest trigger Atlas had ever pulled, but he wouldn't have left the task to anyone else.

He stopped and wiped his brow with the back of his sleeve, and his gaze wandered to where the old gelding lay, so still. Just yesterday Zeus had been almost spry as Atlas rode him across the rolling meadows. Just yesterday. But a disaster of one sort or another was always out there, waiting to strike like a coiled rattler. If it wasn't a blizzard, it was a drought. Or worse.

Atlas grabbed the pick and put all his might into his swing.

The livestock business was much too risky, especially

in these changing times. Somehow he had to convince his father to diversify. Maybe he could get his brothers and brothers-in-law to help him convince their father. They'd all be arriving soon. He patted the notebook in his shirt pocket. He'd start a list of every possible objection.

With dirt piled high on either side, the hole was finally big enough. He tossed out the shovel and pick, then hoisted himself up. Brushing the soil off his jeans, he saw his family's canvas-topped surrey coming through the entrance. Were they home from church already?

Odie didn't stop the team at the barn, but drove across the pasture until they reached Atlas. He glanced from the carcass to the rifle leaning against the fence. His heavy features sagged. "Sorry, son. Have you tried to find out what caused the colic? Did you check the grain for mold?"

"Roper did, but he couldn't find any. Must've been something the old boy ate out on the range."

"Could be it was just ol' Zeus's time, son."

Eyes stinging from unshed tears, Atlas stuffed his hands in his pockets. "I know."

"Oh, by the way," Jane said, fanning herself in the heat as she sat beside Odie. "That youngest Tittle girl said to tell you she was making peach pie again next Saturday. His first trip to town, and the pretty young butterflies are already flitting around our handsome flower."

"*Ma–a.*"

"Well, son," Odie chimed in with a lopsided grin, "you're covered with enough dirt for a dozen flowers to take root."

"Mrs. Clairmore also asked after you," Minerva said from the rear seat.

Glad for the change of topic, Atlas said, "Clairmore? I don't recall the name. Did they buy someone's spread?"

"No, dear. And she's not married. She's that lovely young widow that travels through every other Saturday selling her Professor Puffinwick's Powder. She always lays over for church on Sunday."

"Church? The flimflammer goes to church?"

"She's *not* a flimflammer," his mother insisted. "I'll have you know she's a fine, upstanding Christian. Now, hop in the surrey, and we'll give you a ride back to the house for dinner. You men can bury the horse later, after the temperature cools down."

As he climbed aboard and sat down beside Minerva, she squeezed his knee. "Zeus was such a pet. We'll all miss having his friendly old head hanging over the back fence every day."

"Yeah." Atlas sighed. "He always had to have that carrot."

"But life goes on. And speaking of that, we'll be having the pleasure of spending the whole day with Miss Charlotte next time she comes through. She'll be here just in time for the Independence Day celebration."

"Yes," Jane added, looking over her shoulder. "She's always so much fun. Laughing all the time. And then, with the entire family home again and all the little ones, why, this is going to be the most wonderful Fourth of July ever."

Atlas settled back on the padded leather seat. Charlotte the Christian. Fine—he'd have the entire day to watch her, discover her game.

## ‮ﱒ‬ 4 ‮ﱒ‬

The next two weeks flew by in a flurry of preparations. Instead of helping his brother, C.J., and their ranch hands build fences and winter shelters for the livestock, Atlas was kept home to help Odie construct a tree house for the grandchildren out back in a big-limbed oak. Except, of course, when Jane was dragging him away to set up extra beds in the attic bedrooms or insisting that he not only repaint the kitchen, but also the stairwell wall *before* the grandchildren arrived to run their grubby little hands up and down it.

But Atlas didn't really mind. The thought that this big old house would be filled with noise and laughter again spurred him on. He even seemed to have more energy and speed during his early-morning practices for the upcoming footrace.

The day before Atlas's birthday, Lee met the eastbound train and picked up his sister Venus, and Buck. World travelers, they had come from Los Angeles this time.

By the next afternoon, when Atlas's other brother, C.J., fetched Persy and Jake, their two little ones, *and* a barrel full of lobsters in seawater, everyone had converged. And from that moment on, all the grandchildren tumbled, screeched, ran, and wrestled across the sprawling lawn while his mother and sisters and sisters-in-law circled up the gazebo, buzzing faster and louder than a nest of fired-up hornets. The men lounged in the shade of the wide veranda, mostly listening to Buck spin yarns of their latest adventures in India, Tahiti, and now California. Buck, who'd been blind since the war, never ceased to amaze Atlas with the wonders he could experience.

But Atlas was given little time to enjoy these tales since Minerva, running around like a chicken with her head cut off, kept him hopping, fetching and carrying.

Even after the six little ones had been fed and bedded down for the night, the excitement of the special day— the day of Atlas's "labor" birthday—hadn't calmed. He listened to the other thirteen adults, all dressed in their finery, chatter as fast as ever as they crowded around a table meant to seat twelve.

As he pulled out the chair at the head of the table—the honored spot for his birthday—he realized he had yet to broach the subject of his plan for a meatpacking plant with any of the other men. Glancing around at all the beaming faces, he decided to wait to discuss business until the next morning. He'd try to find some time alone with each of them before they all departed for the town festivities.

Three crystal candelabras lined the center of the lace-covered table, garlands of Jane's prettiest flowers circling them. The tall flaming tapers illuminated a creamy green soup contained in Jane's best china, and Persy's gift of French champagne sparked in crystal flutes. The family's only true cook and connoisseur of fine dining, Persephone always gave this talent as her gift. And, oh, the aroma of her freshly baked sesame rolls . . .

"Very nice, sis," he said to Persy, who with her quiet beauty looked as elegant as the table. "It looks like Michigan Avenue or even New York. It's too beautiful to touch. Almost," he added with a grin. Picking up his glass, he glanced around the table. "To all you lovely ladies. And you, too, Allie," he teased. "In that brown chiffon, any passing stranger would easily mistake you for one."

Undaunted, she made a face, then mouthed, "Labor, labor, labor."

Ignoring the bearbaiting, Jake smiled at his wife. "And wait till you taste my Persy's cream of asparagus soup." A rugged yet sophisticated man, he kissed three of his fingers for emphasis. "And the sauce your sister has created to go with the lobster is fit for the gods."

At the mention of gods, Atlas, along with everyone else, eyed Minerva and burst out laughing . . . except for Lee, who spouted, "Then what are we waiting for?" He picked up his spoon, never a shy one when it came to feeding his face.

During the leisurely meal, whispered secrets passed from ear to ear, along with giggles and smiles in Atlas's direction. Atlas just hoped their gifts to him would not be as silly as the presenters were acting at the moment.

Finally, after the last lobster tail had been cracked, the last artichoke heart eaten, and everyone's glasses had been refilled with champagne, Odie lumbered to his feet and raised his stemmed flute. He smiled down at Jane. "I wish to offer this toast to you, my darling Janie, for being with me thirty unforgettable years and for giving me this wonderful family."

Tears glistened in her soft blue-gray eyes as she lifted her champagne in a returning salute.

"And," he continued, "to all at this table who have come to celebrate the year of our youngest's labor. And most of all," he said, turning to Atlas, "I wish to toast my son, returning home with scholastic honors. May your future be filled with just as much promise."

"Hear, hear," Jake, Persy's darkly handsome New Yorker, cheered, and everyone brought their drinks to their lips.

"Well, now that that's over with," Venus said, her voice as rich and melodious as ever, "let's adjourn to the living room." Rising, she smoothed the wrinkles from a stunning Chinese costume of red. "I want to be first to present my gift. I mean—Buck's and mine," she amended with a loving glance at her blind husband. "This being the first year we've been allowed to buy instead of make them, I've had such fun digging through the most exotic marketplaces."

Reaching the large living room that had been the gathering place for so many years, Atlas sat in the big leather chair nearest the stone hearth, its soot-blackened opening hidden for the summer by a fancy oriental screen that Venus had sent Jane last Christmas.

As everyone else settled around him, Minerva came to perch on the arm of his chair. She hovered over him with that ominous twinkle in her eye.

The time for the announcement of his labor had arrived—his supposed fate for the next year. His stomach clenched tighter than a knotted fist as he recalled some of the others.

"Grandmother, you go first with Bub's labor." Allie's mobile expression held as much of a tease as it did curiosity.

"Yeah, Grandmother," C.J. goaded, hugging his wife, Lizzy, to him. He, too, smiled with as much devilment as ever. "Tell us."

Minerva rested her arm along the back of Atlas's chair and toyed with him by smoothing the small cowlick at his crown. "No, I think I'll wait until you've all offered your presents."

An icy chill snaked up Atlas's spine. It was going to be an awful labor. Awful.

He had a hard time concentrating as Venus gave him an elaborate ivory and jade chess set from Hong Kong and hoped his words of appreciation conveyed the sincerity he truly meant.

Lee and his schoolmarm wife, Meredith, presented him with a wonderfully illustrated book on astronomy and a telescope mounted on a tripod. Very professional looking.

"That calls for an observatory," Odie said, his gaze chasing out the big bay window, no doubt searching the darkness for the perfect spot to start building. Again.

Next, C.J.'s blond head barely peaked over the pile of packages in his arms as he plunked them onto Atlas's lap, his mouth sliding into another lopsided grin. "After all that stargazing, I thought you might need something to bring you back down to earth."

Atlas untied the bow on the first box and found a new set of spurs . . . not a fancy dress set, but everyday ones with the rowels filed down to avoid scouring a cow pony's flanks. He cracked into laughter at his older brother. "Been missing me, have you?" It came as no surprise that the other packages contained a pair of batwing chaps and a rain slicker.

Then Allie knelt down beside him, her eyes full of emotion, so uncharacteristically serious.

He couldn't resist ruffling her mop of short brown curls.

"We heard about ol' Zeus," she said softly. "And I can't tell you how sorry we are. Hal and I brought over a blaze-faced sorrel that's turning into a top cow pony. We'd like you to have him. He's got a real friendly nature, too. Like Zeus."

Atlas swallowed down the tightness in his throat. "Thanks, sis." He turned to her husband, seated on one of the two facing sofas. "You, too, Hal. Thanks."

Hal seemed a bit embarrassed by all the family sentiment as he ran fingers through his sandy hair and shrugged. "We'll all miss Zeus."

"Well, darling," his mother said, coming forward in a cloud of pink chiffon and bearing a box covered in maroon satin, "you've certainly received some wonderful gifts on this, your special birthday. I hope you'll treasure mine as well."

Inside, on a cushion of black velvet, lay a gold ink pen with his initials scrolled on the side. Beside it sat a cut-crystal inkwell with a lid as lustrous as the pen.

"And," his father added, "we thought you'd need something to put them on. In the morning I'll take you out to my office and show you the mahogany desk I built you. With no more than one or two hernias, the boys and

I moved it in there this afternoon while your grandmother was keeping you busy. It's right across the room from mine."

Atlas stood up, satin box still in hand, and looked from one dear family member to another, his chest tight with emotion. "I never thought you all really knew who I'd grown up to be. But each gift was so . . . you seemed to know exactly what I'd want. I—"

"Sweetie," Minerva had come up behind him. "You still have one more surprise."

The blood drained from his face.

"Yeah, Bub," Allie hooted, back to her old self, "the labor."

He was surrounded by wall-to-wall grinning teeth. No quarter would be given. Especially not from Grams.

She looked innocent as a lamb in her ivory silk and the string of pearls Grandfather had given her just before he died. She walked to the hearth and leisurely turned to face him. There was no doubt from whom Venus inherited her flare for the dramatic. "Well, my dear," Grandmother purred. "I've given this a great deal of thought. Even so, you will probably think this too simple a task for a man of your capabilities. . . ."

He sucked in a breath. It was going to be even worse than he'd thought.

"But after all your hard work at school, something of a more pleasant nature was called for; yet at the same time, your labor will be giving someone else a hand who is in need of a little nudging."

Much worse.

"Your labor is to escort that sweet Charlotte Clairmore to five social functions this year."

*"What?"*

Minerva flinched at his outburst. "Now, dear, compared to Lee's labor of teaching school for a year, or Venus's task of traveling throughout the wilds of Nevada as a writer's assistant, yours is but a few friendly courtesies to a withdrawn young widow."

*"Withdrawn?"* Atlas stepped closer and loomed over the much shorter woman. "You call a caterwauling flimflammer withdrawn? Well, it won't work this time. Not even for one of your precious prizes will I be seen in public with some strumpet of a charlatan. I'd be the laughingstock of three counties."

Someone placed a hand on Atlas's arm . . . Persy, alarm widening her blue-gray eyes. "Who is this Charlotte?"

"She's a lovely young widow with a delightful child," Minerva supplied. "But she's been uncommonly shy about accepting social invitations."

Atlas snorted. "To call that woman shy is like calling a strutting rooster shy."

"It may seem that way on the surface, dear," Grandmother said, stretching to her tallest. "But all of us ladies at the church are worried about her. And I think if you can convince her to accompany you to a few casual social gatherings—say, Mother Spooler's ninetieth birthday celebration later this month—Charlotte might start considering marriage again."

Atlas backed up. "Oh, no, you don't."

"No one's asking you to marry her, dear. Just get her out and about." Minerva turned to Persy. "Charlotte has a darling little girl named Opal just about your Diana's age. And sweet little Opal needs a father as much as her mother needs someone to look after her. They travel alone throughout the countryside all the time, and everyone at the church worries about them. We pray for their safety every week."

Buck tapped his cane on the floor. "She travels? Whereabouts?"

"She's a snake oil saleswoman by day," Atlas said. "And by night? I'll leave to your imagination what goes on inside that carnival wagon of hers after the lights go out."

"*That's about enough.*" Lee's freckle-faced redhead, Meredith, sprang to her feet, wagging her finger as if Atlas were still her student. "Shame on you."

"Bub." Lizzy, touching the faint scar lining the side of her face, quietly added her two cents worth. "You really shouldn't judge a person by her appearance, but by what's in her heart."

C.J. placed a protective arm around his wife's slight shoulders. "Yeah, Bub. Don't be such a snob."

Exasperated, Atlas spread his hands. "What's the matter with everyone? The woman dresses like a wild gypsy."

"Sounds marvelously colorful to me," Buck said, his sightless eyes crinkling with mirth.

Atlas plopped back down in his chair. Everyone was acting as if he, Atlas, were the villain. "*All right.* I give up. But this public association with a questionable woman better not impede any of my own pursuits."

"Impede?" Odie, who'd been quietly observing the scene, stood up and ambled over. He wore a disarming grin. "Set up that chess set, and I'll teach you the truest meaning of impede."

"Yeah," Jake added, his own expression betraying far too much amusement. "Then perhaps tomorrow you can introduce me to this most interesting young woman. I don't believe I've ever met a virtuous charlatan before."

## ෩ 5 ෨

Atlas pulled his pocket watch from his waistcoat. Eleven-forty. They'd missed the parade and no telling how many other events, not to mention he'd have far less time to investigate the Clairmore woman.

But what could one expect with this mob of a family? The entire morning had been chaos. He hadn't even been able to manage five minutes alone with the men to propose his plan.

Approaching Paradise Plains on Red Jack, his gift from Hal and Allie, he looked behind him and noted that the trailing Daltry clan was a parade unto itself. Patriotic festoons and garlands fluttered from the surrey, the buggy, and the two wagonloads of excited parents and squealing children. And, thanks to Jane and Minerva, every fidgeting grandchild sported either a paper top hat, parasol, or one of those fans the flimflammer had been selling.

Bypassing crowded Main Street, he led the way to the tall grass behind the church where more vehicles than Atlas thought existed in the county were already parked. He reined in his new sorrel beneath the spraddling limbs of a pecan tree and dismounted to go help the others down.

"Atlas! Quick! Quick!" Persy stood at the back of a still-moving wagon, motioning for him to come. In her other hand, she held out that blasted pie that had taken her half the morning to bake. "Run fast. Find where they're having the pie contest. Mama said it starts at a quarter to twelve."

Atlas pitched Persy's husband a glance.

Towering over his wife, Jake shrugged. "Persy says you're faster."

Rolling his eyes, Atlas accepted the confection with its gold-kissed meringue topping puffing a good five inches high. He balanced it aloft and took off at a run.

As he zigzagged through the maze of rigs, Persy's cry chased after him. "Don't drop it!"

He spotted Charlotte Clairmore's wagon sitting beside the school, but not its questionable owner, as he ran past a crowd gathered to watch a horseshoe-throwing contest in front of the barbershop. Weaving his way on down the crowded street, he passed the newspaper office, where tables of canned preserves waited to be judged, continued past the boardinghouse, patchwork quilts displayed on its walls, their jumbled mix of colors so like the gypsy's skirt . . . that skirt that swam so seductively around her hips, her ankles. . . .

"Yikes!" Holding the pie aloft, he leaped to one side, narrowly missing a lemonade stand that seemed to have popped up out of nowhere. Then, thank goodness, he spotted the table of pies in front of the restaurant. Veering to it, he squeezed past a couple of stout ladies and glided his sister's entry into an empty spot.

"In the nick of time," Rosy Tittle, the mother of the Buccaneer's bunch, said with her hint of a German accent. "The judges, they come now."

Maybelle, from the store, handed him a scrap of paper and smiled sweetly. "Nice to see you home, Bub. Please write your grandmother's name and put it under her pie."

"It's not Grams'," he said, catching his breath. "It's Persy's."

*"Persy's?"* Maybelle wailed, her Southern manners slipping several notches before she recouped. "Oh, my, I didn't know Persy was back, too."

"Just for a few days." Atlas tucked the paper under Persy's pie.

"Well," Mrs. Thornton from the Double T groused, "not much sense waiting around to hear what the judges have to say."

*Sour grapes,* Atlas would've teased if he wasn't so attached to ears the good ladies would've surely twisted off. He wheeled around to survey the street.

Bunting-draped booths crowded between every building, some selling refreshments, while others had folks out front hawking games of chance.

The crack of rifle fire drew his attention to a shooting range set up between the boardinghouse and the sheriff's office. Men held up fistfuls of greenbacks and called out bets as one of the Carpenter boys raised a newer model Winchester to his shoulder.

Atlas was tempted to join them. His stomach thought differently. Maybe after lunch.

He started back toward the library lawn, where the family had agreed to gather for their picnic lunch at twelve.

Approaching the Hatbox, he noticed one booth surrounded by nothing but young men. They hooted and crowed, jockeying for position, blocking Atlas's view.

Then he saw the sign nailed to the top of the stand.

KISSES — 50¢.

Atlas had little doubt who was selling them—that *shy Miss Charlotte*. Maybe if he dragged his grandmother over to get a look at the wanton, she'd relent and not force this particular labor. It was one thing to have a back street dalliance with one of her sort, but quite another to be seen in public with her.

He caught a glimpse of his grandmother through the meandering crowd. Across the road, she and Mama were spreading a checkered cloth in a shady spot. He started toward them, then stopped. Maybe he'd better first make sure the female in the booth actually was the flimflammer. He strode to the millinery shop and stepped up on its boardwalk for a gander over the young bucks' heads.

One cowpoke, hanging onto his hat for dear life, was leaning into the booth, obviously getting all he'd paid for. With a whoop, the fellow fell back and threw his hat into the air as someone else pushed him aside.

In that one quick second before the next customer took his place, Atlas saw . . . *Venus*? *Venus*! That flirty sister of his was standing there blithely selling kisses.

"Bub! Bub Daltry!" Jody Spears, one of Frank's sons, headed his way with a fashionable young lady on his arm. She could just as easily have been strolling along Michigan Avenue in Chicago. Everything about her, from her stylish bonnet to her hemline, bespoke big-city sophistication.

Stepping off the boardwalk to greet his school chum,

Atlas wondered how that beanpole, whose trousers never seemed quite long enough, ever managed to latch onto her.

"Heard you was back." With a friendly, toothy grin, Jody gripped Atlas's hand. "You plannin' to toe the mark with me this afternoon?"

"You ready to get beat?" Atlas fired back, knowing Jody referred to the footrace. "Again?" Laughing, he turned his attention to the auburn-haired beauty. "I don't believe I've had the pleasure."

Jody lost his smile. "Oh, yeah. Elizabeth Blakely, this is Bub Daltry from over to Mount Olympus. You know," he added with sarcasm, "where all them *Greek gods* live."

Despite Jody's put-down, Miss Blakely was apparently intrigued. She offered her hand, and, if she'd been peeking from behind a fan, her smile couldn't have been more coy. "Greek gods." She looked him up and down, then purred, "My friends call me Beth."

He took her hand and returned his most ardent smile. "And goddesses usually call me Atlas."

"I see your feet aren't the only things that are fast these days," Jody said, steering Beth away. "See you later."

Atlas chuckled as he watched them disappear into the throng. So, that was one of the Blakely girls Miss Lavender spoke of the other day. Young ladies of breeding with connections to St. Louis banking. He could hardly wait to see what the other sister looked like.

Starting across the road to join his family, Atlas caught snatches of a rousing rendition of "Onward Christian Soldiers." Curious, he passed a couple of stands that gave way to the lawn in front of the school, then stopped dead in his tracks.

There she was. The charlatan, dressed in the boldest red and white stripes he'd ever seen, the biggest bustle, and the gayest smile. She strutted around a large circle, bellowing the song at the top of her lungs and banging on a tambourine. Marching directly behind, her little one wore a dress of identical fabric and sang and banged her own smaller tambourine. Bringing up the rear, children and adults of all ages sang with almost as much exuberance as Charlotte, while bystanders cheered them on.

Someone on the sidelines blew a whistle.

Everyone halted, and a boy of about eight jumped up and down, squealing, "I won! I won!"

While everyone clapped, Charlotte took the youngster's hand and led him to a table under an elm . . . a table loaded with cakes.

The boy pointed to one frosted with chocolate.

She handed it to him, ruffled his shaggy hair, then hurried back to the circle. "Five cents," she called. "Just one plug nickel for a chance on the best cakes in the county."

Folks crowded around, shoving money at her, which she took while hollering for them to "Circle up! Circle up!"

Within seconds another cakewalk had been formed, and Charlotte started belting out the march again. If not genteel in her enthusiasm, the woman certainly appeared civic-minded, since profits from the Fourth of July activities were always earmarked for some worthy project.

Atlas snorted, not believing her act for one second, and

turned away, leaving the spectacle behind. The woman probably considered herself this year's community cause and was pocketing a good portion of the money for herself.

As he cut across the road, Minerva walked out to meet him. "I *like* that girl," she said, looking past him at Charlotte. "She always brings such life to everything."

In spite of his resolve, he glanced back at the woman . . . her slender figure, so lively and lithe. Her shining curls, caught up in a cascade, bounced with wild abandon. And he could almost feel what it would be like to have all that effervescence in his arms . . . in his bed. . . .

"I'll introduce you when Charlotte is through over there," his grandmother said, rescuing Atlas from his wayward urges just as Hal and Allie joined them.

"We're going over to the registration table, Bub," Allie said, wearing her usual jeans today. "Have you signed up for any events yet?"

"No. I thought it was time to eat."

"Go along, dear," Minerva said. " Everyone was so excited to get a gander at everything first, we won't be sitting down until twelve-thirty."

Outside the mercantile, Hank sat behind the registration table, his bald head turning red from too much sun. He was jawing with a couple of ranchers who had spreads to the south.

"How's it goin'?" Hal asked the men, while hitching his Levi's up over his slim hips.

"'Spect you haven't talked to Collins yet." Mr. Walker from the Lazy W had an ominous note in his gravelly voice.

Hal frowned. "Nope."

Mr. Walker folded work-hardened hands. "Grafton, the cattle buyer out of New Orleans, dropped by Collins's place. Said he wouldn't go any higher than half a cent less than last year. Less, not more. But he acted like he was sweetenin' the pot by sayin' the Montereau Meat-packing House was willing to advance money on next year's herd."

Instantly anger shot through Atlas. "I'll just bet they are—the greedy bastards. Collins didn't agree to anything, did he?"

"Not yet," Mr. Walker said. "But for us smaller spreads, it may be all we can do."

"Don't you believe it." Atlas scanned the schedule again. "I see here that there's nothing planned for five o'clock, and we'll never have a better chance of getting all the ranchers together than today. Pass the word. Five sharp at the church."

"I know you mean well, son," Milburn, the other rancher, said. "But if you're thinkin' on us holdin' out till we get a better price, we can't do that. We was already scrapin' bottom after last year's winter."

"Gentlemen," Atlas said, trying to convey confidence in his tone, "we have options. Don't ever let 'em fool you into thinking we don't. I kept my eyes and ears open while I was at school in Chicago, and, trust me, they're running just as scared as we are."

"Bu–ub," Allie whined. "We didn't come here to talk dreary business. We came to sign Hal up for bronc riding. I'd sign up, too, if girls were allowed," she sniped.

Atlas wanted to say more about the meeting, but it

would have to wait. "Five o'clock," he repeated, then asked for the entry sheet for the men's footrace.

Grinning, Hank rubbed his double chin. "Are you sure you wouldn't rather get yourself bucked off a bronc or two first? Maybe then the other fellas'd have a better chance."

Allie swung around to face Atlas. "Don't you dare." She then turned to Hank and winked. "Bub can't afford to get all stove up today. He has a *very important* personal matter to take care of this afternoon."

Atlas did his best to ignore her remark, knowing she referred to his proposed introduction to Charlotte Clairmore. He concentrated on signing up for the footrace. But it wasn't easy, since Hal was braying like a damned jackass.

"I don't know what you're laughing about, Hal," Hank said, his fleshy cheeks plumping with a smirk. "Married less than a year, and your missus already don't care if *you* get trampled or not."

Allie snagged Hal's arm, then eyed Atlas. "My husband no longer has *personal matters* to take care of, unlike some unmarried brothers I know."

"Well, boy," Milburn drawled as he turned to Atlas. The craggy old range rider looked overdressed in his Sunday bowler . . . especially while wearing a prankish grin. "Sounds to me like you're going to have your hands full today, in more ways than one."

On his return to the Daltry picnic spot, Atlas made a point of stopping every rancher he passed to inform him of the meeting. Everyone's response was so promising, perhaps he'd even mention his plan for the meatpacking operation—one that would always give the rancher a fair price.

By the time he reached the family, they had already congregated and were sitting on the grass with full plates—even Venus, flushed and smiling like a three-year-old who'd raided the cookie jar and gotten away clean. He picked up an empty plate and started piling it with ham and fried chicken and all the fixings. Then he noticed one person was missing.

Grams.

His heart lurched.

At this very minute, she was probably trying to round up the flimflammer.

But it wouldn't work this time. Not on him. His grandmother's matchmaking days were over. He refused to let himself be any more affected by the gypsy's heart-stopping green eyes than if he were as blind as his brother-in-law.

The matter settled in his mind, Atlas sat down between his mother and Buck. He'd managed only a few bites when Grandmother returned with the woman in tow. But then, who could miss Charlotte or her tiny daughter? They looked like a couple of striped barbershop poles.

The other men began to rise, and he put his plate down to do likewise.

"No, please," Charlotte said. "You all look too comfortable."

As everyone settled down again, Minerva introduced Charlotte to those who were visiting. And, except for the fact that the woman didn't look his way once, she was as overly friendly as ever with the others. His grandmother had saved him for last, Atlas noted. But that was all right. It gave him more time to brace himself.

Without realizing he'd gotten up, he found himself on his feet when Grandmother turned to him. "And this is my youngest grandson, Atlas."

As Charlotte tilted her head up to reveal those eyes, as inviting as two emerald pools on a hot, hot day, he held his breath.

"How do you do," she said, scarcely above a whisper.

Entranced by her soft, sultry voice, he caught himself just before reaching for her hand. "Fine, thank you. And yourself?" His own voice came out raspy. He cleared his throat.

"Wonderful." Her gaze, so open, so deadly, held his.

His palms began to sweat.

"Atlas," Minerva was saying, "has just come home from college, all full of ambitious business plans. He's always been the industrious one of the family."

"Oh?" Before Charlotte shifted her attention, Atlas could've sworn he saw disappointment in her eyes. Or was it merely dismay because an educated man wouldn't be so easily duped?

"And this," Minerva said, bringing the small child to the fore, "is our little Opal, who, as you can see, is the spitting image of her mama."

A spritely grin dimpled her cheeks as the imp swept out her gathered skirt and executed a pretty fair curtsy.

Not to be outdone by the cute little tyke, Atlas bowed from the waist. "Charmed, I'm sure."

Obviously delighted by his overture, she stuck out her thumb. It barely missed his lowered nose. "See? I have a splinter."

"Let me check." Her mother reached for her hand.

Opal quickly snatched it away. "No! You'll poke me with a needle." Her eyes were every bit as expressive as her mother's, and the wariness in them tore at Atlas.

"I'll bet I can get it out without poking or hurting you." He softened his dare with a gentle smile.

As he pulled his all-purpose pocketknife out of his trouser pocket, Persy's oldest daughter, Diana, skipped up to Opal. "Let me see?"

At that moment Atlas became aware that all other conversation had ceased, and everyone sat watching the "show." Even Minerva had stepped back for a better view.

After a few seconds' hesitation, Opal stuck out her thumb for five-year-old Diana to inspect.

"It'll hurt," Diana said matter-of-factly, then flounced back to her lunch.

"No, it won't." Atlas peeled out a small pair of pointed tweezers. Kneeling down before Opal, he pressed the tips together. "See? I'll just catch hold of the end of that sliver and pull it out."

The little one reached out with her uninjured hand and placed two of her tiny fingers over his.

He pressed the tweezers tight again and watched her eyes widen, then soften. "Trust me," he said, and held out his other hand.

She inched her thumb forward until he had it in his grasp. She flinched.

"Close those beautiful green eyes," he whispered . . . eyes that were the spitting image of her mother's. "I'll have it out before you can count to ten."

The tip of the splinter was above the surface, and Atlas

was able to remove it with one swift pull. "You can open your eyes now."

Her lids sprang up, and he deposited the splinter into the palm of her hand.

"It is! It's out!" Staring at him with adoration, she grabbed his arm and gave it a fierce hug.

Everyone applauded, and Jake called, "Bravo!" much to Opal's delight.

Hanging onto Atlas's shirtsleeve, Opal giggled.

"Thank you," Charlotte said, stepping forward . . . her eyes now dangerously close. "Opal simply won't let me take a splinter out."

The woman seemed so genuinely grateful, her expression so incredibly vulnerable. Atlas rose from a crouch, but for the life of him, he couldn't think of a reply in the silence that wove around them. He smiled and shrugged.

Then, thank heavens, Persy came over to them, bearing two plates of food. She handed one to Charlotte and the other to Opal, giving Atlas desperately needed time to collect himself.

"Now, sit down, you three," Minerva added, "and eat up."

He didn't miss his grandmother's ploy to lump him with Charlotte and her daughter.

Charlotte, however, found a spot between his two sisters-in-law. Settling onto the grass, her taffeta skirt rustled, and dapples of sun drops danced through the leaves and across hair the lightest shade of red; and he could swear her essence . . . her very feminine essence . . . drifted toward him.

Seated beside her, bespectacled Meredith's deep red locks, mostly covered by a wide-brimmed hat, unaccountably now seemed too dark, too ordinary. On the other side of Charlotte, Lizzy's shiny black hair merely made hers seem more dazzling, like gold on velvet.

Charlotte shot him a quick glance, then turned to Meredith and asked how she liked teaching school—a subject Lee's wife relished and could expound upon for hours.

Atlas experienced a twinge of disappointment, but quickly squelched it by reminding himself that his energies should be spent on the imminently more suitable Blakely sisters. And why in hell didn't the woman cover her hair with a hat, like the other women, instead of merely catching it up with a saucy navy bow—a bow that lifted the tresses off the palest, creamiest neck?

Realizing he was just standing there, surrounded by his entire gawking family, he started to take his seat again, then noticed that Opal's hand was tucked within his. He looked down at her ponytail of springy curls and smiled. She sure was a cute little thing.

He took her plate from her and helped her sit beside him before placing her lunch in her lap. Then, while he cut Opal's meat for her, he noticed the others had resumed chatting with one another. Finally he and his so-called labor were no longer the center of attention. At least, not for the moment.

## ∽ 6 ∾

"Are you married?"

Opal's question shouldn't have come as a shock—since she'd sat down beside Atlas, she'd spent more time talking than eating. Not only had she told him of her every accomplishment, from being able to tie her shoelaces to driving their wagon team, but she'd also asked him questions only a four-year-old could, like *Where do clouds come from?* and *How come birds can fly, and we can't?*

"No, I'm not married," he answered, catching his grandmother watching. Sitting between Lee and Jake a few feet away, Minerva had most likely been listening to Opal's every question. *And* his every answer.

Opal was obviously pleased that he didn't have a wife. She set her plate aside and with that dimpled smile she tipped her freckled nose up at him. "Well, then, do you have a sweetheart?"

She was becoming as cheeky as Grams. Was the child matchmaking for her mother, too? Grams, of course, sat there smiling like a cat at milking time.

"*Opal*," Charlotte rebuked from across the circle. "It's not polite to ask personal questions."

"But I had to know before I ask him to be my partner at the dance tonight." If anything, Opal's reply sounded a bit impatient.

A small frown creased Charlotte's brow above her own pert nose, and Atlas thought she would reprimand the child. But instead she shifted her gaze to him, and her expression softened. "Please forgive her manners, she's—"

"Oh, pshaw," Minerva said as she glanced from Charlotte to Atlas, pinning him with a nudging stare and lift of a graying eyebrow.

*Very well, Grams*, he agreed silently. But if he spent the evening with Charlotte and her daughter, he was determined that it would count as the first social function. He looked down at little Opal and picked up her hand. "Miss Opal, I'd be honored to escort you to the dance tonight."

Before he could read Charlotte's reaction, Opal flung herself into his lap and wrapped her arms around his neck, her animated face mere inches from his own. "You won't be sorry. I can do 'Put Your Little Foot' better than anyone."

He couldn't help chuckling at this soft little ball of lightning. "I'm sure you can. Maybe you can teach me this evening."

"Oh, yes. It's real easy." She turned around, snuggled down on his lap, and looked across at Persy's Diana and Lee's oldest kids. "Do you have a dance partner yet?"

Jupiter, at six, screwed up his face. "Not me!"

But Cynthia and Diana both had their anticipatory every-male-within-miles-better-watch-out look, and started whispering to each other and giggling.

"I heard you have a bandwagon, Miss Charlotte,"

Buck said, sitting next to Atlas. "Whereabouts have you traveled? I'm sure your adventures would make for interesting stories."

She lifted her mesmerizing gaze to the blind yet capable-looking novelist as all other conversation ceased. Her expression looked guarded. Then she broke into one of those wide smiles that made Atlas's pulse quicken. "I'm not the story. The people I meet—they're the story. Every day I hear their dreams, their successes, and, I'm afraid, their sorrows. The funny things—those are my favorite."

"I know exactly what you mean," Buck said. "Venus and I are also privileged. Because of my profession and Grandmother Daltry's generous gift, we're able to travel around the globe, meeting people, sharing their lives in a small way, too. Where have you traveled? Grandmother Daltry said you've only been coming through here this past year."

Yes, Atlas thought, just where did she come from, or, more likely, *run from*? He tried to keep his expression impassive as he waited for her answer.

"Mostly Texas." Her gaze faltered but quickly steadied. "But with the railroad so handy now, I've been thinking maybe I'll put my wagon on a flat car, and Opal and I will ride on out to California. See for ourselves what all the talk is about."

"You wouldn't just take off like that," Jane said in a worried tone. "All alone? Not knowing anyone?"

"We didn't know anyone when we came to this area, and now we have scores of wonderful friends. I've discovered there are good people everywhere."

"A girl after my own heart," Buck said. He wrapped an

arm around Venus. "My wife and I couldn't be happier. Could we, sweetheart?" He smiled in her direction and gave her shoulder a squeeze.

Venus placed her pale, slender hand over his much larger, browner one, then turned to Charlotte. "Actually, my Sanford's more of an adventure than anyone else I've ever met." Venus was the only one who called Buck by his given name.

Chuckling, Buck nuzzled her neck.

Atlas's eyes gravitated toward Charlotte's own kiss-able neck. Catching himself, he swiftly lifted his gaze and found her staring back at him.

Her eyes actually seemed to be begging him to do the same to her. Slowly she rose to her feet, her gaze never wavering. A smile tipped the corners of her lips. As she moved toward him, her striped skirt swayed with the motion of her tantalizing hips.

His heart lurched, then crashed around in his chest like a mad bull. His mouth went dry, and his trousers suddenly became too tight.

She knelt down before him.

One of the men cleared his throat.

*My God, the whole family was watching . . . and the woman didn't care.*

She reached out to him, then whispered, "I'll take her back to the wagon now."

*Her*? Atlas looked down.

Cute little Opal was curled up in his lap, sound asleep.

"Come over here, Bub, and sit with us," his father called.

Atlas had been so preoccupied, watching Charlotte

stroll away with her daughter cuddled in her arms, that he hadn't noticed the men had moved from the spread of food while the women cleaned up. Odie lounged against the dark bark of an elm, ankles crossed, rolling a cigarette.

Rising to his feet, Atlas pulled out his notebook. Finally he'd have his chance to propose his meatpacking plant to the others. Surely they wouldn't be as short-sighted as his father.

"What's this Hal's saying about you calling a ranchers' meeting?" Odie asked, his heavy features hardening along with his sharp blue eyes. "You're not trying to go over my head about that slaughterhouse you want to build, are you?"

"Slaughterhouse? What slaughterhouse?" C.J. sat up from where he'd stretched out on the grass.

Atlas refused to be intimidated as he surveyed the men. Jake, a fat cigar in his mouth, was a gambler—he'd probably side with Atlas when he learned the facts. Hal, C.J., and Buck could go either way, but Lee and Pa were like two peas in a pod. They'd be the tough ones. "I didn't call the meeting about the meatpacking plant. But that's not to say I don't think we should diversify. Marketing the meat is where the money is." He flipped open his notebook. "I have some figures to prove it right here."

"Forget that for now," C.J. said. Sitting Indian-style next to Jake, he leaned forward. "You've sure got a lot of nerve, Bub, lolling away at school for three years, then showing up one week and trying to run our business the next."

"Why don't we give the lad a chance to tell his side of

it before we hang him?" Buck said, then took a long, lazy drag of his aromatic pipe.

Except for calling him "lad," Atlas appreciated his brother-in-law's calm reasoning. Atlas sat down next to him. "The cattle buyer for Montereau's Meatpacking House offered Collins a half cent less than last year. Not more, less."

C.J. stiffened. "That's crazy. There's a vast shortage."

"Oh, but our friends in New Orleans are *sweetening* the pot. They've offered to loan Collins money on next year's herd. And it doesn't take a genius to figure out what Montereau will want for collateral—a mortgage on his ranch. The bloodsucker."

Lee turned to Odie. "Did you know about this?"

"No." He looked as concerned as Lee. "Did he take the deal?"

"Not yet." Atlas gained confidence, knowing he'd now gotten their full attention. "And before Collins has a chance to, it's important to remind everyone the slaughterhouses need us as much as we need them. This year, with so little available beef, a lot of meat packers will be forced to lay off workers. But on the plus side, the shortage will drive up the prices to the customers back East. If we stick together, force them to bid for our beef, we can get our fair share of those profits."

"What do you mean," Lee asked, "make the meat packers bid for our beef?"

"Yeah, what do you mean?" C.J. echoed.

For once they looked at him as if he were something more than the baby brother, and it felt damn good. He sat up straighter. "If all the ranchers in this part of Texas will sign an agreement to sell as a block, we can contact the various packing houses and get them to submit bids. If they're so afraid of having to shut down for lack of cattle, they'll be more than agreeable. And generous."

"Are you sure?" Odie asked, his worried expression adding age to his face.

"My marketing professor was having dinner with a couple of them last month. He mentioned that they were worried about keeping their doors open. But if they thought they could get a lion's share, have the best year ever, trust me, they'll be chomping at the bit."

"The boy's right," Jake said. "I've been in enough New York smokers to know which way they'll jump. If there's enough at stake, they'd cut their own mothers' throats. And it sounds to me like there is."

"Sounds reasonable," Lee said. "What do you think, Pa?"

A slow grin spilled across his father's burly face. "It'll work *if* we stick together." He turned to Atlas and nodded. "I'm real proud of you, son, real proud. And, Jake, would you consider being our representative, since you're used to dealing in those circles?"

"Sure. I could start on it right away. That is, if you can give me a rough figure on the number of cattle you're talking about."

Atlas wanted to protest. *He* had the knowledge. *He'd* followed the market, knew shipping prices—prices that weren't nearly as set as folks might believe. But he had no doubt the other ranchers would trust Jake, the older, experienced man, over him, unless he could somehow convince them of his own expertise.

"You know, Pa, we can't let Bub propose this plan," C.J. said, adding insult to injury. "You or Lee will have to do it. The ranchers aren't going to listen to some college kid who's still wet behind the ears."

*"Wet behind the ears?"* That was the last straw. Atlas sprang to his feet, fists clenched and ready. "Stand up, Cupid! We'll just find out who's wet behind the ears."

"Cool down, son." Odie lumbered up from the ground. "No one's trying to get your dander up. I'm sorry, but that's just the way it is. You gotta get a few more years under your belt." Odie squeezed his shoulder and stared at him until he uncoiled. "Now if you'll write it all down for me, I'll do my best to get it right."

"Me, too," Jake added. "I'll need all your facts and figures about shipping costs and beef prices."

*Nothing ever changed.* Atlas whipped out his pencil. He opened the notepad to an empty page and strode away. Facts and figures. *That* they would trust him with.

"Hey, Bub," Hal called after him. "What was that about some slaughterhouse you wanted to build?"

Atlas shot him the barest glance without stopping. "Some other time. Maybe."

Two hours later, Atlas sat at the far end of town on the sheriff's porch, lacing up his lightweight running shoes, his thoughts a jumble. How would he ever concentrate on the race? He bounced from belittling himself for falling under the woman's spell every time she looked at him to berating himself for not standing up to his family when they were bent on passing him over again. He'd come home, hoping they'd see his hard-gained strengths, but all they saw was "Bub." And worse, all he could see were the sultry green eyes of a gaudy gypsy.

"Got yourself some fancy shoes there, Bub," called

Billy Gains from Box G. "They ain't gonna do you no good."

Atlas was in no mood for bantering. Propping a smile into place, he noticed Jody Spears hadn't shown up to race. Probably didn't want to lose in front of Beth Blakely.

A couple of other ranchers' sons Atlas had gone to school with had shown up, though, along with four cowpokes who had drifted in while he was away at college. They all prepared for the race with muscle-stretching squats and lunges. Clustered around them, their friends and sweethearts gave them support and advice.

It didn't bother Atlas that none of his family had walked down to the starting post to encourage him. They were always confident he would win. . . . Facts, figures, and racing, that's all they thought he was good for. They'd all be at the finish line, taking bets, giving odds.

He refused to wonder where Charlotte was. Refused.

While tying the laces of a soft kid shoes, a flash of red and white stripes caught his eye. He jerked his head up.

It wasn't Charlotte, but little Opal, running pell-mell with Lee's Cynthia and Persy's Diana close behind. Opal slammed into his leg to stop herself, gasping for breath. "I was . . . afraid you'd . . . start without me," she gushed as she sagged into him.

Giving her ponytail a gentle tug, he couldn't help grinning. "I wouldn't let them start the race without my dance partner here to root me on."

"Oh, look." Opal's eyes lit up as she pointed to a young gal.

One of the runners' sweethearts tied a ribbon around

her beau's arm, then gave him a good luck kiss on the cheek.

Opal ripped her own navy bow from her ponytail. Ignoring the toppling of her long curls, she wrapped the strand around Atlas's white shirtsleeve and very painstakingly fashioned a not-quite-so-perfect bow.

But he didn't care. The imp was priceless, especially with his sagging spirits so in need of a lift.

She leaned close and smacked his cheek with her moist, puckered lips.

"Well," he said, rising to his feet. "The ribbon and most definitely your kiss will sprout wings on my feet, even if my name isn't Mercury."

"Wings? I don't see no wings."

"Tell you what." He picked up the street shoes he'd just removed and handed them to her. "You and your buddies take these down to the finish line and watch. By the time I get there, I'll be in full flight."

After his two nieces crowded close with outstretched arms for their own chance to kiss him, he sent the threesome running toward the church at the end of the road. On the way, Cynthia and Diana tried to pull the shoes from Opal, but she clutched them to herself all the more tightly. Obviously certain rights came with being a dance partner.

Stretching out his leg muscles, Atlas continued to watch until they reached the finish line . . . Lee's and Persy's little darlings, and the bouncy strawberry blond. For the first time in his life, he wondered what it would be like to have a daughter of his own—one as precocious and lovable as Opal. Too bad she was relegated to such a precarious life . . . traveling the countryside with a questionable woman, one who would most likely end up behind bars. Poor little Opal would probably spend her childhood in an orphanage. Or worse.

"On your mark!" Sheriff Sampson yelled.

Atlas shook off the morose thought and strode to the starting line along with the others.

A string bean of a fellow who toed the mark right beside him flipped Opal's dangling ribbon with his finger. "Ain't that from Charlotte Clairmore's sprout?"

Looking down at the lopsided bow, Atlas chuckled. "Yeah."

"Nothing quite like a lonely widow, now, is there?" the man said, winking, his fool mouth cocked.

Atlas tensed, ready to knock the sneer off the bastard's face.

Just as quickly, he relaxed his grip. The man probably had firsthand knowledge.

"Get set!" the sheriff shouted, his .45 raised to the sky.

Atlas crouched, rocking onto his toes.

The revolver exploded, and he sprang forward.

## ❧ 7 ❧

Face lifted, catching the wind, Atlas crossed the finish line yards ahead of the competition. As he slowed his course-eating strides to a halt, the whole county seemed to be cheering along with his family. They delighted in thumping him on the back while he struggled to regain his breath.

Hank from the mercantile wedged his bulk through the crowd and pinned a large blue silk button to Atlas's shirt. "Congratulations, Bub. *Again.*"

Several streamers hung from the prize, and at its center, FIRST PLACE was boldly printed in red-trimmed white.

Allie stepped close and flipped it, then leveled a snubbing glance Hank's way. "Maybe if women were allowed to race, too, Bub wouldn't be winning *again.*"

"Hal," Hank said, eyeing Allie's husband, who had walked up behind and was looking over her head. "Don't you think it's time you got this female in the family way? She needs to understand what she's supposed to be about."

"*About*?" Allie's face reddened, and Atlas caught sight of a balled fist cocking to strike.

Laughing, Hal snagged her to him and hauled her away before she could do any damage.

Atlas felt a tug on his pant leg. He looked down to a tiny freckled nose upturned between two sparkling pools of emerald.

"You won," Opal cried in that high-pitched thin voice, a voice as fragile as she looked amid the forest of legs and tromping boots of folks walking by to the next event.

Atlas swept her up, along with the shoes she clutched to her chest. "I told you my feet had wings."

She grinned, her entire mouthful of baby teeth gleaming. "The road was dusty, but I saw them. I did." A not-so-clean hand smoothed across his silky prize. "That's purty."

"It's yours." Shifting her to the crook of his left arm, he unpinned the blue ribbon and attached it to the shoulder of her dress.

"For me?" She looked from it to him with worshipful eyes.

"Absolutely. It's fair exchange for the lucky ribbon you gave me."

She glanced from winner's blue to the navy one she'd tied around his shirtsleeve. "For keeps?"

"Forever and ever." He couldn't resist giving her a squeeze before he put her down so he could change into his regular shoes.

C.J., with Thalia, his three-year-old, perched on his shoulders, stepped up as Atlas finished. "Bronc riding is next, and Hal drew the first mustang."

"Be right with you." Atlas shoved the soft racing shoes into his back pockets, then tossed Opal onto his own shoulders, her full striped skirt around his neck looking like a patriotic bunting. He then followed behind C.J., whose own little doll had hair as blond as her daddy's.

Heading for the Horse Hotel, Atlas felt an occasional slap on the back, along with hearty congratulations from well-wishers who also hurried to the livery's big corral.

Opal weaved back and forth, blinding him with her skirts more often than not. "See my blue ribbon?" she called out to each person by name. "Atlas won it for me."

From their beaming expressions and remarks, it was obvious that folks around Paradise Plains were as taken with Opal as Atlas was.

Rounding the corner of the livery, she bounced up and down on his neck. "Big Whitey! Goliath! Look at my ribbon!"

Atlas tightened his grip on her legs as Opal leaned precariously toward the paddock they now passed.

Her two huge white draft horses stood within, their necks craning over the fence. Low whinnies rumbled from their rubbery lips. Obviously, the animals were as enthralled with her as everyone else . . . these animals that pulled her mother's wagon.

But where was the woman? Where was Charlotte?

Reaching the corral in which the bronc riding would take place, Atlas scanned the spectators for her bold red and white dress. Not spotting it, the remark of his fellow racer came back to harry him. *Nothing quite like a lonely widow, now, is there*?

"C.J.! Atlas! Over here!" Allie beckoned them from her perch on the top fence rail. She waited near the livestock chute on the far side.

"Giddyap!" Thalia squealed, leaning forward on her

father's shoulders, her blond banana curls bouncing like worn-out wagon springs.

"Yeah, giddyap, horsey." Opal rammed her heels into Atlas's chest.

Obliging the imp, he broke into an exaggerated gallop and sped past C.J. and Thalia.

Opal's shrieking laughter was ample proof the rough ride thrilled her, as she grabbed a fistful of his hair and hung on.

Reaching Allie, he unseated Opal and plopped her on the railing beside his sister, then stood directly behind in case a wild horse stampeded too close. C.J. did the same with Thalia.

A couple of cowboys leaned over either side of the chute, their lassos around a rough-coated dun's neck. They hauled the walleyed, snorting, kicking mustang into the narrow space. Another worker closed the gate behind the angry animal, trapping him.

Atlas reached up and tousled Allie's hair. "Looks like Hal's drawn himself a *real friendly* one."

She slapped his hand away. "That's Dust Devil. Sometimes he spins worse than a dog chasing its tail. Tries to bite a chunk out of your leg."

Hal climbed the chute's railing and attempted to ease himself into the ever-moving saddle.

"Good luck, sweetheart," Allie yelled. "Stick like a burr."

The brave smile Hal returned didn't match his worried expression as he rammed his boots into the stirrups of the bucking animal and wrapped the reins around his hand. He nodded to the wrangler waiting to open the gate into the corral.

The gate swung back with a bang and out they spilled, man and lunging, humping, twirling horse. Hal's butt hit the saddle no more than half a dozen times before he went sailing off the back of one of the wildest broncs Atlas had ever seen. He hit the dirt. Hard.

Atlas shook his head. Dust Devil was too mild a name for that thrashing machine.

The spectators who had gasped only a second ago now laughed when Hal scrambled to his feet, cussing and dusting off his pants, while the dun trotted away in victory.

A high-pitched laugh rose above the roar of the crowd.

Atlas wheeled toward the sound.

Charlotte!

From across the enclosure, she waved at Hal and flashed a smile so brilliant it outshined her hair.

Opal saw her, too. "Mama!" she cried, waving her arms back and forth over her head.

Charlotte's expression softened, and she blew the child a kiss. Then, spotting Atlas, her smile faded, leaving her lips parted, her gaze puzzled . . . or was it disturbed? Before he could decide, she turned her attention to Persy, who stood beside her.

The chute gate banged open again, and another ferociously bucking horse charged forth with its clinging rider. The cowboy held one hand valiantly aloft, while the crowd cheered him on.

"Who's that?" Atlas asked C.J.

"One of the hands from the Walker place."

But before C.J. had finished answering, Atlas had already lost interest. He again shifted his attention to Charlotte. How could he not? The bold red in her dress couldn't have attracted him more if he'd been a bull. The thought caused an abrupt crowding in his pants.

Although separated by a large stock pen, Charlotte met his gaze with crashing force.

And he couldn't tear his own away.

Neither did she.

The distance between them seemed to shrink. His mouth felt dry. He licked his lips.

The discharge of a gun announced the end of the eight-second riding time.

"Ouch!" C.J. yelped in empathy. "Great ride, but a gnarly dismount. I doubt if anyone will beat him."

"Probably not," Atlas answered, reluctantly dragging his attention from Charlotte.

"Me, neither," piped Opal, as if she could actually judge the man's performance.

"Me, neither," Thalia mimicked, and the two little ones looked at each other atop the railing and giggled.

Atlas waited impatiently for everyone's attention to focus on the next bronc rider. He wanted to study that sexy female some more. And, who knew, maybe his grandmother was right. Maybe Charlotte didn't look at anyone else the way she did him.

At the thought, he felt himself grin from the inside out.

But even if she did, why not just relax and enjoy what came his way? It wasn't every grandmother who would allow, let alone insist, her grandson socialize with a medicine-show hawker who most likely specialized in night work. For starters, he'd hold her in his arms tonight, whirl her around the dance floor. Then, who knew?

He could almost feel his hand at Charlotte's tiny waist,

feel the rhythm of a passionate waltz reverberate through her as he swung her into a dizzying whirl. Feel her breath on his cheek, see her lush breasts rapidly rising and falling as they pressed against her deeply scooped neckline. Could see perspiration trickling into the dark, warm valley between them. Smell her store-bought cologne as it mingled with her own musky scent . . . a scent that begged to be explored much more closely.

Not caring if anyone noticed, Atlas trained his eyes on Charlotte—and found her conversing with a man. Ed Harper, one of the many nesters who'd swarmed in to homestead on the open range since the railroad came through.

Harper leaned close, the expression on his lean face intent, seeking.

*Charlotte did not step back.*

Harper, a man with a wife and at least three children, took her hand and led her away into the crowd.

She gave no sign of resistance, nor did she so much as glance back at Atlas or her daughter as she disappeared with the heel.

Atlas gripped the railing on either side of Opal, as anger spiked its way through his veins. The woman would even go with a married man. She was the commonest kind of whore.

"Watch out!" C.J. yelled, ripping Thalia off the top railing.

A walleyed, flat-eared mustang charged straight for them.

Opal shrieked, and Atlas snagged her around the waist, hauling her to him. The tiny thing buried her face against his shirt and clung to him for dear life as the bronc spun at the last second, grazing the rider's leg against the fence.

Atlas wrapped his arms around her. "It's all right— you're safe."

For the moment.

But with a mother like hers, for how much longer? He hugged the sweet little thing closer. Poor little Opal.


For the rest of the afternoon, Atlas doggedly devoted himself to the child, buying her treats, entering the few father/daughter contests available. The last thing he wanted was for her to return to her wagon and find that mother of hers *entertaining* some man. And Atlas had no doubt Charlotte's favors were now being enjoyed by others, since he'd seen Ed Harper walking arm in arm with his wife not more than an hour after he'd slunk off with Charlotte. Yet the tart had never reappeared.

As the afternoon faded to evening and Charlotte still hadn't shown her face, Atlas had no trouble at all envisioning her lying with one man after another, particularly that smart-mouth from the footrace. Atlas could just imagine the upstart's bony arms and legs wrapped all around her, kissing those full lips, that creamy throat. . . .

He would've given anything to erase the very existence of her from his mind, but every time he saw one of those patriotic top hats or parasols, they reminded him of what else she had for sale.

With Opal in hand, Atlas stalked back to his family's staked-out spot under the elms as the sun dipped behind the church steeple.

The women were bustling about, filling their children's plates with leftovers for a quick supper before the fireworks began. They chatted happily as if nothing were amiss—and his grandmother smiled more sweetly than clover honey when she spotted Opal with him. How could they possibly not have noticed that Charlotte had been conspicuously absent for a good four hours? Especially Grams, who for some strange reason had also kept her distance all afternoon.

Well, before this night was over, he'd set her straight about the type of woman Charlotte Clairmore was.

As he stepped into the family circle, his grandmother wagged her finger at him as if *he* were the wrongdoer, the floozy. "I do hope you haven't bought Opal so many treats she'll get a tummyache." Dipping the end of a towel in a water bucket, she then stooped down before the child and started washing the sticky spots from her face and hands.

Opal scrunched her freckled nose and tried to dodge the damp cloth. "Swarter tarfy won't make me sick. It's too good. Huh, Atlas?"

"Saltwater taffy," he corrected, while staring holes into his grandmother. He had some choice remarks on the tip of his tongue, but couldn't say them in front of the poor child.

Blithely ignoring him, Minerva swiped at Opal's dress front. "If I'm not mistaken, these are watermelon stains. And didn't I see you and Atlas eating ice cream, too?"

"But I didn't get any on my blue ribbon." She jutted out her spindly shoulder. "See? And that was a long time ago. Your potato salad sure looks good."

Minerva chuckled and gave her a swat. "Then you and Atlas better sit on down and fill yourselves a plate."

"After that," Atlas said to his grandmother with pointed clarity, "you and I will be having a serious talk."

She glanced away, but for just an instant before propping up a buoyant smile. "Oh, pshaw, this isn't a day for *serious* talk."

"Yeah," Atlas's father said. Leaning on an elbow, he lounged on the grass with a plate of food in front of him. "I just got back from that confab you harnessed me into. I've had enough serious talk to last me a week."

Lee, sitting beside him, grunted in agreement as he bit off a chunk of chicken leg.

Atlas couldn't believe he'd totally forgotten about the ranchers' meeting. "How'd it go?"

"I think it's going to work out just fine," Jake said, joining the conversation. He and Persy sat placidly with their toddler, Apollo, tucked safely between them, seemingly oblivious to the fact that another small child had been abandoned by her mother. "The men have formed a committee, and we're going to meet again tomorrow to iron out the details. It may very well save some of the smaller ranchers their spreads."

"Thanks to Atlas." Hal winked at him—giving him his due recognition, which Atlas appreciated, considering everything else.

"I don't want to hear another word about business today," Jane said as she settled down beside Odie. Still looking quite fresh and cool in her white lawn frock, she surveyed this rare gathering of her offspring. "Everyone eat up. Your father has ordered some absolutely spectacular fireworks for tonight, and it's almost dark."

Opal squealed along with the other children as if she were part of the family, then started dragging Atlas toward the food . . . while Minerva said she had to go see about something and conveniently scurried away. Any excuse to avoid facing her grievous error *or* Atlas's wrath.

The evening had long since darkened to a balmy night, and Charlotte still hadn't returned for her daughter. Atlas's anger was tempered only by the fact that Opal never once asked for her mother. The little one sat between his legs in the open field behind the Buc, watching the colorful explosions lighting the sky above. And though awed by the sight, she never ceased talking about the upcoming dance—her excitement over having her very own date had never abated. The little sweetheart also continued to hold onto his knee, making certain as she'd done all day that he didn't get away from her.

As the last spectacular spray of brilliant color faded in the starry sky, Atlas rose and pulled Opal to her feet. Again he searched the many faces for Charlotte. Fruitlessly. His gaze then settled on his mother and grandmother as they ambled toward him.

"Darling," Mama said, "it's been a long day for us old folks. We're not staying for the dance."

*"You're going, too, Grandmother?"* Atlas wanted to shock that smug smile off her cherubic face.

"Yes, dear. I'm really exhausted." She heaved an exaggerated sigh.

"But what about—" Atlas bit off his words before bellowing out his thoughts on Charlotte's shame in front of Opal.

"Why, sweetheart, there's not a thing in the world to

worry about. Everything's coming along quite nicely. Quite nicely." Turning, she strolled away with Jane.

Was that old gal truly that featherbrained? That blind? If Opal hadn't been there, looking up at him with those big, innocent eyes, he would've caught up with Minerva and made her eat her words. Sometimes he wondered if there was anything at all rattling around in her head.

Adding insult to injury, his grandmother paused a few yards away and looked over her shoulder. "Opal, dear," she called. "Do take good care of our Atlas."

The tot giggled and shouted back in her shrill voice, "I will, Mrs. Daltry. I will." She started forward, tugging on Atlas's hand. "Come on, or the band'll start before we get there."

Atlas released a long, resigned sigh and let her drag him toward the restaurant.

Overflowing with young people, the Buc's floor had been cleared of tables. Chairs lined the bare-board walls, except for one end where the band was busy tuning their instruments. Every window and door stood wide open to catch the breeze, and out of them spewed enough noise to rival any Abilene dance hall on a Saturday night.

And, as he'd expected, Charlotte was nowhere to be seen.

But Beth Blakely was, along with another lovely belle who closely resembled her. They stood in a corner with a bouquet of other tittering young misses, anticipating the start of the music.

Not more than twenty feet away, a cluster of eager bachelors also waited as they slicked back their hair and elbowed each other in the ribs. Atlas knew that was where he, too, should be, instead of minding an abandoned four-year-old.

"Atlas," Opal cried, drawing his attention down to her bubbly gaze. "Can we go up and ask the band to start with 'Put Your Little Foot'? Huh? Can we?"

Atlas relaxed muscles he hadn't realized were strung as tight as Abe Caulder's violin bow. "Sure, sweetie. Let's go talk to them."

"Pickin' 'em kinda young, ain't you, Bub?" Jody Spears hooted from the rowdy knot of bachelors.

Atlas slowed. He'd have no problem at all plowing into someone about now, even a beanpole like Jody.

Opal grabbed onto his clenched fist with both hands. "Don't pay that Jody Spears no mind." She turned menacing eyes on the rancher's son and hiked her snub nose into the air. "We're real sorry to hear about that mule what kicked you senseless, Jody."

Atlas cracked into laughter at the snippet's audacity, and so did everyone else within hearing range. And before Opal dragged him toward the band platform again, he was rewarded with a quick glimpse of Jody's face going beet-red.

Abe Caulder was more than glad for the four-member band to play Opal's request. The song was always a good starter, not requiring the formation of squares. As soon as he announced the selection, folks poured onto the floor to form a giant circle of pairs. Atlas noticed that Lee's four-year-old, Cynthia, had commandeered her father while Persy's Diana managed to snag her cousin Jupiter.

"*Atlas*." Sounding rather impatient, Opal stood with her back to him, holding out her arms. "Take my hands before the music starts, then follow me. It's real easy. You'll catch on in no time."

Taking her wee fingers into his, he did his darnedest not to let her catch him grinning as the opening strains of the bouncy tune began. She was trying so desperately to act grown up.

"Now!" she cried and stepped forth, singing the simple words with the rest of the dancers. "Put your little foot, put your little foot, put your little foot right here."

Atlas pretended to lose his step a couple of times. He didn't want to let on he'd known the dance for as long as he could remember.

By the end of the first hour, Opal was yawning almost nonstop. It had been a very big day for the precocious tyke, and if she'd had a decent mother, the woman would've been here by now to see her safely tucked into bed.

Picking her up, he headed for the door, his earlier rage settling into cold, hard determination. He'd take Opal back to the carnival wagon, and if the woman was still inside *entertaining*, he'd report her to the sheriff and take Opal home with him.

Opal's warm head nestled beneath his chin as he walked out and crossed the veranda. Halfway down the steps, he heard his name being called from behind. He swung around. "Yes?"

One of the older Tittle girls, a Nordic-looking blond, pushed past a couple and stopped at the edge of the steps. "Where are you taking Opal?" Inga demanded, as if he were the culprit.

That was the last straw. "To find her mother," he grated. "If that's possible."

"You needn't bother." She held out her long, thin arms. "I'll take her. I'm supposed to be keeping an eye on her for Charlotte."

"Hi, Inga," Opal slurred sleepily and spilled into the girl's arms, snuggling close.

"*You were supposed to be watching her?*" Atlas felt like throttling the irresponsible girl right along with the wanton.

Inga stiffened her narrow shoulders. "And I have been. I may've been dancing and . . . and other things, but Opal hasn't been out of my sight all evening."

"And just where is her mother?"

"I don't know off hand, but I was told to take Opal back to the medicine wagon when she got tired."

"You do that, girl. And don't leave her there alone if her mother's still missing." He shot her his sternest look, while pulling a half-dollar from his pocket. He placed it in her hand. "You got that?"

Eyeing her windfall, Inga's thin lips split into a wide smile. "Yes, sir!"

Atlas wasn't totally satisfied. But it really wasn't his business. He leaned down and, brushing Opal's bangs aside, kissed her forehead above her closed eyes. "Good night, pumpkin."

He waited until the Tittle girl had disappeared with Opal into the darkness, then glanced back at the Buc. He knew he should return inside and join the other young people, check out the Blakely sisters. But he was drained from wanting to throttle Opal's mother. He wouldn't be fit company.

A cool night breeze flapped the ends of the navy ribbon the imp had tied around his sleeve so many hours ago. He toyed with it a second; then, taking a deep breath, he started for the stable with the first words he planned to say to his grandmother already burning into his brain.

*Now, about your so-called shy Charlotte . . .*

## ∽ 8 ∾

Atlas had been staring out his bedroom window for the past few minutes, urging the sun to peek over the rolling meadows to the east. He'd done little more than catnap during the night, and knew tonight would be no better unless he got this Charlotte Clairmore business settled with Grams.

When at last the first rays trimmed the hills, he inhaled deeply of the flower-scented morn and patted the notebook in the pocket of his work shirt. Grams always bragged about rising with the dawn, so there was no need to wait any longer. He wheeled from the window and strode across the Oriental rug.

The hair ribbon he'd tied to the bedpost last night caught his eyes. Opal's. He stopped and let a satin strand slide across his fingers. Poor little Opal.

No. He couldn't weaken. No matter how enchanting the child was, she was not his concern. *And he was going to make certain Grams understood that once and for all.*

When he stepped into the hall he heard no stirrings in the house. Undeterred, he walked to the room next to his and rapped lightly on the door.

He had to knock twice before he heard a groggy, "Who's there?"

"Atlas. May I come in."

"I suppose." Her answer didn't sound all that certain.

*Good*. He walked in and right up to her lace-canopied bed.

Minerva propped herself up on pillows trimmed with eyelet ruffles and violet ribbons. Settling back, she tucked a coverlet of appliqued irises around her pink satin and lace nightgown—the woman actually slept in a room as frilly as one of her hats.

"Dressed already," she mused, while smoothing her hands over her hair. "My, aren't you the early bird this morning."

"I wanted to speak to you privately. About my labor."

Minerva rolled her eyes . . . as if he were merely some bothersome squirt.

So be it. He pulled out his notebook and flipped it open. "I have made a list of my observations, *these facts*, and when I'm through reading them, you'll see the folly of my pursuing any sort of association with this—the woman in question."

She raised a brow but remained silent as she waved her hand for him to continue.

He cleared his throat. "Number one. Charlotte Clairmore dresses like a loose woman. Two. She is loud, and her laughter is most unladylike. Three. The first time I saw her, she disappeared into a darkened boxcar with a brakeman. *Laughing uproariously*," he ad-libbed. "Four. A man I raced yesterday made an insinuating remark about her. And I do believe you'll find five quite enlightening. She left the bronc-riding contest in the company of a married nester who shall remain nameless, *and never returned*. And, last but far from least, she cares so little about her daughter that she abandoned her all afternoon to consort with this married man and most probably several others." Flipping his notepad closed, he looked up, wholly expecting to see his grandmother's shocked expression.

Yet she appeared totally calm. "Is that everything? You've left nothing out?"

"Isn't that enough for you?"

"Come sit down." She patted the spot next to her until he complied. "Yes, I would say that was a very damning list. You should've taken up the law. Except, my dear, it's not accurate. That nameless nester you spoke of was Ed Harper. *I* sent him to find Charlotte. His and Lucy's baby had become real croupy. And, you see, those powders Charlotte sells have menthol in them. Inhaled with steam, they work wonders on the croup. And, as for Charlotte being gone all afternoon, she volunteered to turn her wagon into a steam room—and on such a hot day, too—till little Arty was breathing better."

Charlotte *hadn't* gone for a roll in the hay with Harper? An odd feeling of relief stole through Atlas. Yet one kind deed didn't erase everything else. "That accounts for a couple of hours. But the woman never returned the rest of the day, not even to check on her daughter."

"Sweetheart, when baby Arty fell asleep on her bunk, Charlotte didn't have the heart to move him. She told Lucy and me to pass the word that she'd keep an eye on any other little sleepyheads. The woman is a saint, Atlas.

She spent the rest of the Fourth of July tending the babies so everyone else could have a good time."

"I wouldn't bestow sainthood on her just yet. As I read to you from my list, she never once checked on her own daughter. I didn't even know someone was keeping track of Opal until I was setting out to take her in search of her mother."

Minerva's grin was just short of cherubic. "I'm afraid that's my doing, dear. I reported back to Charlotte from time to time, and, well, seeing the bosom buddies you and Opal had become, I sincerely thought the child was doing just fine in your care. Just fine."

Atlas lunged off the bed. "So, it was your doing all along. You pulling the strings, and me, just another one of your puppets."

For once she wore an appropriate expression—one of dismay. "I truly thought you were enjoying Opal."

"That isn't the point. You saw to it that I had no choice."

"But surely you can see the benefit of winning the child's affection in fulfilling your labor."

"Yes, the labor. Let's get back to that." He faced her squarely. "Mrs. Clairmore may not have been with a man last night, but what about at the train station? Her laughter left no room for doubt that day."

The infernal woman smiled again. "No, there's absolutely no doubt that those red-and-white-striped top hats are laughable. Absolutely. I laughed every time I saw one of the grandchildren strutting around in them yesterday."

"Hats! We're not talking hats."

"Yes, we are. Charlotte always has Clem Tucker and all the other railroad men along the Texas and Pacific on the lookout for amusing items to entertain us with. I happen to think Tucker outdid himself this time. And judging from Charlotte's hoots, she must've thought so, too."

Grandmother was knocking more holes into his arguments than buckshot through a paper target. But he still wasn't convinced. "What about that fellow's remark just before the race?"

Stiffening, Minerva looked as protective as a mama bear. "And what exactly was that, dear?"

"It's not *what* he said, but *how* he said it."

"Yes?"

"He said there was nothing quite like a lonely widow."

"That's it?" Minerva burst out laughing. "Don't you know she's every young cowpoke's dream—a pretty young widow who might be generous with her charms? He was just snorting wind and hoping. Anyone who knows Charlotte knows how skittish she is when it comes to men. Why do you think I gave you this labor? Either her husband—God rest his soul—was so wonderful that she hasn't met anyone to compare, or he treated her so badly she's afraid to take another chance. I'm inclined to believe it's the latter, but since she's never talked about her dear departed, I can't be certain. And, of course, I wouldn't dream of prying."

"*Heaven forbid,*" he sniped. "Well, one thing's sure— you've managed to make her sound pure as springwater and timid as a morning glory on a cloudy day."

"Hand me my robe off the foot of the bed." When he did, she angrily thrust her arms into the sleeves. "I realize you think I'm trying to match you with Charlotte. But, truly, Atlas, I know you are fully capable of organizing every detail, every nuance of your life. And, fine, you do that. I find your stuffy attitude toward Charlotte most uncharitable, however. The least you could do is spare a wee bit of time to give this fine lady a hand when she can't seem to take that first step for herself."

"Oh, really, Grams? The woman lives out of a medicine-show wagon. Wears outrageous clothes . . . and that *laugh* . . ."

Glowering up at him, Minerva threw back her covers and stepped out of bed. "You mean because it's not some practiced little titter behind a lacy fan? It's an honest laugh. Free. Spirited. Not caged and muffled like a bird in a bustle." Her eyes narrowed. "The labor stands, young man. And, if you continue with this snobbish behavior, you'll fail."

Atlas snorted and turned for the door. Grams was impossible.

"*Atlas.*" Her voice, lowered commandingly, halted his departure. "I suggest you remember that I have a coveted prize awaiting you."

"Then perhaps my failure would be for the best. You are entirely too free with your money."

Her plump cheeks flamed red. "Young man, what I choose to do with my money is my business. *So*, I think I'll add another twist to your labor. If you fail, this most *extravagant* prize will go to Charlotte."

By the time the second Saturday rolled around again, Atlas couldn't believe the muddled mess his thoughts had become. Every discreet inquiry he'd made about Charlotte had borne out his grandmother's words. Apparently she had a prearranged safe place to park every night along her route, and she and Opal always took their meals in specific eating establishments or in the homes of friends. And, beautiful as she was, she'd never once been seen in the company of a man since the day she arrived two summers ago. In fact, she'd become a challenge to every young buck for miles around. As Minerva and Jane had both stated, folks at church were beginning to worry that one of her admirers might become too insistent, too forceful.

Above all, everyone refused to believe Charlotte had a dishonest bone in her body. Despite her flamboyance and loud voice, she was considered every inch a lady.

By rural Texas standards, that is.

But he had big-city plans for his life, and she simply would not fit in. As attracted as he was to her, he could never allow himself to succumb.

Reaching the edge of town, Atlas guided Red Jack, his sorrel, around a muddy spot in the road caused by last night's summer storm. It was barely past noon, but he might need considerable time to study the situation, come up with the right approach. He'd keep the invitation very casual. Maybe even businesslike. Ease her into accepting. Because from the way his grandmother had said coveted prize, he was sure she intended to award him the badly needed meatpacking house.

He turned onto Main Street, his gaze going instantly to the far end where the church stood flanked on either side by the library and the school . . . and in the grassy area in between, Charlotte's wagon was already parked.

Folks crowded around it. She stood above them, taking money from a customer, her uncovered hair a blazing reflection of the midday sun.

Atlas's mouth went dry. His fingers itched to bury themselves in that wild mop.

Instead, he wiped his sweaty palms on his pant legs and checked his wayward thoughts, reminding himself of his steadfast purpose. The meatpacking plant. And if she was as skittish as everyone said, he'd have to approach her slowly, carefully.

He reined his sorrel off the street and into the passage-way between the livery and the general store. He'd better watch her unnoticed for a while. He needed to absorb her every move until his heart didn't buck with each glance. He couldn't afford to lay bare his baser desires. Perhaps he'd start by giving her some business tips.

Yes, some business tips.


"Charlotte, honey, do you have an *S*?" Mrs. Spears edged closer to the bandwagon. She waved a silver dollar at Charlotte.

"Do frogs jump?" Laughing, Charlotte took the money, then began rifling through a box on the fold-up table beside her. "I ordered one 'specially for you. I know what pride you take in your home." She found a brass door knocker in the shape of Mrs. Spears's initial and handed it to the matronly ranch wife.

"Miss Charlotte!" a familiar young voice called.

She searched the crowd of upturned faces until she found its owner—one of Mr. Carpenter's passel of boys.

"My granny needs some more of your powders."

"Didn't she send you in for some last time I was through?" Charlotte questioned, reaching for a bottle from the shelf-lined door.

"Yes, ma'am." He swiped off his misshapen hat. "But

she ain't swallowin' down all that medicine. She's mixin' it in some sorta concoction to make up a plaster for her rheumatism. Says it's workin' real good, too."

"Is that right? Well, you have to get her recipe, and I'll write it on the slate." Charlotte pointed to the blackboard on the side where she let folks post their needs, whether something to buy, rent, or sell. "If her plaster works like you say, there are plenty of folks along my circuit with cranky joints and whatnot who'd be tickled pink to get some relief." Taking his two bits, she handed the boy a square, stoppered bottle of her Professor Puffinwick's Powder.

As she straightened she caught a flash of movement across the road. Her heart stopped, then started again with a hard thunk. It was that good-looking Daltry . . . the one who stole Opal's heart on the Fourth of July. He was tying his horse to the hitching rail in front of the library.

She felt a moment's disappointment that he hadn't stopped at her wagon like the rest of the folks. But, being a college graduate fresh from Chicago, he undoubtedly had other pursuits to entertain him.

He didn't go inside the library, however. He sat down on the porch steps between two Grecian pillars. She saw his head turn in her direction and instinctively knew he'd come because of her.

She quickly glanced away. If she dared look into his eyes, she knew they'd be staring back, making her forget everything else.

She began straightening the door knockers in the box, busying herself. Even if she could afford to have men in her life, she knew better than to pick one with an ambitious business mind like his. Never again would she be trapped by a man like that.

"Miss Charlotte," Maybelle from the mercantile drawled in her soft Southern voice, pulling Charlotte back to her own livelihood. "Do y'all have any more jars of that pomegranate jelly you was sellin' last month? If you do, I'll take 'em off your hands. Folks around here were mighty partial to it."

"Sorry. I've nary a one. But I've already put in double the order with Mrs. Haskell for next year. But you know what . . . ?" With a sidelong glance at Maybelle and the others gathered around, she stooped, wearing a conspiratorial grin. "I've put out the word for some pomegranate saplings. I have the railroad workers on the lookout. I'm hoping to have you folks some bareroots before next spring."

"That's our gal," Mrs. Bennet from the boardinghouse said, her blue eyes twinkling. "Always got another little surprise tucked up your sleeve."

Taking pleasure in the praise, Charlotte rose to her feet again, but her gaze slipped away to the library steps and Atlas Daltry.

He wasn't watching her after all. Head down, he was writing something in a notebook. Then suddenly he did look up, and he caught her staring.

Oh, dear. He'd think she was interested. And even if it weren't too dangerous, his own grandmother had warned her about him.

"Atlas!" With a high squeal and a blur of color, Opal ran across the expanse of lawn toward Mr. Daltry.

Charlotte knew she should call her back. But Opal had talked of nothing but her dashing new beau for the past two weeks, had insisted on wearing his blue ribbon every single day. And didn't everyone always say Opal was just like her mama? Well, it was true—right down to the men who caught their fancy.

While Charlotte looked for the correct door knocker for another customer, she sneaked another peek at her daughter and Mr. Daltry.

Opal now stood between his legs, bobbing up and down, and even at this distance Charlotte could tell the child was talking a blue streak. And Daltry? His brilliant white teeth fairly sparkled as he pushed back his hat and laughed. Such a delightful sight.

After that, Charlotte had a difficult time concentrating on her customers. Although she tried to listen to Miss Lavender, the milliner, with her latest physical complaints, her gaze wandered time and again to the library steps. Her little Opal was hopelessly smitten. Judging from Daltry's expression, so was he.

Opal's springy orange curls spilled across Mr. Daltry's sunny brown hair as she bent to watch him write something.

Charlotte chuckled. She supposed she'd just have to let Opal have him when the imp grew up.

*No! Absolutely not.* What was she thinking?

According to what his grandmother had said about his ambitions, Atlas Daltry would be just as stodgy in a few years as Cecil, her husband, had ever been, just as unfeeling. No time for the little pleasures or an afternoon's adventure. He'd never see the hills covered with springtime's bluebonnets or hear the call of the meadowlark. He'd only be full of himself and his enterprises.

No, she wouldn't wish him on anyone, especially not a daughter of hers.

"*Miss Charlotte*," the bonnet-maker scolded, her bird-like face scrunched in a frown. "I don't believe you heard a word I said."

During the next half hour while Charlotte attended the last of her customers, she began to wonder what Atlas Daltry and a four-year-old could still be talking about. She knew Opal was capable of jabbering on like a magpie, but just how much could a grown man have to say to a child?

*And what is he forever jotting down in that notebook?*

A chill coursed through her body in spite of the day's sultry warmth. Mrs. Daltry had said her grandson had spent the last few years in Chicago, hadn't she? Not snooping around in Austin or San Antonio—Chicago. And Mrs. Daltry had always seemed a truthful person . . . a little eccentric, perhaps, but honest. But what if her grandson had lied to Mrs. Daltry? As long as he'd been gone from home, he could have taken up the business of detecting. And was searching for her.

As her last customer walked away, clacking the hinged letter *R* against its brass plate, Charlotte saw Daltry get up.

He stuffed his ominous notebook into his shirt pocket and, taking Opal's hand, ambled nonchalantly across the street toward her—as nonchalantly as a wolf stalking a lone sheep.

Determined not to let him suspect she was uneasy, Charlotte climbed down the wagon wheel and fetched herself a dipper of water from the bucket hanging beneath the wagon bed. Still, she couldn't help watching him approach as she took a sip.

For one supposedly as young as Daltry, he certainly had a mature sureness about him. With that holstered revolver riding his hip, he looked every inch the seasoned gunman. Without his city-slicker clothes, no one would ever guess he'd lived in Chicago . . . if, indeed, he actually had.

Another anxious chill shimmied up her spine.

He closed the distance between them.

Desperately she tried to concentrate on her thirst.

He and Opal stopped before her, forcing her to face him. She looked up . . . and was stunned again by eyes that seemed transparent, depthless—the lightest gray rimmed with blue. His eyes held hers.

"Mama, Mama!"

She wrenched her attention away to her child.

Opal was all freckles and shine. "Guess what? Atlas said there's gonna be races for us kids. And big blue prizes better than this one." She smeared her hand down the one pinned to her yellow peasant blouse. "And Atlas says if I practice every day, he's got a lucky ribbon he'll tie around my arm." She swung back to Daltry. "Ain't that so?"

"Isn't," Charlotte automatically corrected as she, too, turned to him. What was he up to? She hadn't heard of any upcoming racing events.

"The church is giving Mother Spooler a big birthday party Sunday after next," Daltry said. "It's her ninetieth. And, well, I thought it would be fun if we also had games and prizes. Especially," he said, smiling down at Opal, "for curly-headed little girls."

"I see." She relaxed slightly, knowing there actually was a big party coming up. Was it possible that he was simply a kind young man? Nothing else? His face did seem incapable of deceit and trickery. Of ugliness.

"In fact—" Daltry's gaze wavered slightly. "My family enjoyed your company so much on Independence Day that we'd all be delighted if you would join us for the birthday barbecue." He patted his shirt pocket, his hesitant expression giving way to a grin. "You have to come. Opal and I have been planning some very exciting games, haven't we, pumpkin?"

Opal clutched Charlotte's skirt and jumped up and down. "Please, Mama. Say yes. Atlas writed it all down."

"Wrote it." Charlotte's fear melted away. His notes— they were merely plans for the day's festivities. She really had to stop suspecting every capable-looking stranger who took notice of her. If no one had been sent to cause trouble by now, they probably never would be.

"Grams, in particular wanted me to ask you," he added. "You don't want to disappoint her, do you?" He tilted his head, and his crystalline eyes pleaded disarmingly.

And charmingly. Too charmingly to be rebuffed. Perhaps this once. Just this once. "No, we certainly wouldn't want to disappoint *Grams*. Opal and I will be pleased to join your family."

"Good." Daltry exhaled noticeably. One would think he'd been anxiously awaiting her answer. "The pleasure will be all ours. But before I go, could I see one of those door knockers you're selling? I think Father would like one. He's a frustrated architect and loves adding fancy gewgaws to our house."

"Ah, yes, I've heard about your place. Folks say he's trying to compete with the glory of ancient Greece."

Daltry chuckled in a pleasing low rumble. "Not exactly. It's Grams who likes anything Greek."

Starting to climb onto the wagon again, Charlotte placed a foot on the hubcap of the back wheel. But before she could hoist herself up, his hands encircled her waist, and he lifted her to the platform.

After thanking him, she could still feel the warmth and strength of his grip, and the oddest tingling sensation whirled around inside of her. Avoiding his gaze, she started rummaging through the crate.

"Me, too. Me, too," Opal cried out.

Curious, Charlotte turned back with the door knocker to see Atlas sweep Opal up and swing her high over his head before landing her alongside Charlotte, to Opal's screeching delight.

Charlotte couldn't help smiling as she handed the brass knocker to the handsome young man. She loved nothing better than hearing her daughter's laughter. "One dollar, please."

He pulled a silver dollar from his pants pocket and placed it in her palm. "Two weeks."

The coin was warm from pressing against his body. At the thought, Charlotte felt her own cheeks heat up.

"I'll see you in two weeks."

"No!" Opal wedged in front of Charlotte. "Tomorrow, Atlas. Ain't you going to church?"

Flashing Opal a grin, he stepped back. "You bet. Unless something comes up at the ranch that can't wait." He turned to go. "See you tomorrow."

Forgetting herself, Charlotte watched after Atlas until

he mounted his horse and rode out of sight. It had been a long time since she'd allowed herself the pleasure of a man's company . . . or the pleasure of freely dwelling on such a pleasing countenance. She sighed. A very long time.

"Mama. Look." Opal dropped down on her belly and scooted backward off the wagon bed. As soon as her feet hit the ground, she stooped, and when she came up she held a small notebook in her hand. "Atlas dropped it."

Charlotte shot a glance down the road. "Too late to catch him. But we'll see him tomorrow. Let me have it."

Opal flung it up to her, and Charlotte caught the fluttering pages. She started smoothing them down.

The words Daltry had written jumped out at her. Slapped her in the face.

## ை 9 ை

"Hmm, wonder why Miss Charlotte has her horses hitched up?" Odie said as he maneuvered the Daltrys' surrey into an empty spot between two buggies parked in front of the church.

Atlas hadn't noticed. From the moment the family's canopied conveyance had turned onto the main street, his thoughts had been centered only on the hope of catching a glimpse of the woman, not her rig.

"That is odd," Minerva mused as she adjusted the position of her flamboyant feathered and flowered bonnet. "Charlotte usually stays here until Monday morning." She turned to Atlas, sitting beside her on the backseat. "Dear, did she mention anything to you yesterday when she accepted your invitation—*and* you took that wonderful first step toward your prize?"

"No, she didn't say anything, so you'll have to contain your curiosity until after services, since you two women have made us late. *Again.*"

The angelic twinkle in Minerva's eyes was really full of the devil, making her severe black church dress her only concession to the Sabbath.

Reining the horse to a stop, Odie placed a hand on his

wife's knee and looked back at Atlas. "Don't you know the most important thing your mother can teach you is patience for that day when you, too, marry? It's important to learn early on that wives are never ready on time. It must be the eleventh commandment."

"Oh, pshaw." Minerva leaned forward and rapped Odie on the shoulder. "You boys stop your jawing and help us down, or we'll be that much later."

Atlas had hoped the congregation would all be standing up and singing when they walked in to cover their untimely entrance. But no such luck.

From behind the pulpit, Reverend Baxter paused midsentence and peered over his spectacles as the foursome stepped inside the little church. Standing directly beneath the large brass cross, he seemed even more imperious.

There was an empty pew near the back. Atlas pointed to it.

Minerva shook her head and followed her son and daughter-in-law down the center aisle toward their usual places near the front.

Lagging behind, Atlas scanned those gathered for the unruly curls of Charlotte and Opal. But no strawberry locks were in evidence. He felt a wave of disappointment.

An instant later he spotted Charlotte. Her hair was completely covered by a simple wide-brimmed straw hat, its only adornment being a pale green ribbon that matched her dress. Very subdued, very unlike Charlotte.

Beside her, Opal's wild hair had also been tamed. Hers was in braids that fell over a dress of the same conservative linen as her mother's.

It was probably best there was no empty space beside Charlotte, or he might have found himself sitting there uninvited. Ever since he'd first seen the woman, his impulses had been overtaking his good sense. Striding past as noiselessly as possible, he tried not to stare openly at the surprisingly prim twosome.

"Atlas!" came a loud whisper.

He paused and looked back to see little Opal and her dimpled grin. She waved excitedly.

Charlotte captured her child's hand and spoke in her ear. Even a fleeting glance his way would have been appreciated, but none was forthcoming.

He continued down the aisle beneath the scathing scowl of the black-robed minister, then quickly slid onto the hard bench beside Minerva.

Before long, Atlas realized the theme of the sermon was, of all things, King David's lust for Bathsheba. And he was sure the reverend spoke directly to him. Had everyone in the county seen him lusting after Charlotte? Sweat began to prickle the skin beneath his starched collar.

Life had been so much easier at college. He'd been simply one of many young men feeling their oats, flirting with the young ladies who strolled Michigan Avenue. And the professors had turned blind eyes to the occasional foray to a house of ill repute.

After what seemed like hours, Reverend Baxter announced the closing hymn, and Atlas rose to his feet along with the rest of the congregation as Miss Lavender at the pump organ wheezed out the opening chords of "God Be With You Till We Meet Again," and everyone began to sing. Soon he would be free of the pastor's censuring scowl.

Suddenly he caught a flash of movement beside him and turned to find Opal clambering onto his pew.

Standing up on the bench, she rose onto her toes and pulled him close by the jacket sleeve, her round emerald eyes peering up with open concern. He bent down, and she put her lips to his ear. "My mama says we can't go to the birthday party."

Atlas stopped singing and leaned down to her ear. "Why?"

She shrugged the puffed sleeves of her pastel green dress.

After the benediction, he waited until his family had filed out past him before leaning down to question the child further. But Opal spoke first.

"I think Mama's mad at you about something."

"Nice to see you here," Miss Lavender broke in as she walked past, bringing an end to the departing stream of people.

"You, too, ma'am," he replied absently, scarcely looking at her. He turned back to Opal, thoroughly confused. "Mad? About what?"

"Musta been something you wrote in your notebook. Maybe she doesn't like some of the games we planned."

His notebook. That's where he'd lost it.

*His notebook!*

The blood drained from his face before he remembered he'd torn out the accusatory list he'd read to his grandmother. But, still, Charlotte would've seen his comments on how unprofessionally she handled her customers . . .

comments meant only to help him formulate a list of suggestions to improve her business.

Atlas plucked Opal up from the pew and started toward the entrance while searching his brain for the most tactful explanation. He scooted past the people clogging the entrance, and moved out onto the porch.

Charlotte waited just beyond a group of chatting women. She looked every inch the haughty young matron, her usually capricious expression now frozen into one of indignation—an apt frame for eyes of green ice. She looked from Opal to him, her arms tightly folded—and strangled within her white-knuckled grasp was the notebook.

If he'd had a choice, Atlas knew he'd rather take on a wild Texas longhorn than her about now. *If* he had a choice. His legs didn't want to move forward.

Opal wrapped her arms tighter around his neck and whispered, "Don't be scared. She don't bite."

"Doesn't," he corrected absently, hoping the child was right. "I think maybe a present is called for. Do you think she'd like some toilet water, or maybe some candied fruit?"

Opal's eyes lit up like candle points. "A present? I know a present. A good present. Mama loves kittens. Kittens with lots of fluffy hair. Lots and lots."

The women who'd shielded Atlas from Charlotte moved away, leaving nothing but a gaping distance between them. He took a steeling breath, then walked down the steps to take his medicine.

She took a few jerky but swift strides toward him, then stopped abruptly. Before he had a chance to say so much as, "How do you do?" she whisked Opal from him, slapped the notebook into his hand, and stormed away in thunderous silence.

Watching her stalk off to her rig, he fervently wanted to check his list to determine just how damning the words really were. But he couldn't let her catch him doing it. Or anyone else, for that matter. As it was, he could feel any number of curious eyes boring into the back of his head—the minister's in particular.

Minerva moved alongside him and took his arm. "Well, my dear, it would seem Mrs. Clairmore is somewhat miffed with you."

He watched Charlotte scoop her skirts above trim ankles and climb aboard her wagon. She picked up her whip and snapped it above her horses' backs, and they lunged forward, their bangled harness chiming cheerily. She guided them onto the street and drove away, her pert nose high in the air, her spine arrow-straight.

"Whatever did you do?" Minerva asked accusingly.

Feeling defeated, Atlas turned back to her. "I dropped my notebook yesterday, and Charlotte found it. She must have read the list I was compiling about her—"

"Surely not the list you read to me last week." His grandmother's fingers dug into his arm.

Attempting a smile, he patted her hand. "No. One I was making to assist her in—"

"You and your lists. Don't you know you can't keep people on lists? They'll jump off every time." Relaxing her grip, she nodded her head toward their surrey. "I suppose it was too much to hope that all my grandchildren would fulfill their labors. But I guess it's all right, my dear. I'm sure Charlotte and little Opal will put the prize to good use if you fail."

* * *

"Clem," Charlotte sputtered, unable to control her laughter, "you've—outdone yourself—this time. Peacock feathers!"

Striking an outrageously feminine pose, the brakeman swayed against the door frame of the boxcar. He fanned himself with one of the colorful plumes as if he were some dainty debutante.

She laughed all the louder—the man was big enough to wrestle a full-grown bull to the ground, not to mention he had a bushy mustache a walrus would be proud of.

"And don't forget the orders for peachicks." Lowering the feather, he composed himself. "It ain't easy comin' up with something new and different all the time. But then, I've become real famous. Every railroad man up and down the lines knows there's a brakeman on the Texas and Pacific with very strange and exotic tastes. But they do come through for us, don't they?"

"They sure do. And with your daughter getting married in a few weeks, I'm sure you can always use the extra cash."

"Ain't that the truth. Between her and the missus, I never saw so much fixin' and fussin' going on in my life. You are comin', ain't you?"

"Oh, I'll be there, all right. I wouldn't miss the chance to see that thick neck of yours choking in a starched collar." Lifting her skirt, Charlotte unpinned a small cloth purse from her petticoat and opened it. "How much do I owe you this time?"

After she paid Clem Tucker for the merchandise, he piled her arms so high with bundles of the long feathers, she had to blow one away from her eyes merely to see a small piece of the floor as she led the way onto the loading dock . . . and ran smack into someone.

The person caught her by the arms to steady her as she blindly mumbled a muffled apology from behind a mountain of turquoise and green iridescence.

The hands released her and parted the feathers. Atlas Daltry's face appeared. *That handsome Atlas Daltry*, his golden tan set off by a brown-and-white plaid shirt.

Her heart leaped, then froze. This was the man who'd been sent to spy on her. To gather evidence against her.

He smiled benignly, deceptively benignly. "Ma'am, I'd like a word with you. About a private matter." Stepping past her, he took the brakeman's load of feathers. "Perhaps we can talk while I help you take these to your wagon."

She knew Tucker couldn't protect her from this enemy. With this one she was on her own. "See you next time, Clem," she barely managed before her throat closed. She sucked in a breath and started toward her rig parked at the end of the loading dock, grateful now that the plumes shielded her face. She needed time to compose herself.

Daltry's boot heels tapped one after the other, right behind her, unnervingly close.

Her every instinct cried out for her to flee, but she knew it would be better to face him and get it over with. She'd hardly slept the past week and a half, wondering when he'd pop up again.

Reaching the end of the dock, she tossed her bundles onto the platform at the rear of the wagon, then stepped aside while Daltry did the same. Feeling cornered, she had a sudden urge to strike back. She balled her fists and jammed them onto her waist. "Well, get it over with."

"I'd like to explain about the notebook. I'm sure you must have thought it rude of me to be studying you and your business, but I assure you there's an explanation." His last words trailed off, and he gave her one of those embarrassed, I-don't-want-to-be-here looks.

And rightly so. He was nothing but a snoop, a paid tattletale. "Just say your piece and get it over with."

"Where's Opal? Is she inside?"

"What's the matter? You afraid she'll hear what a lily-livered sneak you are?"

She enjoyed seeing his cool gray eyes flare . . . from guilt, no doubt.

"Never fear," she continued before he could find his tongue. "Opal is playing at a friend's house. I'll be picking her up on the way out of town."

His gaze faltered for a second. He took a step back. "As you know, my grandmother is particularly fond of anything that has to do with the ancient Greek myths, and one in particular, the Labors of Hercules. She has taken it upon herself to assign a labor, or task, for each of her grandchildren on their twentieth birthday. If it's successfully completed, she awards that person a grand surprise. And as it would happen—"

"What is all this gibberish? Just admit you're spying on me for Edgar. But let me warn you, if you so much as lay one finger on me, I'll—"

"I don't know anything about an Edgar." Daltry spread his arms with the expertise of an accomplished actor. "I'm here because of my grandmother. And if you'll just calm down long enough for me to explain, not only will you not be mad as a wet hen, but you'll consider this your lucky day."

"I'll be the judge of that."

A slow grin softened the perfectly hewn planes of his face, and he nodded, seemingly amused. "Oh, by the way, are those your only horses?"

What a strange question at a time like this. "Yes," she snapped.

His expression turned serious again. "One could easily come up lame or sick."

"Are you threatening me?"

"Of course not! I'm merely concerned about your welfare. Truly."

"Well, you needn't be. I've had good luck with my horses so far."

"It's not good business to rely on luck."

So that was his game. "If you think," she said, wagging a finger under his nose, "that you can come here, talking gloom and doom, then try to buy me out with some two-bit offer, you've got another think coming."

He caught her finger and stepped close. "And if you'd just shut your pretty little mouth long enough for me to get my piece said, we could both get on about our business in a much happier frame of mind." He released her finger. "To begin with, I'm not interested in buying your outfit."

Charlotte cocked her head in disbelief. "Remember, I saw your notes. How many customers I had. What they bought."

He shifted his weight. She had him dead to rights, and he knew it. "I was just jotting down a few observations. I wanted to show you how much more efficient you could be. How to make better use of your time. Time is money, you know."

"Hmm," she snorted. She'd pegged him right from the very first. He *was* just like Cecil. "Did any of my customers walk away empty-handed?"

"No. But—" He halted midsentence and frowned. "That's not why I'm here. I have a proposition I'd like to make."

"*That's* what this is all about? *How dare you!*" She stepped back, outraged. "You're no better than the rest of the useless two-legged mavericks around here." She started down the dock stairs.

Daltry caught her arm. "Lady, you can be so exasperating. Not *that* kind of a proposition. If you'll just give me two measly minutes, I'll explain my invasion into your life to your complete satisfaction. And then some."

Daltry glanced off to the side, drawing Charlotte's attention to a couple of elderly women. They sat on a bench in front of the station hotel, gawking at them like a couple of old crows perched on a backyard fence.

"Let's go around to the other side of your wagon," Daltry said. He stepped back, allowing Charlotte to precede him down the steps.

By the time they reached the far side of her outfit, he looked so serious, Charlotte wasn't sure if she wanted to hear what he had to say. "I really need to be going. As you said, time is money."

"And if you will just take the time to listen, you're sure to profit quite handsomely."

"Very well, say your piece. I won't interrupt again."

And say it he did. For the next several minutes, Atlas explained about Grandmother Daltry's labors in detail, from Lee's to Allie's. "This year it's my turn. I'm almost certain my reward will be funding for a meatpacking house I want to build here in Abilene. It would keep most of the profits of the cattle industry here in Texas where it belongs. Not to mention putting all those useless two-legged mavericks of yours back to work."

"That all sounds so very admirable of you," Charlotte answered with only a slight touch of sarcasm. "But what could all of this possibly have to do with me?"

His chest expanded as he sucked in a breath. "I'm afraid, Mrs. Clairmore, that *you* are my labor."

"*Me?*" What mischief had that old woman cooked up? "Just exactly what does Mrs. Daltry want you to do for me? Take over my daughter? My business? What?"

He slipped her a pained grin. "It seems Grams and the rest of the busybodies at church think you should start socializing."

"*Socializing*! That's all I do. Every day with my customers."

"That's not the kind they think you lack. They think it's time you started . . ." Shrugging, he glanced away.

"Yes?"

He looked back at her and squared his shoulders. "Started keeping company. I think my grandmother thought I'd make a safe person for you to start with. To fulfill my labor, I'm required to escort you to five social functions this year."

*How dare she!* Charlotte wanted to scream. She did. "*How dare she! And you!*" She jabbed a fist at his wall of a chest. "You went along with it?"

"Not willingly."

That jarred her into silence—but not for long. "Oh, you find me too common? Too offensive?"

"No, not at all. But I don't like the way my grand-mother is always trying to manipulate our lives. That's why I'm here, telling you all of this. You see, one of the rules of this labor is that I'm not allowed to tell you or anyone else. Only the family is in on these secrets, *these games*. If Grams finds out I've told you, my prize will be forfeited."

"So, it sounds as if you've lost before you began."

"Only if you tell. But I'm hoping you won't. For the sake of Texas. After two years of killing blizzards, and then last summer's drought, the ranchers are in dire straits. We need to get top dollar for the few steers we can spare during the next few years in order to recoup. Having our own meatpacking plant would ensure that. If you'll cooperate and let me escort you to five social functions, not only will I not overstep my gentlemanly bounds, but also I will buy you a second team of horses—another good, sturdy pair so you can switch off. Let each team go out to pasture for a couple of weeks and rest up between trips."

Charlotte glanced at her gentle white giants. "I'm sure the boys would like that a lot. But to feed and care for an extra team—I don't think I could afford it."

"That's no problem. You can leave them with Hal and Allie. And if there's any added expense, I'd gladly foot the bill. A small price for a meatpacking plant."

Of course. No one would ever accuse this economics graduate of proposing an unprofitable deal. Charlotte turned back to the horses and muttered, "No, sir, can't let anything stand in the way of that meatpacking plant."

"I'm sorry, I didn't hear what you said."

"Oh, nothing important. Being the thorough business-man you are, you've made it almost impossible for me to refuse your offer. As you said, my accompanying you will be strictly business."

"Absolutely." As he took her hand, his fathomless gray eyes softened, enveloping her in a warmth she hadn't thought possible. Quietly he added, "You have my solemn word."

Gradually she became aware that everything about his look, the sound of his voice, his touch, erased his promise. She doubted anything between them could ever be simply business. Her heart lurched with unexpected joy. Why not take a chance? Why not? After all, it had been two years since she left Austin, and the trouble she'd expected hadn't followed, no matter how many times her mind had played tricks on her.

Giving his hand a squeeze, Charlotte smiled up into that princely face. "Well, Mr. Daltry, I suppose Opal and I will be joining you for Mother Spooler's birthday."

He laughed—the most delightful deep laugh, and, reaching up behind her, he plucked one of the plumes from out of the bundle. "You won't be able to miss me. I'll be the one wearing the peacock feather."

## ∽ 10 ∾

Mounted on Red Jack, Atlas rode beside the railroad tracks. He didn't know when he'd been in a better mood. He'd been right to be frank with Charlotte. More right than Grams, who insisted on dallying in people's lives. And as long as he and Charlotte kept their arrangement secret, what difference could it possibly make? This way everyone came out ahead.

Him most of all. Imagine being *required* to keep company with that gorgeous strawberry blond. Laughing out loud, he wished all the chores in his life would be so pleasant.

Over and over as he rode past the stockyards, he recaptured the moment when she'd peeked up at him from behind that rainbow of feathers, so glad to see him . . . before she remembered to be mad. And even if she was gun-shy with men, her eyes had flashed in that one second a world of unconcealed interest. He had no doubt of that. And later, the way her expression had turned shy when he took her hand . . . and her pulse, how it had throbbed at the base of her throat. She'd quite liberally stolen his breath away.

Atlas was hard-pressed to stop smiling as he redirected

his thoughts to the business at hand—a location for the meatpacking plant.

Past the cattle pens and their lingering stench, the landscape opened to a gently rolling plain of prematurely dry grass. Again this year the rains had failed to come often enough to keep the meadows green in the hot months. Another of the many reasons to diversify. He reined in his sorrel and surveyed a field that was relatively flat and treeless. A perfect spot for the buildings. A perfect spot on a perfect day.

After crisscrossing the acreage a couple of times, he headed back to the depot. He wanted to share his find with someone. Namely Charlotte. But when he reached the loading platform, she and her wagon were already gone.

Disappointed, he turned Red Jack toward Abilene's business district and headed for the land office. But, despite telling himself not to, he listened for the tinkle of harness bells and looked for her brightly painted wagon down every cross street.

Even while he gave the title clerk the location of the property he'd selected, he found himself glancing out the window at every sound, every flash of movement.

Lo and behold, Charlotte did drive by, and cute little Opal was sitting up on the high seat beside her.

Atlas charged to the door. Then, his hand on the doorknob, he halted. He couldn't go running out into the street, yelling after her like some rutting young buck. She'd think he was no better than the rest of them. Or worse, some lovesick kid, now that she knew he was only twenty. He'd have plenty of opportunities to tell her about the property at the barbecue.

By the time Charlotte's wagon disappeared around the corner, lust had again overridden logic. He literally ached to go after her.

His overheated gaze landed on the Cattle Exchange Saloon. The perfect place to put the rutting buck in him back to sleep. He'd go over there, have a celebratory drink, and pick out one of the "ladies"—the most surefire way he knew to take his mind off Charlotte.

The idea should have excited him. Instead it left him cold. Had Charlotte become his sole object of desire?

Grinning like that lovesick fool he knew he surely was becoming, he turned back to the title clerk, who was searching through a sloppy pile of papers . . . obviously a very disorganized man. "I'm going across the street for a drink. About how long do you think it'll be before you have the information I need?"

The stoop-shouldered man, whose collar had wilted hours ago, looked up. He licked his lips nervously. "Ten minutes, fifteen at the most."

"Fine." Atlas opened the door. "I'll be back then." He dipped the brim of his hat against the afternoon sun and headed for the saloon. The wood frame building had an impressive front, and its second-story balcony provided plenty of shade for the boardwalk. No one could deny it was one of the most noticeable structures on the main street, a testament to the town's main attraction aside from the railroad. And soon, he reminded himself, there'd be a much larger building. One that would change people's image of Abilene from now on. He smiled. Damn, he felt good today.

As he stepped up on the boardwalk in front of the saloon, the batwing doors banged open, and two saddle tramps spilled out, bouncing off each other. They plowed into Atlas, stinking of sour whiskey, then barreled past as if he didn't exist.

Atlas wheeled around to confront the rude bastards. But from the way they grabbed the reins and swung onto their horses, a person would think they were running from a prairie fire. Or worse, he chuckled to himself, an irate husband with a shotgun. Putting the spurs to their mounts, they rode out in a cloud of dust.

Resettling the holster strapped to his thigh, Atlas turned back and pushed through the swinging doors and strode into the dim, cavernous saloon. Almost empty on this hot Wednesday afternoon, it appeared even larger. The only patrons sat in a haze of smoke at the back, playing cards. Two saloon girls, in gowns cut so low they'd be arrested if they stepped outside, lounged in a careless sprawl at a table near the front. One was in orange satin, the other in purple, and judging from their rumpled appearances, it looked as if they'd worn them day and night for a week. They each gave him a quick glance, then put their heads together and began to speak in tense whispers. They seemed to be arguing quietly about something. Perhaps which would have the honor of approaching him.

After another assessing look, he knew he'd give neither the honor. He walked up to the long and empty oak bar and came face-to-face with a life-size portrait of a naked woman lying on red satin. She was creamy white, curvaceous. Soft . . . too soft for his taste. He glanced away.

A rough cob of a bartender, one who looked capable of

quelling any disturbance, approached him from the far end. "What'll you have, son?"

*Son.* "Beer." Maybe it was time to grow a mustache. Laying a dime on the bar in exchange for the tapped brew, Atlas turned to watch the cardplayers. His attention, however, was again captured by the gaudily clad women as the one in orange rose swiftly.

Her chair screeched against the plank floor as she pushed it back. She patted down her messy hair knot, peroxided to a brassy yellow. It almost outshined her dress.

"I wouldn't," the other woman said with disdain, grabbing her arm.

How Atlas had ever thought Charlotte could be one of them, he'd never know. By contrast, in her bright gypsy costume, she looked clean and fresh and gay as a morning glory kissed with dew. These two looked like yesterday's beer, shiny in the glass, but foul to the taste.

Suddenly wanting to leave the stale-smelling place, he blew a hole in the foam of his brew and downed a sizable amount.

"I have to," the one in orange said and pulled out of the other's grasp.

"He'll agree with me." The purple-clad one stood and smoothed the skintight bodice over her ribs as she followed the brassy blond to where the bartender leaned against the counter. Neither woman took time for the usual saloon-girl slink.

The bartender's mouth curled downward as he straightened to his full height. "What are you two gals arguing about now?"

"I say we should go tell the sheriff, just in case," said the one in orange.

"And I say," the brunet challenged, "if we start calling in the sheriff over every little suspicion, we'll lose our regulars."

"And *I* say," spewed the first even louder, "that she's so well liked that we'd probably receive a medal and more customers than we can handle."

Grabbing the bar edge with both hands, the bartender jutted forward, eyeing them menacingly. "Judas Priest, women! Spit it out!"

The girls shied back.

The one in purple spoke first. "You know those two good-for-nothings that just left, Bobby Lee and Rooster? Well, they was tryin' to get us to go upstairs with 'em. On credit."

The bartender's eyes narrowed more. "I told you not to do that."

"We didn't," she snapped back.

"But they was startin' to get real ornery about it," the blond added. "That's when the medicine-wagon woman drove by."

"Miss Charlotte?" the bartender asked.

*Charlotte*? Atlas stepped closer.

"Yeah, her," the blond continued. "That's when Bobby Lee grinned and said he knew where they could get took care of for nothin'. Then he whispered something in Rooster's ear, and the two took off like they was shot out of a cannon. I say they plan to catch up to Miss Charlotte out on some lonely stretch and have their way with her."

Atlas wheeled around and tore out the door, scarcely

hearing the brunet as she spouted, "And I say it's none of our business."

At the hitching rail he halted.

Where the hell was his horse?

Then he remembered and sprinted across the street to the land office. Leaping onto Red Jack's back, he spurred the sorrel in the direction he'd seen Charlotte go—down a road that, once it left town behind, ran alongside a creek for several miles before reaching Buffalo Gap . . . a road where trees and brush crowded between it and the bank. Miles of places where a big wagon could be driven into the dense foliage, be hidden completely, with no one passing by any the wiser.

His right hand went instinctively to the butt of his revolver. "I'll kill the bastards if they touch a hair on her head. A single hair," he muttered.

Sitting beside Charlotte on the wagon seat, Opal swished a satin streamer of her prized blue ribbon across her rag doll's face, shooing off a pesky fly . . . a smudged and stained streamer she would not be without.

Charlotte smiled. The little imp certainly was taken with Atlas Daltry. But then, she herself could hardly wait until next Sunday, when she'd see him with a peacock feather in his hat. Not only did he have flawless good looks, he'd surprised her with that bit of humor. Despite his penchant for business affairs, so much else about him was unlike Cecil. Cecil had rarely smiled, let alone joked. And where Cecil had been more than twenty years older than Charlotte, Atlas had just turned twenty, younger by months than she. Cecil had been very gaunt, with that annoying Adam's apple always bobbing up and down, hands that . . .

An icy shudder drizzled down her spine.

His hands had always smelled of lye soap and formaldehyde, always a constant reminder that he was a mortician. If living above his funeral parlor wasn't bad enough, she'd hated even more having him touch her. . . . Hated lying beneath him while he panted and sweated. Hated the wait until he finished and rolled his bone-sharp body off her.

Yet the way she'd felt today when Atlas merely took her hand had been incredibly different. It had been exciting. Thrilling. So thrilling it was scary. Her lips had actually tingled with the desire to touch his.

She traced them with her tongue and set them tingling again. Perhaps affairs of the heart really were as the dime novels portrayed them.

Maybe.

If only Papa had lived, he could've told her, and she wouldn't have so many doubts. He'd always been good about that, as well as making everything exciting and fun. Even when a wheel came off the medicine wagon or when a horse came up lame. With him, every day was rainbow-fresh and sunny. If he'd lived, she wouldn't have been left alone in a strange town with only the mortician who'd laid Papa out to take pity on a frightened fifteen-year-old girl.

Opal scooted back on the seat and held up her rag doll, then touched her nose to its pink one, nuzzling it.

Charlotte shifted her reins in one hand—she couldn't resist giving her daughter a hug.

Smiling at her mother with those winning green eyes, Opal began plaiting the doll's red yarn hair.

They neared a deep rut that cut across the road, and Charlotte reined the horses to a walk, her thoughts returning to the past.

No matter how much guilt she'd endured, she was mightily grateful to be free of Cecil Clairmore these last two years. Glad she'd had the courage to take the tarp off her father's wagon and strike out on the road again. Of course, she reassured herself, she wasn't glad that Cecil had suffered terribly with galloping consumption—yet she was pleased to be free, nonetheless.

Cecil had always treated her more like a child than her own father had. Never would he give her so much as a penny unless she first accounted to his satisfaction for its expenditure. Never was a cent to be spent on anything frivolous, only the absolute necessities. All profits were invested . . . and only with the most solvent banking houses. Cecil took his survival very seriously. Perhaps the fact that he dealt with death on a daily basis was the reason.

And after living the gypsy life with her father, being cooped up in three sparsely furnished, utterly plain rooms above Cecil's business was akin to being trapped in one of his caskets. She reached such a desperate point that one night she even dreamed that Cecil, his Adam's apple working grotesquely, had come upstairs with a bolt of black satin to line their walls.

And there'd been no one she could talk to. How could she invite someone up for tea when she knew her guest would have to pass a dead body to get to the stairway?

During those three years in Austin—years that had

seemed an eternity—she'd come to understand how truly necessary a little fun and friendly laughter were for the soul. And the importance of a frivolous trinket now and then. Without them, the spirit shriveled up to nothing.

Charlotte's gaze wandered from the rolling plains to the east to the birds flitting through cottonwoods and willows on the other side. Thanks heavens, she was free of that casket and the skeleton who'd lived in it with her. Never would she allow herself to be possessed by an overbearing skinflint again.

And lest she be fooled, it wouldn't hurt to be aware that Cecil at twenty may have been just as charming as Atlas Daltry. Before his rigor mortis set in. She doubted it, but it was possible. Worth keeping in mind.

She set her mouth in a determined line . . . until she remembered her daughter.

She could never totally regret her marriage to Cecil. Opal meant everything to her. Everything. And no matter what, she couldn't lose her child. Now that she'd agreed to accompany Mr. Daltry, she'd have to be more careful than ever.

Charlotte looked down at her ragamuffin's curls and said the exact words she knew would light up the darling's freckled face. "Baby doll, I spoke to Mr. Daltry today when I was at the train depot. We'll be going with him to the birthday picnic after all."

Opal shrieked and flung her arms around her mother's neck.

The horses started and picked up the pace. Charlotte tried to loosen the child's stranglehold with one hand while keeping the team in check with the other. "Settle down," she scolded, "or you'll stampede the boys."

"And the races," Opal piped in her high, thin voice, her arms still around Charlotte's neck, her nose inches from her mother's. "Will there still be races?"

Charlotte tweaked the freckled button. "You're such a silly goose. Of course, there'll still be races."

"Then you have to get me the most prettiest hair ribbon in the whole of Texas to tie on Atlas's arm. I want everyone to admire it when he wins."

"My, but aren't we confident about our Atlas."

Opal's excited smile vanished, and the imp actually managed a snooty air as she returned to her place on the box bench. "Atlas always wins. And he says I will, too. I just have to practice."

"Well, then, I suppose I'd better keep my eye out for a very special hair ribbon between now and Saturday. But, Opal, I don't want you pestering Atlas all day the way you did on the Fourth of July. Grown men have other things to do besides play with little girls."

Opal picked up her forgotten doll from where it had fallen on the floorboard. "You mean like what Simon Bennet said? He said he likes to play with big girls. 'Specially ones with big—you know . . ." The audacious tot cupped her hands in front of her chest at the strategic spots.

"Opal!"

"Well, he did. Ask Pepper Tittle."

"Nonetheless, it's not ladylike to repeat such things. Now, getting back to Mr. Daltry. We'll be attending five parties with him in the next few months. Won't that be fun?"

From the way Opal's eyes lit up, a body would think

she'd just been told there'd be five Christmases this year. "Five. How many's that?"

"Hold up your fingers." When the child did, Charlotte counted off the numbers, then wiggled Opal's thumb. "And this little piggy is going all the way to Mother Spooler's birthday picnic."

Opal giggled, and her gaze skipped around as much as her bottom did on the wagon seat.

Charlotte had no doubt that little brain was whirring with plans. "Now, I don't want you to think there's more to this than there is. So don't start thinking you own Atlas. After the five outings, we'll most likely never accompany him anyplace again. Is that understood?"

Opal clambered up to her knees again and grabbed Charlotte's face in her little hands. "But, Mama, you—" Her mouth gaped, and she stared past her mother.

Instantly Charlotte swung around.

A horseman rode alongside, almost close enough to touch. The sweat-streaked cowhand smelled of "devil brew" and had a smile to match.

How could she have been so careless? She'd let him catch her off guard. And, heaven help her, she'd forgotten to take the rifle out of the box seat upon which she and Opal now sat.

"Howdy, Miss Charlotte."

She'd seen the redhead's shock of hair somewhere. Without a hat, it stuck out like red straw. "Afternoon," she answered smoothly. She didn't want him to know she was suspicious.

His Adam's apple bobbed up and down along with his sun-bleached brows. He continued to grin as if he had a big secret.

My God, how she hated a bobbing Adam's apple. Tearing her eyes from his lanky neck, she knew she'd have to act fast. "My, but it's a hot day. Would you care for something coo—"

"Hey, Rooster."

Charlotte's gaze darted to the other side of the wagon.

Another rider leered at her from beneath close-set, droopy eyelids. "The lady says she's hot . . . and thirsty," he drawled out of one side of his mouth.

"That so?" The redhead unhooked his canteen from around his pommel. "Well, reckon we can fix that right now." He unscrewed the top and tipped back his own head first, letting some vile amber liquid pour past his florid lips.

Fighting down nausea, Charlotte grasped Opal's arm. "I have something much more quenching." She lifted Opal up and stood her on the seat. "Sweetie," she said, looking her daughter in the eye. "Go inside and get the jug of lemonade from under the counter."

For once Opal kept her mouth shut and did as she was told. She unlatched and pushed open the half door above her seat and crawled inside.

"Let me help her." The redhead flung his leg over his saddle horn and leaped aboard.

"No!" Charlotte's heart raced with panic. "You can't go in there."

He stopped in front of her, balancing himself with the brake stick. "I'm only tryin' to be helpful," he said with a mocking smile.

She reached for her whip. *It was gone.* Feeling his hot whiskey-breath on her face, she glanced up.

His smile was gone, replaced by a fiery look in his bloodshot eyes. He pushed her toward the opening.

Releasing the reins, she blocked the way with her back and yelled, "Shut the door, Opal! Bar it!"

The wagon lurched.

The man sprawled on top of her, started pawing her chest.

She heard the door slam and the bar drop into place. Thank God, Opal was safe. Charlotte shoved the oaf off, then, to her horror, saw that the other man had Goliath's halter and was pulling the team off the road.

The red-haired scum threw a leg over her, and his slobbery mouth came after hers.

She jerked her head to the side.

The handle of his revolver banged against the back of the bench.

She scrambled for it.

His hand slapped down on top of hers.

She tightened her grip and jammed her finger through the trigger ring.

As he clawed at her hand, he screeched, "She's got my—"

The gun bucked out of her palm with an explosion that splintered the seat.

He slammed her up against the wagon wall. Held her. His brows formed an angry red ridge above his narrowed eyes as he swung back his hand and slapped her. Hard.

Her head crashed against the unyielding wood. Her vision dimmed.

"Mama!"

Opal's cry from inside renewed Charlotte's determination. She lunged.


Halfway up a rise, Atlas reined in his horse. He'd heard a gunshot. But he couldn't gauge the distance or the exact direction. He sat as quietly as his pounding pulse would allow and listened.

Nothing.

It was probably just some kid shooting squirrels.

He spurred his horse into a trot and scanned the edge of the road for wagon tracks cutting into the dense foliage. Reaching the top of the hill, he could see a good half mile of straight road. Empty road.

What if he'd been wrong? His throat went dry. What if Charlotte had taken another road out of town? The woman had a route she followed, so why hadn't he taken one lousy minute to see for sure where she'd gone?

He looked to the road behind him. He'd been riding hard for at least fifteen minutes. He should've caught up by now. He needed to go back *now*. Sweet Jesus, he'd be another half hour behind them.

His chest knotted. He'd never make it in time to save her.

But he had to try.

He yanked the reins hard across Red Jack's neck.

The sorrel, a well-trained cow pony, spun on his hind legs.

Then he heard them. *Voices.* Harsh, angry voices.

Atlas reined the horse around again and spurred him into a gallop.

Within seconds, Atlas spotted wagon tracks and a path of trampled brush. He jerked Red Jack onto it and plunged into the maze of willows and cottonwoods.

An excited voice rang out, clear and close. "Hold the bitch's arms. I'll get her legs."

A woman screamed. Charlotte.

Spurring the sorrel on, he drew his .45.

The wagon came into view. Beside it, Charlotte flailed in the dirt. One bastard trapped her hands. The other dove for her kicking feet.

Atlas hit the ground, firing a round.

The men spun on their haunches . . . the same scum-sucking pigs he'd seen leaving the saloon. Not so brave now, their eyes were wide with panic.

"Let her go." Atlas pointed his revolver at the one with shifty eyes.

Instantly the weasel released her, and Charlotte rolled away.

"Put your hands up. In the air where I can see them."

The cowards couldn't wait to comply. The skinny redhead tried a smile. "We didn't mean no harm. We was just funnin' with her."

The other jerked an agreeing nod. "Yeah. We wasn't doin' nothin'."

"*Lying sons of bitches*." Atlas's finger itched to blow their heads off. "On your feet."

They started to lower their arms.

"Without the hands."

Both raised their hands again. They knew better than to tempt him.

Any other time, watching two swill bellies stumble and fall several times before gaining their feet would've been humorous. Not today.

Atlas judged the lazy-eyed one to be the more dangerous. Shorter, more powerfully built, he moved quicker. Atlas kept his .45 trained on a button dead center of the saddle tramp's dirty gray shirt. "With your left hand, reach down and unbuckle your gun belt."

The man stared back at Atlas without moving, obviously weighing the odds.

"Go for it. I'd purely love to blow a hole clean through you."

"For chrissake, Bobby Lee," the redhead screeched. "You tryin' to get us kilt?"

His partner's reluctance still showed in the hard set of his jaw as he slowly lowered the one hand and unbuckled his belt.

"Let it drop to the ground."

The man balked again.

"Do it!" his partner grated through clenched teeth.

The weapon hit the dirt.

"You're next." Atlas waved his revolver at the skinny one, who quickly followed suit.

"Now, move back." As they complied, Atlas kicked the gun belts out of their reach, then leaned down to retrieve them—not for a minute relaxing his challenging stare.

Charlotte stood several yards away, holding onto a tree trunk, looking dazed. She shook as if she had a fever, and blood trickled from her nose.

The sight inflamed his rage even more. If she hadn't been through enough already, he would've shot the filthy scum where they stood.

Then, in a surge of panic, he remembered her little one. "Where's Opal?"

"Who?" the redhead croaked.

Atlas ripped his attention back to the men. "Charlotte's daughter."

"Inside. She's inside," the bolder one spewed, his courage slipping. "We didn't touch her."

Keeping them pinned with his revolver, Atlas backed up to the wagon. "Opal, honey, it's Atlas. Are you okay?"

After a couple seconds of silence, a tiny voice squeaked, "Is it really you?"

His throat tightened at the sound of the wee frightened child. "Yes, it's me, pumpkin. And everything's all right. Your mama's fine. But I want you to stay put for now. Will you do that for me?"

"Uh-huh."

Satisfied she was safe, he strode back to the men. "Sit down and take off your boots."

"What for?" Shifty Eyes challenged with renewed bravado.

Atlas thumbed back the hammer of his Colt.

At the sound of the click, both men dropped to the ground and frantically started tugging at their boots.

Atlas glanced back at Charlotte. She looked so pale, so frail and vulnerable. But at least she had stopped that fearful trembling.

She took a hesitant step toward him.

"Sweetheart," he said in as gentle a tone as he could muster under the circumstances. "Do you think you could round up their horses and tie them to the back of your wagon?"

Her gaze wandered to where the cow ponies were munching on some water grass. "I guess. . . ."

His stomach clenched at the dull whisper. He returned his attention to the men struggling to get their sweaty feet out of their boots.

The redhead noticed Charlotte collecting their mounts and let out an ear-piercing yelp. "No! You can't take our boots *and* our horses."

"If you don't shut up, I'll take your heads, too." The big toe sticking out of the other weasel's dirty sock made a tempting target . . . one that was hard to resist.

From behind came Charlotte's almost soundless words. "It's done."

He glanced over his shoulder and smiled, hoping to reassure her, then turned back to the men. "Now, Charlotte, if you wouldn't mind, I'd like for you to climb up on your wagon and take it on out of here. I'll catch up after me and the boys swap a few more lies."

Atlas dwelled on the pleasure he'd take in shooting the sniveling snakes. But as time passed, with Charlotte and Opal riding safely away, and as the two miserable drunks stared up at him like whipped dogs, his blood began to cool. He draped the confiscated holsters across his cow pony's neck, then went back for the boots.

Taking their guns and horses had been one thing, but when he got to the footwear, he unleashed stares of pure hatred from the men.

Let them try something, he thought. Now that Charlotte was safely gone, he'd have no problem blowing a few holes in them. With a menacing smile, he tipped his hat and holstered his revolver. Then retrieving the sorrel's reins, he swung up into the saddle.

Like a sudden squall, the two were on their feet, charging.

At the sound of their war whoops, Red Jack reared up.

Tightening his grip, Atlas whipped out his .45 and fired . . . at the one thing he couldn't resist. The big toe sticking out of the weasel's stocking.

The man's droopy eyes sprang wide with horror. "*You shot me.*" He fell to the ground and grabbed his bloody foot.

The long-legged redhead deserted his friend, crashing away through the brush as fast as his bootless feet would take him.

Atlas wagged his head and grinned. "Doesn't look like your partner wants to get his own remembrance of today.

But I guess one souvenir toe's enough. *For now.*"
Reining Red Jack toward the road, Atlas took one last
satisfying look at the man furiously wrapping a bandanna
around his foot. "You be sure and make a stranger of
yourself, now. Ya hear?"

# ∽ 12 ∾

Atlas breathed easier when he rounded a curve and spotted Charlotte's wagon moving slowly down the road, the two cow ponies tied behind. Of course, he told himself, where else would she be?

He nudged Red Jack into a gallop and sped after them.

As he reached the front of the wagon, Charlotte was watching him with eyes streaming with tears. They fell unchecked and mingled with the blood from her nose. In one hand she held the team's reins, in the other she clutched a rifle that lay across her knees.

And Opal clung to her like a frightened monkey.

The sight broke his heart.

Opal lifted her face from her mother's shoulder. Giving him a tremulous smile, she wiped a small, dirty hand across her own tear-streaked cheek. "Hi, Atlas."

"Hi, my little pumpkin." Then quietly he said, "Charlotte, I'd like for you to bring the rig to a stop so I can tie my horse on. I'll drive the rest of the way to Buffalo Gap."

She opened her mouth to speak, then only nodded as she complied.

Dismounting, he tied Red Jack to the rear axle beside

the other two horses. Then, after stashing the confiscated gun belts on the nearest pony, he unhooked the covered water bucket and dipper that hung beneath the wagon and brought them to the front.

His strawberry blonds watched him with their mournful, wet eyes as he climbed up and poured them a dipper of water. It was obvious how grateful Charlotte was for the drink. Her eyes fell shut as she took in a goodly portion.

After they'd all had their fill and Opal snuggled down between her mama and Atlas, he pulled a red bandanna from his back pocket, wet it in the water, and raised it to Charlotte's face.

Her eyes flared. Was she afraid of him?

"I just want to clean you up a little. I would never hurt you. Ever."

Her gaze fell to her hands. "I know," she whispered and turned to him.

Atlas couldn't believe how much the simple act of washing that sweet face pleasured him. Wiping away the dirt, blood, and tears spiking her copper lashes was like unwrapping a beautiful gift. Her skin was fine and smooth, yet supple to the touch, and except for some puffy redness along her nose and a scratch over her eye, it truly did look like a sun-kissed peach. And her lips were as soft and inviting as one of his mother's pink satin pillows.

He took an extra-long time caressing that face with his kerchief, wishing the cloth were his thumbs, fingers . . . his lips . . . his tongue.

Gradually he became aware that she was staring at him with eyes that were now dry.

He withdrew the cloth, feeling guilty for his thoughts and wondering if she'd read them. Swinging away, he busied himself by rolling his sleeves above his elbows. He then poured some more water onto the bandanna. After wringing it out, he lifted Opal onto his lap and did his best to wash away her dirt streaks as well as her fear.

When he finished, Opal rose up swiftly and wrapped her arms around his neck, nearly knocking off his hat, and kissed him square on the mouth. Then, rearing back, she looked up at him with round, adoring eyes. "You knew we needed you, and you came. Just like Robin Hood. You came and saved us."

That did it. He blinked back wetness of his own—wetness he would never admit were tears. He pulled both of his girls into the protection of his arms.

Atlas spotted the first buildings of Buffalo Gap—a farmhouse and barn nestled in a shady grove of pecan trees . . . quiet, peaceful.

The wagon team also seemed pleased. They picked up their pace just as Charlotte climbed out from the interior of the wagon where she'd gone minutes before to bed down her napping tot.

Closing the hatch behind her, she took her seat beside Atlas. Brush in hand, she began running it through her hair.

Absently, Atlas reached over and pulled a twig from a tangled curl.

She glanced furtively at him, then resumed her task.

He wasn't sure if he'd frightened her again or merely startled her. One thing was certain—he'd have to stop making sudden moves around her until she settled down.

"I didn't want to ask before . . ." She spoke quietly, yet her voice jolted him. They were her first unsolicited words since he'd joined her. ". . . not in front of Opal. But I have to know. I heard a gunshot back there—did you kill one of them?"

He was tempted to take her hand. But he dared not. "No, just slowed them up a bit. The sheriff shouldn't have any trouble catching up to them."

Her brush froze halfway through a stroke. "The sheriff? Does he have to know? It's so—I'm so—ashamed."

Atlas cupped her chin and turned her to face him. "We have their horses. There'll be questions."

Her gaze wavered, then settled somewhere below his chin. "Couldn't you—I mean—would you go tell the sheriff? I—I—"

"Don't give it another thought, sweet Charlotte." He couldn't resist running his thumb down her cheek. "I'll take care of it. When we get there, I'll deliver the horses to him. You ride on with the wagon to wherever you park for the night."

"Next to the smithy's house."

"When I'm through, I'll meet you there. And don't worry. What happened is in the past now."

Those big green eyes swept up to his with such pain that he wondered how long she would be haunted by today's terrible ordeal.

"Howdy, Charlotte."

An older couple walking at the edge of the road waved.

Glancing their way, Charlotte shielded her swollen nose and called a greeting. She needn't have worried about her appearance though, because their attention was glued to Atlas. Judging by the presumptive glee in the stout woman's eyes, he knew the gossip mill would be grinding tonight.

At the jailhouse, Atlas leaped down, untied the horses, and went in, while Charlotte continued on. When he told the sheriff, a lean man who looked tough as rawhide, that she'd been attacked, the man bellowed an obscenity and charged toward the door.

Atlas had to physically restrain him.

"Where are they?" he growled, pulling away from Atlas. "I *will* be dragging their asses back here. The circuit judge is due any day now. We'll have 'em tried and hung before the week is out." He drew his Peacemaker and checked the chambers for bullets. "*If* they live that long. Folks round here are mighty fond of Miss Charlotte."

"Sheriff." Atlas motioned toward the desk. "You better take a seat. We need to talk."

Atlas gave him most of the details, then spent several minutes convincing him that Charlotte wasn't up to facing folks if they knew, let alone testifying at a trial. "Personally," he added, "I'd like to put the nooses around their necks myself, but not at her expense. But I'm sure you'd have no trouble catching up with them if you'd like to have your own *private* talk with them. I brought their horses, gun belts, *and* boots in with me."

The sheriff leaned his chair back on two legs and grinned, displaying a jumble of crooked teeth. "You don't say. And how far back did you say they were?"

"About three or four miles. Oh, and I guess I ought to mention I did find it necessary to shoot one of them in the foot."

The sheriff's chair thumped down on all four legs, and he whacked his knee. "If you're looking for a job, boy, you got one right here with me."

"Thanks, but my folks have a ranch out of Paradise Plains. Keeps me pretty busy. And, well, I've got to see to Mrs. Clairmore's safety. See that this sort of thing doesn't happen again."

"You just might have your hands full there, son. When it comes to her independence, she's one stubborn woman."

As Atlas unlashed Red Jack's reins from the hitching rail and mounted, three men watched him from across the street. A visit to the sheriff's office after riding into town leading two riderless mounts was bound to cause a stir. He pretended not to notice them, hoping to make a clean getaway.

No such luck. Before he'd managed to turn the sorrel into the road, a butterball of a man waddled toward him, blood on his butcher's apron and a headless chicken dangling from his hand. "Run into some trouble out there on the road?"

"Yeah," another old geezer called out to him. "Who do them two saddle horses belong to? And what was you in talkin' to Sheriff Wilcox about?"

Atlas tipped back his hat nonchalantly, hoping he looked unconcerned. "The horses were wandering loose. Found 'em grazing three or four miles back. Thought I'd better bring 'em in."

"Don't recognize the brands," said another with a pencil and paper in hands that were smudged with printer's ink.

That's all Atlas needed—a snoopy newspaperman.

"But they're rigged for cattle," the slightly built journalist continued.

"Yep," Atlas agreed, tapping the flanks of his sorrel. "Lot of drifters passing through lately."

The newspaperman caught hold of Red Jack's bridle and looked up with weak eyes. "Miss Charlotte didn't seem her usual cheery self when she rode by. Is she ailing?"

"Nothing serious. She must've eaten something in Abilene that didn't sit well, so I obliged her by driving her wagon here. I need to catch up to her now." Atlas stared squarely at the man until he released Red Jack's bridle. With a cluck, he urged the sorrel into a leisurely walk down the dusty street . . . his heart leaping ahead to Charlotte.

"Lucky you did," the butcher called as he jogged alongside. *Stubborn man.* "Two riderless horses seems a mite suspicious."

"I wouldn't know about that," he lied in a casual tone.

"You don't seem to know much of anything. Do you at least know what surprise Charlotte brung this time?"

In disbelief at the butcher's abrupt change of interest, Atlas shook his head and grinned. "Isn't my place to tell." Glancing at the feather he'd twined in Red Jack's golden mane what now seemed like days ago, he heeled the horse into a trot and left the meddlesome man behind.

Riding toward the smithy's shop, he saw folks loitering in front of nearly every business. Charlotte undoubtedly drew folks out in Buffalo Gap just as she did in Paradise.

But now it was he they were staring at.

Riding through a gauntlet of stabbing eyes, he kept his

own forward and his face within the shadow of his Stetson. He passed the blacksmith shop, which had MCCUTCHEON & SONS printed boldly across the false front, then saw Charlotte's wagon in a shady meadow on the other side.

People waited at the back. But Charlotte was missing.

A stout woman with a severe bun barged past the others to reach Atlas as he dismounted. "What's this all about?" she demanded with the finesse of a drill sergeant. "You bringin' in two riderless horses, and her actin' all queersome. Not speakin' to anyone and lockin' herself away in that hot wagon."

Old and young alike surged toward him.

Atlas raised a hand to stave them off. "You're all getting yourselves worked up for nothing. Charlotte and her little one aren't feeling quite up to snuff today. And as for the horses, they're just some strays we found along the way. Now if you'll leave them to their rest this evening, I'm sure Charlotte will be her old cheery self by morning." He stared pointedly at them and added, "Good evening to you all."

His not-so-subtle hint worked—everyone dispersed with the exception of one person, a short but powerfully built man who stepped forward and thrust out his hand. "Name's Gil McCutcheon." The man's grip was firm, honest. "I own this pasture. And if Charlotte didn't think to tell you, she takes a scoopful of my grain for each of her horses before she stakes 'em out to graze. The feed bin's in the lean-to next to the chicken coop. And the well's between the shop and the house."

"Do I pay you first?"

"No, we settle up once a month."

"If you don't mind me using some for my own horse, I'll pay for the extra grain now." Atlas reached for his money clip.

"Wouldn't think of it." The expression on the smithy's square face hardened. "Somethin' bad happened out there today. You ain't foolin' any of us. But if Miss Charlotte wants us to think she's just feelin' poorly, then that's what we'll do. And since the sheriff didn't lock you up, I figure you had a hand in gettin' her here safe. We're all mighty grateful. All us here in town worry about her and her young'un, riding around out there alone. Keep 'em in our prayers all the time." Unexpectedly he grabbed Atlas's shoulder and gave it a squeeze. "Yes, sir, we're mighty grateful."

Atlas took his time feeding, watering, and rubbing down the big work team, then his own smaller quarter horse, hoping Charlotte was taking a much-needed nap. But he couldn't help wondering if she really was in a restful, cleansing sleep or just hiding out in the closed-up wagon, reliving the horror of the day.

His own thoughts returned time and again to the picture of her writhing helplessly beneath those drunken saddle tramps. Sweat beaded his temples. *Just one minute later.* One minute, and he would've gotten there too late to stop them from doing their worst.

Across the street a dinner bell clanged at the local boardinghouse, reminding Atlas that it was dusk and he hadn't eaten since before dawn. Gathering the water bucket and rags, he walked back to the wagon. He hung them on their hooks, then hoisted himself up on the rear platform. Hesitating only a moment, he rapped lightly on the door.

The bottles on the inside of the door tinkled softly as Charlotte opened it a few inches, wide enough for him to see that she'd pulled her hair back into a single braid. It fell over a flowered silk kimono, and she looked more fragile than he would have ever imagined.

"Yes?" Her eyes seemed to take up half her face.

Fleetingly he noticed that the swelling on the side of her nose had turned purple, then he returned his gaze to her eyes, so invitingly dark in the shadows. Gradually he remembered why he'd knocked. "I thought I'd go over to the boardinghouse and bring us back some supper. If that's all right with you."

"Would you? I really don't feel up to facing folks over there tonight. Just tell Sister Elliot the plates are for us. She knows what Opal and I like. We eat there every time we come through."

Her voice was so hushed, it tore at his gut. He would've given anything to hear one of those loud, happy laughs he'd stupidly thought unladylike. Tempted to pull her close, feel the press of her delicate curves against him, he placed his hands on the doorjamb and took a disciplining breath. "I'll be back quick as I can."

"Wait." She reached out to stop his departure, then just as quickly retrieved her hand. "The sheriff. Is he . . . ?"

"No. We talked, and he understands."

"Good," she whispered on a sigh, then quietly closed the door.

Atlas returned through the growing darkness, balancing three plates and in much lighter spirits. While waiting for their food, he'd run into a former ranch employee and the solution to his problem—at least a temporary one. He set the food on the back deck.

Before he could reach up to knock, Charlotte pushed open the door. The bottles of medicine tinkled again—a happy chiming—as she stepped out, carrying a lantern turned to a low flame. Setting it beside the plates, she hooked the back door to the wall and moved to the edge of the platform. "Would you help me down?" she asked softly. "Opal is still asleep, so I thought it would be best to eat on our sitting log."

Atlas reached up and placed his hands around her waist . . . a waist covered by nothing more than a thin layer of silk. He prayed his hands wouldn't react.

"The log is beside where I make my fire for coffee in the mornings," she said in a rush . . . as if the uprooted tree didn't stick out like a sore thumb.

He lowered her to the ground . . . too slowly.

Her gaze nervously flitted away. In the soft lantern light, her hair shimmered angel-gold, and he couldn't take his eyes off of it.

She stepped out of his hands and picked up two of the plates. "Would you mind getting the lamp and bringing a dipper of water to share?"

Share the dipper? Put his lips where hers had been? His breath quickened. He could still feel the soft warmth of her body in his palms. They ached to trace the curve of her hips, feel her hasty heartbeat, her moist lips on his, her—

"Mr. Daltry," Charlotte called back to him in a loud whisper, "is there a problem?"

Finding himself just standing there, he snagged the handle of the lantern and went for the water.

He'd managed to get his fantasies under control by the time he joined her on the log.

She handed him his plate, but carefully avoided his eyes as she took the dipper and balanced it in a knothole.

She was so close. He could smell the fragrance of her soap. So near, yet so untouchable.

He wondered how much longer she would remain so timid, so withdrawn. And why was she taunting him by wearing that silk wrapper? It clung to her every curve. He could actually see the tip of one of her breasts as it pressed against midnight-blue silk. And the shape, the fullness of the lower swell.

She reached for the dipper.

Dragging his eyes away, Atlas picked up his fork. "While I was getting supper," he said, breaking out of the heated silence, "I ran into an old friend my family used to hire for cattle drives before the railroad came through. Maybe you know him. He's a tall, older man with a pot belly. And sometimes when he gets to talking too fast, he whistles through a gap in his teeth. So naturally he's called Whistle."

"Yes, I know him. He's that old windbag who used to ride shotgun on the stage to Austin."

"Yep, that's the one."

"What'd he want?" She was beginning to sound apprehensive.

"It was more what I wanted. He'll be escorting you while you make your circuit back to Paradise Plains. I'd do it myself but I need to be getting back. My father wasn't happy as it was when I took off for Abilene in the middle of stringing wire. And then there's the supplies for the contests . . ." He found her looking at him, her lips parted . . . soft, full.

She looked away. "Please tell Whistle I'm obliged, but I won't be needing him. I was careless today, let myself be distracted. It won't happen again."

"He's already hired. It's done."

"I don't accept charity. Like I said, things are fine the way they are. I'm fine."

He knew better. "And Opal? Is she fine, too?"

At the mention of her daughter, any resolve she'd mustered seemed to collapse, along with her shoulders. "I guess you're right. Maybe it would be best for now. As Papa used to say, I could be real pigheaded sometimes." Hesitantly she reached out and put her hand over his. "Truly, thank you for today. For saving me and my baby."

Her abject gratitude caught him by surprise, humbled him into silence. He speared a chunk of pot roast with his fork. After a moment, he realized Charlotte had yet to take a bite. "Eat up," he encouraged. "You'll feel better, and besides, I promised Mrs. Elliot that I'd bring the plates back soon as we're finished. After that, I'll be staying the night there if you need anything."

She took a small bite . . . a very small one. Then she looked up at him again. "What brought you down this way today? You never did say."

"It was just a stroke of luck. When I left you at the depot, I went to take care of some more business, then stopped off for a beer. That's when I heard that those two no-accounts had been in the saloon bragging about what they were planning."

"And you rode out by yourself to save me? Why didn't you fetch the town marshal? You could've been shot."

"It never occurred to me. I just . . ." Feeling even more stupid than when she'd thanked him, he finished with a shrug and took a bite of potato.

She continued to stare at him.

He could feel her gaze burning his cheek. Or was the heat caused by him blushing?

"I don't expect you to keep this from your own family," she said quietly, changing the subject. "When your grandmother learns about the shameful thing that happened today, I'm sure she'll gladly give you another labor. And as for the birthday party, I'm releasing you from escorting me."

He put down his plate and took her face in his hands. "I told you before, nothing happened that my grand-mother or anyone else needs to know about."

The glow from the lantern on the ground reflected the tears welling in her eyes. Atlas had the strongest urge to kiss them away.

Instead he released her and repeated, "Eat up."

# ᦙᦙ 13 ᦙᦙ

Charlotte crawled out of the lower bunk, grateful for the first glow of dawn. Any real rest had been impossible. She'd jumped at every hoot of an owl, every coyote's yip, even though she'd placed her rifle on the floor beside her. She'd always felt safe parked next to the smithy's. She knew he and his family kept watch over her. Sleeping with the doors open on a hot night had never frightened her before.

She checked Opal in the faint light. Curled in a ball on the top bunk, she had kicked down the sheet, as usual. Pulling it up, Charlotte stretched a number of sore muscles . . . more reminders of yesterday's horror. Of clawing hands. The ghastly Adam's apple. Trying to shake off the fact that they'd even invaded her dreams in those rare moments when she'd managed a catnap, she made her way to the small closet at the end of the beds.

She opened the door, started to pull out one of her gypsy work skirts, but couldn't. It, too, reminded her of yesterday. Instead, she removed a shirtwaist and a brown twill skirt and put them on, then slipped into some soft moccasins before leaving for the McCutcheons' outhouse.

Unplaiting her messy night braid on the way back, she saw no lamplight glowing from the family's kitchen. For once she was up before them. Passing their rain barrel, she scooped out some water and splashed her face and bruised nose, wondering how discolored it was now. How noticeable. The thought of trying to put up a cheery front today drained what little energy she had.

Coffee. She needed a good strong cup of Arbuckle's.

Stopping at her ring of firestone, she saw a stack of split logs and some kindling awaiting her and felt a rush of warmth. Most people were kind and friendly. Helpful. That's what she needed to concentrate on. Robby never failed to supply her with firewood. Just as she never failed to renew the youngest McCutcheon's supply of rock candy.

She arranged her wood with practiced expertise, then went back to the wagon for matches and coffee fixings. Reaching under, she unhooked the surprisingly heavy water bucket. Atlas must've filled it to the brim last night.

Beneath the wagon, something growled.

She jumped back and dropped the bucket.

"*Jeez!*"

*Atlas Daltry?* Charlotte's hands flew to her mouth.

He scrambled from under the wagon and came to his feet. Water dripped from his face and hair, down his soaked clothes.

"I'm sorry. I thought you were . . ."

Swiping the wetness from his eyes, he paused, and a smile slowly grew until it tugged at her heart. "And a splashing good morning to you, too, Miss Charlotte."

"You scared the wits out of me," she whispered back

with her own grin, then placed a finger to her lips. "Opal's still asleep."

Atlas picked up the bucket. "And *you're* out of water." He started away, his shirt untucked and his feet . . . bare?

Charlotte glanced from them to a bedroll laid out beneath her wagon. "Wait a minute. What were you doing down there?"

He looked back at her, his mouth open, his eyes shifting away as if he were trying to come up with a good story. "Well, you see . . ."

"Yes?" The man had been sleeping right beneath her bed. She *would* have an answer.

He glanced at his wet feet, muddy now, then looked up again. "There was so much snoring going on at the boardinghouse, I couldn't sleep. So I took my blanket and pillow and went outside—Oh, yes," he added for what sounded like good measure, "it was stuffy in there, too."

She stepped closer in the predawn light to avoid whispering so loud. "That still doesn't explain why you were under my wagon."

"It looked like rain?" With that, he made an about-face and marched away, wringing water from his shirttail. But his shoulders were convulsing, and she knew he was laughing. Drenched and still laughing.

Atlas Daltry did have a good sense of humor. She had to give him that.

Once the fire was going and the coffeepot hung on the tripod over it, Charlotte began to feel awkward. With a relatively unknown man, she sat on the log, waiting for their morning coffee to brew. But even if he was almost a stranger, he'd cared enough to spend the night guarding her and Opal. If she'd only known he was lying mere feet beneath her, she would've slept better. *Or would she have*?

Even as she busied herself, poking at the fire with a stick, she knew his eyes were on her most of the time. And with a day's growth of beard, he looked older, more rugged. Even better.

She realized she couldn't possibly look presentable herself. She hadn't so much as run her fingers through her hair since she'd pulled it from its night braid.

She sprang to her feet. "I'll go get the cups."

When Charlotte climbed down from the wagon a couple of minutes later, she had quickly brushed and contained her hair by tying a yellow scarf at the nape of her neck. Now it was a bit more presentable. But, alas, she'd seen her face quite clearly in the wall mirror, and the bruises looked more pronounced than they had yesterday. Ghastly evidence of the shameful day.

At that instant, a shining edge of the sun gilded the hill behind the boardinghouse, reminding Charlotte that this truly was a new day. The other one was gone.

Yet her palms turned clammy.

Facing the fire, Atlas turned at the sound of her approach, coffeepot in hand.

She stepped up to him and held out the two cups, hoping he wouldn't mind they were unbreakable tin instead of china . . . hoping he wouldn't notice her hands were slightly shaking or that her nose was swollen to double its size.

But she felt his eyes on her more than on the coffee he

poured. Pretending not to be aware, she studied the steam rising up as if her life depended on it.

"Looks like it's going to be another hot day," he said, placing the pot on one of the firestones and stuffing the bandanna he'd used as a pot holder into his back pocket . . . the same bandanna he'd used yesterday to wipe away the ugliness that had been done to her.

She looked up, pretending great interest in a cloudless sky.

Chuckling, he took one of the cups she held. "Guess there really wasn't much chance of rain last night." He continued to stand there, staring at her, looking interested. Too interested.

Why couldn't he just sit down, drink his coffee, and stop staring? Then it suddenly occurred to her—he was being a gentleman.

She settled herself on the log, and sure enough, so did he. Since he'd been the one to broach the noncontroversial subject of the weather, she could certainly find the courage to do that as well. "Yes, it's going to be a warm day. But I think summer is wonderful. For me, everything's so much easier. Freer." That said, she blew on her Arbuckle's to cool it.

"Yes," he agreed, being the amenable guest. "I don't imagine you do much business during a blizzard or in the spring when the mud is deep enough to swallow a cow."

"No, Opal and I boarded with a family in Abilene most of last winter."

Atlas took a sip from his cup. "Couldn't be good for business."

*Business.* It always came back to business. And it wasn't as if she hadn't been told plain enough. Shifting her attention to the small fire, she breathed in the steamy aroma coming from her cup, then took a drink, letting its strengthening warmth flow into her. And she made a decision. "You're right—business isn't good here in the winter. So I think I *will* load my rig on the train and go to California before the weather gets bad. If your sister Venus is right, I should do real well there."

She waited for him to say something, to make a comment about her leaving Texas. Waited while he leisurely lifted his cup to his mouth and took a sip. Then another.

Finally he spoke. "Thinking about going out to California, are you? Well, then, guess we'll have to be on the lookout for every party in the countryside if we're going to manage to work in five before winter." He said it flatly, without the least emotion, then topped off the statement with an earnest smile.

She wanted to scream, or cry, whichever came first.

He took another sip. "There's something about the smell of coffee over a campfire, isn't there? Watching the sun come up in the crisp air of morning."

She swallowed down another mouthful, along with her own foolish disappointment. "Yes, I always enjoy this quiet time before Opal wakes up and my busy day begins."

"It always seems as though you're having a good time with your customers."

"Yes, I do." Remembering her disfigured nose, she touched it. "Usually."

"If you're not up to facing folks today, I'm sure Whistle would gladly take over for you. He probably knows everybody in North Texas. Gabs worse than an old woman."

Charlotte turned toward Atlas and displayed her face. "Honestly, how do I look? Are the bruises too noticeable?"

His gaze roved slowly over her, then stopped at her eyes and stayed . . . the light blue-gray of his own eyes was such a pleasing contrast to his tan. After a time, he lifted a hand and brushed the tips of his fingers across the swollen bridge of her nose. "Don't you know," he whispered, "you'll still be the most beautiful woman there?"

Her breath caught. She knew she should move away. She couldn't let herself be swept up by him . . . not him. . . .

He dipped his head . . . his lips came toward hers—

"Mama!"

Charlotte snapped back and turned toward the wagon to see Opal on her belly, sliding off the edge of the platform. She set aside her cup and opened her arms.

With the joyous innocence of a four-year-old, Opal bunched up the hem of her thin cotton nightgown and ran to her mama.

Charlotte lifted her up and gave her a hug and a kiss . . . a safe kiss. "How's my precious jewel this morning?"

Opal nuzzled her for a second or two, then turned to Atlas, happily displaying all her baby teeth and both dimples.

Atlas returned a grin just as buoyant. "Morning, pumpkin."

Opal scrambled off Charlotte's lap and squatted, studying Atlas's feet—the ones covered in nothing but mud—then looked up at him and wagged her head. "Guess it was just a dream."

"What?" he asked, while Charlotte, suddenly uneasy, tried to remember what she and Atlas had been saying to one another near the wagon. Exactly what had her daughter overheard?

Opal brushed the side of his dirty foot. "I dreamed they'd sprouted wings again." She spread her arms. "This time big as angel wings. And you swooped down from heaven and saved me from a pack of mean dogs. Then we flew up to the clouds, and we rolled around on them all day just like they was a big pile of feathers."

"That so?" Atlas said with just the right amount of enthusiasm as he lifted Opal onto his lap. "We sure must've had fun."

Rising up to her knees, Opal twined her arms around his neck. "We sure did. And that's when I knew Mama was right all along."

"Right about what, sweetheart?" Tears clogged Charlotte's throat at the treasured sight of Opal and Atlas, forehead to forehead.

Opal rolled her head enough to see Charlotte. "About us having a guardian angel." Rearing back a few inches, she stared Atlas in the eyes. "'Cuz there you were yesterday, right when we needed you the most. I'll never be afraid again." She kissed him then, a big, smacking kiss.

Charlotte yearned to be as uninhibited, as bold. Too bad her daughter had awakened when she did.

When Opal pulled away, Charlotte noticed a blush rising up from Atlas's open collar. Sliding her an uneasy glance, he picked up his coffee and downed the remainder. He, too, must've remembered how they'd nearly kissed. "Guess I better saddle up and get on home." He placed Opal on the ground and came to his feet.

Charlotte also rose, already missing him. "I hope you haven't worried your family too much."

"Oh, they know I can take care of myself."

"You sure can!" Opal piped up. "You're better than any old Robin Hood. Better than his whole band of merry men." The child's enthusiasm for Atlas was boundless.

Scooping her up, he tossed her into the air and caught her to him. "And you, my little chickadee, *you're* going to be a blue-ribbon winner. As for your mama, I want to see her back to her old perky self by next Saturday."

He slipped Charlotte a pleading smile.

"And I know just what'll do it." The child then whispered something in his ear, something that made her giggle with excitement.

Opal was a corker, all right. Such a scamp. Charlotte's very own precious jewel.

## ❧ 14 ❧

Atlas sat, leaning against the trunk of the big elm, his legs comfortably stretched out across the cool, shady grass, the schedule for the next day's games in his lap. Yet he had difficulty concentrating as he studied it for missed details. In the last half hour, dust devils and the late afternoon sun had conspired any number of times to trick him into thinking his folks were just over the nearest rise.

But they should be coming back from Paradise Plains any minute. Any second.

Damn, he wished he'd just gone ahead and ridden into town to see for himself if Charlotte had arrived safely.

Actually he wanted to know far more than that. Now that she'd had a few days to think about him, would she still be glad to see him? More important, would her eyes again darken, begging him to kiss her?

That same sensation that excited him every time he thought about that moment shot from his heart to his groin.

Feeling a crowding of his jeans—*again*—he knew his grandmother was right. He'd spent much too much of his life doing the logical, practical, plodding thing.

But, his sensible half warned, if he had gone, he might've appeared too pushy, too eager. He might've scared her off. Everyone said Charlotte was skittish.

He exhaled and glanced down at his schedule, trying to remember where he'd left off.

"I swear, Atlas! You and your lists."

Startled, he swiveled around and found his grandmother looking over his shoulder. How the devil had she sneaked up unnoticed?

"Not that it isn't wonderful of you to volunteer to be in charge of the games." She moved to his side and handed him a welcome glass of lemonade.

"Thanks. This'll really hit the spot." He took a big swig. "Just to set the record straight, there is more to me than lists."

"That's my good boy." Condescendingly she patted him on the head as if he were still five years old. "And I just want to say that for someone who was so dead set against your labor, you certainly have gotten into the spirit of it. But still . . ." She paused, a tiny frown forming creases between her salt-and-pepper eyebrows. "I find it hard to believe that after Charlotte turned down all the young bucks in three counties, she accepted your invitation. Especially after she found herself on one of your infamous lists."

"Like I said, Grams, there *is* more to me than just lists." *Like someone who breaks the most important rule of his labor*, he added to himself in guilty silence.

"Oh, here come Odie and Jane."

Atlas's heart plucked like a guitar string. "Good!" He sprang to his feet, then realized he looked much too exuberant. Resettling his features, he said, "I hope they were able to get everything I need for the games tomorrow."

He strode across the lawn to the slate walk bordered with pink and purple petunias and reached the gate just as his father pulled the horse and buckboard to a stop.

"Here, take this, sweetheart." Jane handed Atlas a tote sack. "And help me down."

He spied peacock feathers poking out of the bag he set on the walk. Immeasurably gladdened, he grasped his mother's still-slim waist and swung her to the hard-packed driveway. "I see Charlotte has arrived."

A knowing smile reached her eyes, and crow's-feet appeared on either side.

"Those feathers," he said lamely.

Before Atlas could get a question in edgewise, Odie, who now stood at the back of the small wagon, chided, "That ain't the half of it." Hoisting a crate onto his shoulder, he glanced at his wife. "The woman ordered half a dozen peachicks. Says, 'A gazebo simply isn't a gazebo without at least one peacock perched on its roof'."

"Odysseus Daltry!" Jane obviously wasn't pleased with his imitation of her voice. "For someone who's always pounding on some newfangled secret out there in your workshop, *you* certainly have no room to talk about a few expenditures for my yard."

Odie's chuckle had a triumphant ring. His locked workroom had always been a prime source of frustration for her. Passing Atlas, he paused. "And concerning that labor of yours. Looks like you've got yourself some competition. And you're not going to believe who."

Atlas stopped breathing. Charlotte had found someone else?

Jane squeezed Atlas's arm. "Your father is just joshing. You remember that drover we used to hire every summer, Whistle McSween? He's driving Charlotte's rig. Temporarily. Until she's feeling better."

By this time, Minerva had joined them. "Why? What's ailing the lass?"

"Doesn't appear to be catching," Jane said. "She didn't look like she had a fever or a cough. But it's something, all right. It's taken the laugh right out of her."

"Our Charlotte not laughing?" Minerva sliced a glance Atlas's way as if it were his fault . . . when no one could possibly be more concerned than he.

Odie started up the walk with the crate of goods. "All I know is it hasn't put a damper on Whistle's high spirits. Says he's havin' more fun than a Saturday night hoedown."

"That reminds me." Atlas picked up the tote sack and turned to his mother. "Did the blue ribbons I ordered come in?"

"They sure did. And don't forget to thank Hank at the store when you see him tomorrow. He ordered them by telegraph wire just to be sure you got them on time. And he didn't get just blue. He got red ones for second place and white for third, so more young'uns can feel important." She and Minerva started up the walk behind Odie. "Everything you wanted," she tossed over her shoulder, "is in that bag you're carrying."

He strode after them, loosening the drawstring. "The rubber balls, too?"

"Here's your list, darling. I know you. Until you've checked each item off for yourself, you won't be happy."

Atlas crumpled the note page beneath his mother's nose. "I trust you."

"Bravo!" Minerva turned back with a laugh. "You're coming along right nicely. Right nicely."

Stifling his first retort, he pressed the paper ball into her hand. "In my own way, Grams. In my own way."

"Oh, it almost slipped my mind." His mother's face brightened. "That little Opal. She *is* a pistol. She ordered me to tell you she's been practicing her running every day, and she's—these are her own words—fast as lightning now."

Starting up the walk again behind the women, Atlas envisioned Opal, her determined little face, skirt bunched above her knees, and her short legs pumping like engine pistons. He reached into the sack and pulled out a prize ribbon. "And we've got exactly what she wants."

But, Atlas thought, it was Opal's mother who needed the real cheering up. He'd assumed she was fine by the time he left her in Buffalo Gap. Still a little shaky, but pretty much back to her old self. He'd been wrong. Perhaps he'd better take Opal's advice. It couldn't hurt. "Mother, do Lee and Meredith have any kittens left from that last litter?"

The next morning, Atlas drove the buckboard into town with all the supplies for the games, from burlap bags, string, balls, and rope for the children to horseshoes, croquet, and baseball equipment for everyone else. The several dozen raw eggs had been the most difficult to transport over the bumpy road, but no day of games was complete if folks didn't get at least a little egg slime somewhere on their person during the egg toss.

Spotting Charlotte's wagon as he turned onto Main Street, Atlas quickly checked his brown string tie to make sure it hadn't shifted from the center of his white shirt, then looked down to see if any dust had settled on his khaki summer suit or his highly polished boots. But nothing had changed since he'd last checked a couple of minutes before.

A soft mewing sounded from the lump in the flour sack beside him.

"Not much longer," he said, gently patting the kitten curled up inside the cotton bag.

Halfway down the street, Atlas spotted Whistle Mc-Sween sitting on the veranda of the dry goods store, his hands working almost as hard as his mouth. He sat in one of several chairs Hank kept outside for folks to congregate and chat. Three other men were there with him, listening, most likely, to one of his animated tales.

Atlas veered the buckboard to the side of the street.

"Well, howdy, there, Bub," Whistle called and lumbered to his feet. Coffee mug in hand, he ambled down the steps.

Atlas waited until the paunchy older man reached the wagon. He'd just as soon the others didn't hear their conversation. "How'd everything go? Was there any kind of trouble after I left Buffalo Gap?"

"Nah. But you know folks. There ain't nothin' a body can do to stop their wonderin'. They was busy, buzzin' all around what might've happened. So I just told Missy Charlotte to stay inside and let me handle things till her bruises faded. Been havin' myself a high ol' time, too.

Yessiree," he drawled with that gap-toothed grin, "we're gonna have so many peacocks a-struttin' round the country-side, folks passin' through's gonna think the tracks of the Texas and Pacific go all the way to India or China. Or whichever place them glorified turkeys come from."

"Well, I'm pleased you've been enjoying yourself, because I was wondering if you'd mind working for Charlotte another couple of weeks. Till she's back to her old self again."

"I'd be plumb tickled." Tucking his chin, he nodded thoughtfully. "Till the little lady's herself again."

"Good." Atlas pulled a couple of banknotes from his money clip and handed them down to Whistle. "And I want to keep this between you and me. Same as before."

Continuing down the street, Atlas found himself hoping to catch a glimpse of Charlotte near her outfit. His collar began to scratch. Was he sweating already?

Passing the medicine-show wagon, he spotted her behind it, and his heart did its usual leapfrog—something he was beginning to take for granted. He set the brake and climbed down with the bagged kitten tucked in the crook of his arm.

"Hold still," he heard Charlotte order as he walked past her colorfully painted back wheels. She sat on a stool, and Opal stood between her legs. As usual, they wore dresses of the same fabric—this time a beige polished cotton with large pink cabbage roses. Charlotte's bustle bobbed crazily off the back of the stool as she struggled to braid her daughter's hair. Her own had been brought up to her crown and was fashioned in a swirl, with just the perfect amount of curls playing around her nape and cheeks to tempt the strongest-willed man.

"Oww!" Opal yelped, her face scrunched in a petulant frown. "You're making it too tight."

"If I don't, it'll be coming loose before . . ." Charlotte must have sensed Atlas was watching because she slowly turned his way until she located him, her emerald eyes wide, her lips parted slightly . . . lush, waiting.

"Atlas!" Opal broke free of her mother and came at a run. She crashed into his legs with her usual exuberance.

Reaching down with his free hand, he pulled her into a hug. "Well, you certainly been practicing for the race. I never saw a four-year-old run as fast as you. Maybe not even someone who's five."

As he took her hand and started toward Charlotte, Opal looked up at him with worshipful eyes. "You really think so? You think I'll win?"

"Absolutely." His own eyes returned to her mother. "Good morning, Charlotte," he said, noting her swollen nose was almost normal again. "I would be honored if you'd allow me to escort the two loveliest ladies in three counties to church this morning."

Her smile was fleeting, but he didn't miss the shy encouragement in it.

"If you think I'm pretty now," Opal crowed, "wait till you see my new ribbons." She backed up to her mother again. "Mama, hurry up and tie them on my braids. Please," she quickly added, but it was no more than a perfunctory afterthought.

With raised brows, Charlotte treated him to one of those patient-mother smiles as she picked up from her lap a pink satin strand with beige lace trim and began to fashion a shapely bow . . . her fingers as graceful as a breeze-blown willow. Fingers that he knew could do such things to his—

"Don't you think they're pretty?" Opal cried, cutting off his thoughts before he could even begin to explore them.

"You bet," he answered with forced enthusiasm. "I didn't know they made ribbons that pretty."

"I'm so glad," she said with total earnestness. "It's the one I'll give you when you race."

"That's very sweet of you, pumpkin, but I'm not racing today. This is your day. I just hope I can find a ribbon half as pretty to tie around your arm."

She sucked in an excited breath. "And the kiss. You have to give me a kiss."

"*Opal*," her mother reprimanded.

Atlas winked at Charlotte. "Oh, yes, the kiss. Now, pumpkin, I forget. Just exactly where do I put it?"

With coy impatience, Opal cocked her head. "Here, silly." She poked a finger in her right dimple.

Atlas bent down. "Maybe I'd better practice, so I get it right."

The closer he came, the harder she giggled. But when he pressed his lips to her cheek, she fell silent.

Glancing over at Charlotte with a wink, he found her looking at him with the same unguarded warmth he'd seen in Opal's eyes. His heart kicked. The two were so alike.

The kitten tucked in his arm mewed and started to wiggle.

"What's that?" Opal's eyes danced with expectation, and she reached for the flour sack.

Atlas straightened to his full height, eluding the child. "Oh, this." He placed the tote in Charlotte's lap. "It's that little present for your mama we talked about."

Opal squealed.

The kitten jumped.

So did Charlotte. She uncinched the top of the sack, and out popped the kitten's calico head. Charlotte laughed nervously. "At least it isn't a rat."

Opal whisked away the fluffy thing. Hugging it to her, she whirled around. Then, stopping, she kissed its nose.

It licked hers.

"Oh, Mama, isn't it the most beautifulest kitten you ever saw? Look at its coat. It has every color."

"I picked that one," Atlas said, "because it reminded me of your and your mama's gypsy skirts."

"Oh, yes. It's just like me and Mama. Our little gypsy cat. Can we call her Gypsy, Mama? Can we?"

Charlotte's lips were pressed tightly together. She was none too happy. "Yes, Opal, she's a beautiful cat. But we've talked about having a kitten before. Kittens like to stay put. They get frightened when they're moved from place to place."

Frowning, Opal hugged the kitten tighter. "My lap is one place. It won't be afraid in my lap. See?" She dropped down onto the grass, her full skirts making a nest for the tiny animal. She started petting it, and Atlas heard it begin to purr.

Charlotte stood abruptly and peered down at Opal.

Atlas had no doubt he'd been tricked . . . and by a four-year-old, no less. But the child was gazing up at her mother with such pleading eyes, he couldn't bear it. "I don't mean to interfere, Charlotte, but couldn't you give it a try? Just two weeks. If it doesn't work out, I'll gladly take it back."

"Oh, yes, Mama, *please*," Opal whined. Then, getting up, she held out the kitten. "Touch Gypsy, Mama. She's so soft."

Charlotte's defeated sigh was all Opal needed. She hugged her mother's leg, then took off with the kitten, shouting over her shoulder, "I'm going to show Gypsy to Whistle."

Charlotte wagged her head and turned back to Atlas. "You certainly know how to make a little girl happy."

"My intent was to brighten your day."

The lace that edged the net inset of her bodice fluttered with a quick intake of breath, drawing his eyes to the thinly veiled swell of her bosom. He told himself it was the fashion, that even his mother had dresses with net insets. But on Charlotte it was more alluring than any saloon gal's daringly low-cut costume.

Her hand edged up to fidget with the satin rose pinned to her lace collar and shielded her exposed flesh.

Quickly bringing his attention up where it belonged, he caught a hint of panic in her eyes before her gaze flitted away. What was the matter with him? She was already spooked enough without him ogling her endowments. He removed his Stetson and nervously raked his fingers through his hair. "I should've known Opal wanted the kitten for herself."

"Kitten? Oh, yes, the kitten. I imagine you're learning that little girls have a way of wrapping great big men around their fingers."

"No more than their mothers." He hadn't intended to say that. It had just popped out. He quickly recouped.

"Has Whistle McSween handled things okay since he's been with you?"

"Yes. You were right about hiring him. I really wasn't up to making the rest of the circuit alone." She moved past him. "I'd better fetch my bonnet. Folks are starting to arrive for church."

He looked toward the building. A couple of buggies had already arrived, and more were coming down the street. "Wait. There's something I need to tell you while we're still alone."

She stopped and turned, standing far enough away for him to view all of her at once.

In that instant, he wished fervently he'd taken up photography instead of economics. He would give anything to have her immortalized in that exact pose . . . the morning light turning her cascade of curls into a glorious frame for her fragile beauty, and the lovely swell of her bosom accentuated to perfection by her bustled skirt.

"Yes?" She took a step toward him, breaking yet another spell.

"Whistle has agreed to accompany you on your next circuit."

"No. I can't afford to pay him, and I won't let you."

"It's already done."

She stiffened. "Just because we have a temporary business arrangement, I didn't give you license to take over my life."

"You're absolutely right." And she was, but . . .

She couldn't seem to make up her mind whether to be glad he agreed or disappointed.

In the breech he pressed his cause. "As soon as I see

roses in your cheeks again instead of merely on your dress, I'll stop meddling."

Her smile won out over the frown. "I doubt that. I ran across a book on Greek mythology yesterday. Do you know what it said about your namesake?"

Rolling his eyes, he groaned.

"My, my. Such a tremendous responsibility you have. The whole world to worry about, no less. If Atlas stops holding up the heavens, all the earth will be crushed. My, my, my."

She was teasing him. It was going to be a good day. Very good. "But even the Lord rested on the Sabbath. So, my fair damsel . . ." He took her hand and placed it on his arm. ". . . it would be my supreme honor to do nothing more than escort you to church."

That panicked look reappeared. She glanced past him to the white steepled church where folks were starting to walk inside. "You haven't said anything about— You didn't say anything to your family, did you?"

He placed his hand on top of hers. "No. I told you I wouldn't. Besides, nothing that happened was your fault. But I do have something I forgot to ask you."

"What?" Her wariness returned.

"I need to buy a length of the prettiest ribbon you've got. For Opal's big race."

Her expression dissolved into a breath-stopping smile, and she whispered, "The very prettiest."

## ⊸ 15 ⊶

Halfway through the afternoon games, Atlas wished he hadn't taken charge of them. Although he was pleased with the results—Opal now sported two blue ribbons of her own—he'd been deprived of spending that time with Charlotte. Earlier, when he'd been with her during church and the dinner for Mother Spooler, she'd been exceptionally quiet. Engaging in the usual small talk with her friends had seemed too difficult for her. The loud, yacky Charlotte they knew simply wasn't there.

Atlas stole glances at her while handing out burlap bags for the boys' sack race. She sat on the far side of a croquet field on which several young couples played.

His mother and grandmother sat under an oak with her, and she wore a polite smile while Grams, as usual, rattled on. Probably telling Charlotte some noxious tale from his childhood . . .

"Bub, are you going to give me a sack or not?" The youngest Carpenter boy stood in front of him, waiting.

"Sure." He shoved one at the kid, then held out another for the next youngster . . . and glanced back at Charlotte.

Grams and Mother rose and walked away, toward the

outhouses behind the church, leaving Charlotte sitting alone on the family's blanket. His fairy princess. His lonely princess.

Atlas willed her to look his way so he could beckon her to join him.

But she didn't. Her legs tucked neatly beneath her, she fiddled with something on the blanket. She looked as delicately beautiful now as she had this morning. And just as vulnerable. Just as desirable.

And he wasn't the only one who'd noticed. A number of young studs—seven, to be exact—had stopped off to speak to her since he'd handed her over to his family. Small wonder. Her unexpected quiet loveliness was like a magnet. She'd given them no encouragement, however, and each had eventually drifted on.

Atlas handed a bag to the last boy, then blew the whistle strung around his neck to get their attention. "Line up and get into your sacks." He waved at the judge at the finish line, one of the twins from the Horse Hotel and pulled his revolver to start the race.

Some of the boys weren't ready. They were still kicking into their sacks . . . which gave Atlas time for another quick glance at Charlotte.

In the few seconds since he'd last checked on her, three men had surrounded Charlotte. One was crouched down before her. Atlas could see from that distance that everyone was smiling.

Everyone except Charlotte. Her back was stiff, and her hands were tightly clasped in her lap, out of easy reach. Atlas couldn't see the expression in her eyes, but he had no doubt she was frightened.

Holstering his .45, he turned to the father of one of the

contestants. "Jack. Take over." He whipped off the whistle and shoved it at the ranch manager, along with the raft of prize ribbons and the list. Without waiting for an answer, he took off at a run.

Circling the croquet players, Atlas noticed a boy walking away from a table loaded with ice cream freezers. He had two bowls of the rare treat.

"Trade you a quarter for those."

"Why? They're free just over yonder." The towheaded boy pointed with one of the bowls.

Atlas fished a coin out of his pocket. "Don't have time to wait my turn."

With a greedy grin, the boy thrust the ice cream at him.

"Thanks," Atlas tossed as he hurried on to save Charlotte, armed with his cold and creamy weapons.

In the time it took to reach her, another of the men had dropped down on the grass beside her.

Her face was now blanched so white, the sprinkle of freckles on her nose stood out above a stiff smile.

Strangers to Atlas, none of the young men were dressed in Sunday clothes, just their usual jeans and neckerchiefs. Most likely they'd heard talk of the barbe-cue and dropped by the way young drifters were apt to do. And he was pretty sure they were merely flirting. But couldn't they see Charlotte's discomfort?

He stepped between the two young men crouched on either side of her and handed her a bowl. "Sorry to take so long getting the ice cream." Grasping her elbow, he helped her to her feet.

The other two scrambled up as well.

"I know how busy you've been." Picking up her cue, Charlotte's voice was a bit too bright.

"Well, I'm all yours now. We can take that stroll I promised you."

She took his arm, then turned to the men. "Thank you for stopping by to chat."

One swept off his hat in a belated polite gesture. "Couldn't pass up a chance to call on our Miss Charlotte."

"Our Miss Charlotte" sounded entirely too possessive, too personal, for Atlas. His own territorial instincts surfaced. But he couldn't very well punch the bum just because he didn't like the way the cowhand said *our*. He bit back his anger. "Sorry to whisk her away, boys, but I did promise."

After leaving the threesome behind, Atlas began to uncoil and allow himself the pleasure of watching the sunlight play across Charlotte's bare head. "Would you like to walk down to the creek to eat our ice cream?"

She looked up at him with an expression that made her look as young and vulnerable as Opal. "That would be nice. Get away from all the prying eyes for a while."

"Charlotte," he said, guiding her toward the line of trees on the far side of the meadow, "no one knows anything about the other day. Folks are just curious and maybe a little worried. They're used to hearing that laugh of yours."

"It's that noticeable? I didn't know I laughed all that much."

"You're kidding! If we could bottle and sell it, you'd be a rich woman."

"Always looking for a business opportunity, aren't you?"

Something in her tone made him uneasy. But it made

no sense, so he dismissed the thought. "Well, actually, I've been thinking of going into the blue-ribbon business, considering the way Opal's been winning them today."

"Where is she? I lost track."

"In the back of Frank Spears's wagon, playing with his granddaughter and"—he added with a grin—"that kitten she bamboozled out of me."

Charlotte didn't relax until she and Atlas started down the bank and into the haven of the willows overhanging the broad, lazy stream. No matter what Atlas had said, she'd felt everyone's eyes crawling all over her since he'd first escorted her inside the church that morning. No one had actually referred to the incident, but she was sure they knew something—no matter how sincerely Atlas tried to reassure her they didn't. Whistle McSween was not noted for having a tight lip.

As they reached the bottom of the bank, the cool air off the water caressed her face and neck, and the deep shade soothed her eyes. So peaceful, so needed. It was enough to make a girl want to cry . . . if she were the sort.

Her errant knight, who'd again come to her rescue, now helped her across ancient roots and boulders until they stepped out on a flat-topped rock surrounded on three sides by the shallows. "Would you like to sit here?" he asked, his voice as gentle as the sound of the water whispering past, gentle as the rustling of the leaves above.

She looked into eyes that had taken on the sultry darkness of the glen. "Yes, this is perfect."

He helped her down, then sat beside her, almost touching. But not quite. "I hope you like blackberry."

Breathing in the faint fragrance of his cologne, she glanced down at her melting ice cream. "Blackberry is one of my favorites."

As he picked up his spoon, she noticed his sleeves were rolled up, exposing his arms. Long, yet ever so masculine, and as flawlessly tanned as his face. If his future children inherited his wonderful skin, they would be lucky indeed.

She shifted her gaze to the opening of his partially unbuttoned shirt. The skin there was also golden brown, and she envisioned him bare-chested, splitting firewood or pounding in fence posts. She saw him pouring a basin of water over himself after a hard day's work, his slicked body gleaming. Saw her hands roving his muscle-padded shoulders, his . . .

Suddenly aware of where her daydream was leading, Charlotte picked up her own spoon. She really couldn't believe those had been her thoughts, her desires. Not after three years of enduring Cecil's demands, and then the horror of last Wednesday. Why was her body longing so for his touch? Wanting him to fill some unnamed emptiness that yawned within her—an emptiness that grew more needy by the second?

Taking a spoonful of ice cream, she closed her eyes and tried to ignore this new kind of hunger.

"It is good, isn't it?"

Atlas must have mistaken her expression. "Yes, very." She looked out over the sun-dappled water, not wanting him to read the yearning in her eyes correctly.

To her relief, he began to concentrate on the dessert.

Yet, as they finished their bowls of ice cream, Charlotte felt a tension in the silence. She should say something, but knew she couldn't mention the outrageous thoughts swimming around in her head. And just how many times could a body discuss the weather?

"I've been asking around about a sound wagon team."

Thank goodness he'd said something. Now it was her turn to answer. "Oh, really?"

"From the look of your horses, I supposed you'd want another matching pair. But so far no one I've talked to knows of a good team for sale."

"If you'd like I could write your request on my slate board. I have it up for folks who want to buy or sell something."

"That's very enterprising of you, Charlotte. How much do you charge for carrying an advertisement?"

"Charge? I don't charge. It's as much of a convenience for me as for everyone else. Since I tacked the slate on the wagon I don't have to keep everybody's needs in my head."

"You're a very nice lady, Charlotte," he said as he took her bowl and stacked it on top of his.

She knew he was merely patronizing her. As a student of economics, his measure of success undoubtedly would be only in the profit. "Thank you, Mr. Daltry. I'd like to think I am a considerate person."

Her answer must have been too stilted. Shifting his weight, he glanced nervously around, and though they sat side by side, a gaping silence came between them again. Finally he turned to her. "Speaking of business, I heard a joke the other day that you might find amusing. There were these two shopkeepers directly across the street from each other, a baker and a candy maker. Each accused the other of being the source of a terrible plague of flies."

He stopped, his forehead scrunching in a puzzled frown. Then, as if suddenly remembering, he brightened and reached into his shirt pocket. He pulled out his notebook and started leafing through the pages. "Yes, here it is."

Charlotte couldn't believe it. Did he even make notes of jokes? She snatched the notepad from him, and sure enough, there they were—the baker, the candy maker, and the flies. She burst into laughter. Uproarious laughter.

"It is a funny joke, isn't it?" He chuckled, too, as she handed the pages back to him.

Laughing all the louder, she shrugged her convulsing shoulders and sputtered, "Not the . . . joke. I'm laughing . . . at you. You even keep . . . a list of . . . jokes." It took a good while before she could swallow down her amusement enough to take a calming breath. "Jokes. Lists for business ventures. Lists for games. Don't you ever just go out and have fun?"

She'd hurt his feelings again—his pained expression told her so. He looked down at his notebook, then back at her.

She reached for his hand. "I'm sorry. That was very rude of me."

"But true. A habit I got into when I was a kid. You see, I'm the youngest in my family, and I've spent my whole life trying to catch up. Trying to get them not to treat me like a baby. I started writing things down so no one could fluster me when I wanted to prove a point, to be taken seriously."

"Well, you certainly have succeeded. I don't know another man your age who has much more on his mind than sowing wild oats. But you—you're not only trying to secure the funds for your first business venture, but you've even picked out its location. Really, Atlas, couldn't you just once throw away your notes and just have fun?"

"You're right. I'm turning into an old stick in the mud. Tell you what . . ." He held up the tablet. "I'll throw this nagging thing in the creek if you'll come back to the party with me and have a good time."

"Me?"

"Yes, you."

She stared up at his infectious smile. "Why not? I've got to stop going around all down in the mouth because of two no-account galoots." She held out her hand. "Help me up, and let's get to it."

"That's my Charlotte." Atlas leaped to his feet and hauled her up to hers. He then pressed his notebook in her hand. "And for our first devil-may-care act, throw this blasted thing in the creek."

"Are you sure?"

"Small price to pay if I can hear you laughing again." He took her wrist, and together they sailed the notebook out across the water.

The tablet, flapping like a many-winged bird, landed with a splash.

Charlotte wondered if she'd pushed Atlas to do something he'd regret as she watched it float downstream and slowly sink out of sight. She looked up at him and found him watching her, not the stream. And more. He had yet to let go of her wrist. She felt herself moving closer, her gaze centering on his mouth. She heard his breathing, felt her own throbbing pulse beneath his fingers.

He was going to kiss her.

She shouldn't let him . . . but what could it hurt?

Abruptly Atlas stepped back, as if he'd been shot. "Then what are we waiting for?" With her in tow, he dashed up the bank. "If we hurry, we'll be in time to enter the wheelbarrow race."

"What?" Charlotte dug in her heels.

Grinning, he turned back. "I'll be the wheelbarrow, of course."

"But it's so unladylike. I mean, can't you just see me? Your feet in my hands, charging across the field, this stupid bustle chugging up and down like a butter churn? Anyone gets too close, it'll knock 'em winding."

"Are you saying Opal's the only one in her family who can win a blue ribbon?"

"Are you daring me?"

"Double."

"You're on, buster!" Wrapping her fingers around his wrist, she let out a whoop and hoistered herself up the last few feet of the bank. "Let's get at it."

## ☙ 16 ❧

The next Saturday, Atlas knotted the second saddle strap across an oilcloth-wrapped bundle. Neatly folded within were his best suit, his dress boots, and other items he'd need to attend a wedding in Abilene—everything except the boil-starched shirt his mother was now ironing.

Although the sun had barely risen, and the wedding Charlotte had invited him to wasn't scheduled until that evening, he was anxious to arrive early. Today would be the first time the two of them would be together without her child or his family watching every move they made.

Leaving Red Jack tied at the hitching ring outside the gate, he started up the walk to the back door to see if his mother was finished with his shirt.

He knew he and Charlotte were set to meet at Langley's Boardinghouse shortly before eight this evening, but who knew, maybe she, too, would come early on the chance of spending more time with him. Just the fact that *she* had been the one to invite him to the wedding of her brakeman-friend's daughter was an encouraging sign.

His more sensible side was less hopeful. She'd probably invited him simply to get his labor out of the way. To rid herself of him and his crazy family.

Shaking off that notion, he walked into the kitchen.

Minerva had come downstairs while he was outside and had that danged busybody gleam in her eyes. She sat at the table, one plump hand wrapped around a china cup. "Where are we off to so early on a Saturday morning? You didn't mention anything at supper last night."

His mother gave him a helpless shrug. She'd been the only one he'd told this morning, and then only because he'd needed the shirt. He hadn't wanted to listen to Grams' endless stream of advice all week, any more than he'd wanted to put up with the men's inevitable teasing.

He also hadn't wanted to give them any more openings to question him about last Sunday. That time with Charlotte had been too precious to share with anyone just yet.

"You'll be pleased to know, Grams, that I'm going to my second social function with Charlotte this evening. A wedding in Abilene." He turned to his mother, who was carefully wrapping his shirt in tissue paper. "Good, you're done."

Minerva raised a suspicious brow. "Why haven't we heard about this wedding before now? And, if it's not until tonight, why are you leaving so early?"

"There's some property I want to check into . . . just in case someone in the family starts seeing the wisdom of the meatpacking plant." It never hurt to keep reminding her of what he wanted for his prize.

"Oh, yes, that slaughterhouse. But let's get back to Charlotte. Since you never mentioned a wedding until this very minute, how can I be sure you're actually taking her to one? Not just trying to put something over on me?"

Although Jane didn't say anything, her expression gave her away. She was on the verge of laughter as she handed him the shirt.

"Thanks, Mother," he said, knowing he'd been right in not telling them before now. At the door, he looked back at his grandmother. "Tell you what—to prove I was with her, I'll bring you a lock of her hair."

"Hmm." Minerva narrowed her gaze.

"Would you prefer the whole scalp?" Jane teased as she walked to the stove.

Not waiting to hear his grandmother's answer, Atlas strode out the door.

As he approached Red Jack, his thoughts drifted to the actuality of lacing his fingers through Charlotte's hair, of snipping off a strand. Just the hope of again breathing in the lilac soap she used spiked the heat of desire downward.

Tying the paper-wrapped shirt on top of the bundle, he mounted and reined the sorrel around, then nudged it into a trot. The sooner he escaped his family, the sooner he could again relive the last time he'd seen Charlotte.

Last Sunday. The two of them had laughed so much during their attempt at wheelbarrow-racing that his arms kept collapsing, sending him face-first into the dirt. Needless to say, they'd come in last. But the silly contest had done the trick. From that moment on, Charlotte was back to her old hooting and joking self. Only when she'd looked directly into his eyes did she forget to laugh.

But *that* he'd liked even more than her merriment. For

he'd seen hunger in those wide green eyes. Hunger for him.

He'd be willing to bet the ranch on it.

Almost.

Tonight he'd make sure. And if it was the last thing he did, he was going to kiss those rose-petal lips.

Looking back now, it was hard to believe he'd actually balked when Grandmother had assigned him the labor. To think he'd been so worried about his reputation. He shook his head at his pretentious audacity.

Everyone loved Charlotte just the way she was. Who cared what some stuffy old bankers in Chicago or New Orleans might think about the match? This was Texas. And she was Texas at its best. Not only did he consider himself lucky to be in her company, the fact that he was falling head over heels for the woman no longer gave him a moment's concern. Hell, he loved every second of it.

Charlotte looked at the slant of the late afternoon sun as she drove a borrowed buggy into Abilene. The wedding was no more than two hours away, and she still had to pick up her gown at the dressmaker's and get ready. She sincerely hoped Mrs. Langley would have a bath drawn and waiting when she reached the boarding-house.

Passing the many saloons, she noticed the cowpunchers were already riding in for their Saturday night hell-raising. Seized by a sudden grip of panic, she shot a glance down the street to the Grand Hotel, the large brick establishment where Atlas had said he would be staying. Thank goodness, he was standing outside.

He must've already seen her because he strode off the

veranda toward her, his hat in hand and looking every inch the dashing gentleman in a charcoal suit and matching plaid waistcoat. But his greeting smile was what she appreciated most.

With her own happy grin, she slowed the horse to a stop . . . then realized what a dirty, wind-tossed mess she must be after spending a couple of hours on hot, dusty roads to get there.

"Howdy," he said, placing a hand on the back of the leather-padded seat. "I was beginning to think something came up and you couldn't make it."

She slipped her fingers up to retuck any strays beneath her straw bonnet. "Actually, we did have a problem. Crossing the railroad tracks this morning, a wheel broke on my wagon. But thanks to you I had Whistle with me. He rounded up a couple of his old cronies in Clyde, and they took care of the whole business for me."

"I'd hoped you'd be able to join me for a light supper at the hotel before the wedding, but I suppose you won't have time."

"That would've been very nice, but as you can see, I'm in much need of repair."

Atlas's gaze roved over her. "Please don't *repair* yourself too much. I like everything I see right now."

His eyes, his words, made her tingle all over. She could stare at him all day. But there simply wasn't time. "That's very flattering, but if I don't get to my seamstress soon, we'll be late." She raised the reins over the bay's back.

"Well, I certainly wouldn't want to cause you to be late for our first wedding." He stepped back from the buggy. "I'll be by for you at a quarter to eight."

As she drove away, she couldn't believe that absolutely gorgeous young man would be her escort. Once Clem Tucker's daughter got a gander at Atlas, she'd probably wish she had a second choice.

Charlotte scarcely believed she'd managed. But just as she looked over the banister at the grandfather clock down in the entry hall, she heard the front door opening.

Seven forty-five precisely.

She started down the stairs in the one and only ball gown she'd ever had made. The green satin rustled with rich elegance along with her every step. It was trimmed in velvet of the same shade, and the skirt drew fashionably to the rear in the most lavish bustle she'd ever worn.

She so hoped a young man who'd spent several years in the big city would find it as up-to-date as the dressmaker had promised. Nervous, she took in as much of a breath as her tightly laced corset would allow, then had a sudden horrifying realization. If she'd been able to inhale more deeply, her breasts would've popped out of the low-cut gown. In fact, the seamstress had fitted the entire bodice so tightly, it hugged her like a second skin. And the skimpy tucker of black lace did little more than draw attention to the problem. "Oh, dear."

She slowed to a stop just as Atlas stepped into view.

He, too, halted. He stared, his mouth gaping open.

Merciful heavens, the dressmaker had been terribly wrong. Terribly.

Seconds passed before Atlas sprang to life again. He leaped up the stairs and stared at her so harshly, she thought she would faint. He grabbed a hand she'd gloved in sinfully black lace. "You must never again wear a gown like this . . . unless you forewarn me. My poor heart can take only so much."

My, God, did he hate it that much? The blood drained from her face.

"You are without a doubt the most ravishing creature I've ever seen."

"What?" The word came out on a feathery whisper. He thought her beautiful?

He lifted her lace-covered fingers to his mouth and kissed them. As he did, his eyes never strayed from her lips.

Her knees threatened to buckle. Grabbing for the banister, she heard a clatter and realized she'd dropped her onyx shell fan.

It bounced down several steps.

Atlas chased after and retrieved it—this gallant Prince Charming who'd come to escort Cinderella to the ball.

"Didn't Clem look every inch the proud papa when he introduced us to his daughter?" Charlotte asked Atlas as they strolled up the wide staircase in the Texas and Pacific's hotel. They were part of a stream of wedding guests, heading for the reception. "And Dulcy, wasn't she the loveliest bride?"

"Yes, very," he answered politely when all he could think was how much lovelier Charlotte would look as a bride. No veil could hide that strawberry hair, those emerald eyes.

The top landing opened onto a long, wide gallery, and Atlas noticed the doors to the guest rooms ran down one side, and chairs lined the opposite wall below a bank of tall windows . . . windows swung wide to draw the southern breeze. The chairs, for the most part, were already taken by the ladies. Men clustered in small groups about the room. Atlas recognized only a few of them whose local business establishments he'd visited during the last couple of summers. He assumed most of the others worked for the railroad.

Seeing tables of food at one end of the hall, he turned to Charlotte. "Did you ever get a chance to eat before the wedding?"

"Yes. Mrs. Langley, the dear, brought me a plate while I was getting ready. But isn't everything wonderful? Like some big-city affair. Crystal chandeliers. Even a string quarter." She pointed with her fan to formally dressed musicians at the other end.

He smiled his approval. "It would seem that Abilene is becoming a city in her own right. Not simply the end of a dusty cattle trail. Which reminds me, whatever possessed you to drive in from Clyde alone?"

Charlotte's first expression was one of guilt, then it turned righteous. "It seemed as good a time as any to start looking after myself again. Besides, my rifle was always within easy reach."

"Maybe so, but I'm driving you back to your wagon tomorrow. You and that dress will have half the men here frothing at the mouth before the evening's over." He made a quick sweep of her charms—charms that couldn't have been displayed more seductively.

The color in her cheeks heightening, Charlotte flipped open her fan, strategically, shielding those lush swells that peeked out above the black lace. "Wasn't it generous of Major Stocking to offer the hotel's gallery for the reception?" The lady was changing the subject to something less provocative. "He told Clem it was small recompense, considering Clem's years of faithful service to the railroad."

The quartet began to play a lovely Vienna waltz, saving Atlas from more dreary polite conversation when all he wanted to do was hold her.

The floor cleared, and Tucker's daughter Dulcy and her bridegroom circled the room alone for the first dance. Dulcy, though large-boned like her father, really was quite graceful as she followed her husband's lead. Atlas knew, however, that when he and Charlotte took to the floor, his strawberry blond's elegance would by far outshine the bride's.

That is, *if* she didn't burst into raucous laughter.

His lips curled into a smile at the thought. Charlotte was so much more than merely pretty.

The parents of the bride and the groom joined the young couple on the dance floor, and Atlas could scarcely wait for his own turn.

He gazed down at Charlotte, making every effort not to stare at her enticements . . . enticements that reminded him of a fortune teller's crystal balls. And, Lord, how he wished he could be the one to set them glowing with the heat of his caress.

But, of course, he couldn't. At least not here, not now.

He rubbed his tingling palms on his pant legs and bowed formally. "Miss Charlotte, would you do me the supreme honor of giving me this dance?"

A mischievous light twinkled in her green eyes. "Why, Mistah Daltry," she drawled, sounding more like a Georgian belle than a Texan, "I'd be plumb honored to do you that honor." She slipped the silk loop of her fan onto her wrist and held out her arms.

Again Atlas used every vestige of willpower to refrain from lowering his gaze to the creamy globes that he knew would be thrusting upward with her arms. Concentrating on the wispy tendrils framing her face, he wrapped his fingers around her waist and took one of her gloved hands as she placed the other on his shoulder.

Mere inches separated them. The very air between them seemed magnetic. The temptation to press her flat against him was almost irresistible. He spotted a pulsing at the base of her throat and wanted to kiss it so badly, his whole body was becoming one giant, throbbing ache.

Then, thank God, before he lost all control, the cello player nodded, and other couples began to move onto the floor. Atlas swept Charlotte into the whirl.

The next hour was like soaring to the heavens on a cloud of music that was sprinkled on occasion with sparkling peals of Charlotte's laughter. Atlas had no doubt he was the envy of every male in the room. On the rare moment when he took his eyes from her, he saw many watching.

But, alas, the musicians stopped for intermission, and the men headed for the refreshment table.

Atlas steered Charlotte toward the row of chairs beneath the open windows. "I'll get us some fruit punch."

Flipping open her shell fan, Charlotte cooled herself as she took a seat between two other young women—neither of which, Atlas decided, could hold a candle to her. He'd never actually measured the length of Charlotte's lashes before, either, until that very moment as she swept them up to gaze at him.

"Hurry back. I'm absolutely parched." Her bosom rose, then fell on a soft sigh.

Striding away, he chuckled to himself. Did she really think he'd dally?

"Pardon me." A middle-aged man with a luxuriant mustache and wearing an impeccable black frock coat stepped in front of Atlas, blocking him. "Aren't you one of Daltry's sons? From the Circle D?" The man offered his hand.

"Yes," he said, shaking it.

"I'm Major Stocking, the railroad's agent in West Texas. I oversee everything from the running of this hotel to shipping cattle."

"I see." Perhaps the clerk at the land office had mentioned he was looking at property adjacent to the tracks? Land that could very well belong to the Texas and Pacific.

"If you have a moment," Major Stocking said, gesturing toward an empty doorway, "I'd like to speak with you about a financial matter."


"I declare, Miss Charlotte," the young woman next to her said, "if I hadn't heard you laughing with that handsome fellow of yours, I never would have recognized you, our very own gypsy drummer. Your hair looks quite tame in that chignon. And that gown . . . wherever did you get it?"

"Mrs. Pritchard over on Pine made it. She has wonderful patterns and fabrics straight from New York."

"Well, it's surely turning the men's heads this evening. Even my Warren made a comment." The brunet's own gown, a blue-and-gray-striped taffeta, was also fashionably cut, yet her tone held a hint of resentment.

"I'll be sure to tell Mrs. Pritchard that you admire her work." Charlotte glanced down the gallery toward the refreshments. Even after several minutes, there was still a crowd of men waiting to fetch drinks. But she couldn't locate Atlas. She fanned herself impatiently. They'd been having such a glorious time, how could he desert her for so long?

The brunet's gentleman friend arrived with punch cups and did little to improve his own lady's disposition. Instead of concentrating on her, he was rudely inclined to sneak glances at Charlotte. In particular, her décolletage.

Thank goodness the string quartet resumed playing, and the girl snatched her escort away to dance.

Charlotte again scanned the end of the hall and finally found Atlas. He was *not* in line for refreshments, but standing empty-handed in a doorway, deep in conversation with the railroad boss. Judging from the serious set of their faces, they were talking business. *Business*.

Here she sat, practically hoarse from thirst, and Atlas had abandoned her to discuss something apparently more important than being with her.

She stood up. She'd fetch her own drink, by gum. Charlotte Clairmore was no longer required to wait on the pleasure of a man. Hadn't been for over two years now. And she liked it that way.

She'd taken no more than two steps when Cauley Dobbs intercepted her. The expressman, whom she passed from time to time when he was out delivering packages, hadn't been the least bit shy about his interest in her.

With a confident smile, the horse-toothed man handed her a cup of punch. "Figured with all your frolickin' around, you'd be a mite thirsty."

She wanted to refuse, give him no opening, but it would be rude if she did so only to go fetch her own. "Thank you," she said, accepting it. She took a much-needed sip . . . and caught him staring where every other man had tonight. Flipping out her fan to cover the exposed area, she knew she'd be having a serious talk with Mrs. Pritchard before the woman sewed her another dress. "The gentleman I'm with seems to have been detained."

"Yes, I noticed you was with someone. I take it that means you're past your mournin' time for your late husband."

Charlotte didn't like the direction the conversation was taking. "More or less," she murmured, then turned and waved at some fictitious person, hoping to distract him.

When she turned back, a second man, Brownie Frye, sidled up.

"Dobbs," he said. Yet as the town's new wheelwright addressed the expressman, he looked straight at her. "Ain't you got no manners? Keepin' this pretty little filly standin' when she come here to dance." He whipped the cup from her and handed it back to Mr. Dobbs. Incredibly bold for someone she scarcely knew.

Then, before she could react, he caught her hand . . . his rough calluses scraping across her lace glove, the sight of his dirty fingernails scraping across her nerves.

Mr. Dobbs snagged her other arm. "Hold your horses, there, Frye. I was here first."

"Gentlemen!" She felt like some poor rabbit caught

between two dogs, and the panic she couldn't seem to quell lately rose again. She jerked free of their grasps. "I do believe I have a say in this."

"Course you do." Frye caught her hand again. Set in a broad face, his small, dark eyes seemed like those of a night hunter. "And 'fore you choose betwixt us, I'd like to say that you couldn't have picked a better dress to set off your—uh—green eyes."

"Yes," came a familiar voice from the side, "that's what I told my fiancée earlier this evening when I escorted her here."

The wheelwright looked as surprised as Charlotte.

But the expressman's narrow face darkened. "So that's the lay of the land, is it? All the time you was playin' the grievin' widow, stringin' me along, you was seeing someone else."

*"I never!"* Remembering where her hand was, she pulled free of the other man and latched onto Atlas's arm.

His muscles felt fighting hard.

She shot a glance at Atlas and saw the same murderous glint she'd seen that day by the creek.

Dobbs must have seen it, too. "No sense getting all het, up, boy. We're here to celebrate Clem's daughter's wedding—not ruin it by raising a ruckus." Doing an about-face, he strode stiffly away, with Frye following close behind.

Atlas stared coldly after them until they'd joined a group in the corner.

And it wasn't until then that she felt his arm relax beneath her grasp.

"Forgive me," he said, turning to her, his expression losing its fierceness. "As alluring as you look this evening, I was a fool to leave you unattended even for a few minutes."

But he had. To talk business. Cecil all over again.

She felt the beginnings of a headache . . . and felt weary, disheartened. "If you don't mind, I'm feeling quite tired. I'd like to leave now." Without waiting for his response, she brushed past a couple moving onto the dance floor and headed for the stairway.

Atlas was quick, however. Within seconds he reached her side, pacing his strides to hers as if their departure had been a joint decision.

It wasn't until they were down the stairs that Charlotte realized she'd left the reception without thanking her host and hostess. She paused at the bottom and looked up, wondering if she should return.

Atlas took that opportunity to step in front of her and grasp both her arms. "Now that we're far enough away not to disturb the wedding party, I have to know. What did those men say? You're obviously very upset. Did they insult you?"

Glaring up at him, Charlotte removed his hands. "No more than you." She spun away toward the entrance and rushed out the open doorway to the faintly lit boardwalk.

Undeterred, he caught up with her as she hurried toward the borrowed buggy. "Charlotte, truly, the second I saw you were being bothered, I came."

"What an inconvenience that must've been," she sniped. "Interrupting your important talk with Major Stocking." Reaching the buggy, she grabbed the brake to hoist herself up.

Before she could, Atlas lifted her into the small rig and started around to the other side.

"You needn't bother seeing me to the boardinghouse. I wouldn't want to interrupt your business dealings any further."

Atlas stared steadily at her for several seconds. "I *will* be seeing you back to your lodgings." He hoisted himself up and sat down beside her, his sudden weight causing the cushioned bench to tilt in his direction.

She caught hold of the buggy bonnet. She had no intention of falling into him.

He picked up the reins and snapped them lightly across the horse's back, then guided the rig to the center of the road.

That was when she felt the burn of his eyes upon her, but she wouldn't give him the satisfaction of acknowledging it.

He spoke anyway. "I've heard the men in my family complaining about how hard it is to understand their women, and now I know what they mean. I could've sworn you were having a good time. How could you possibly be upset about me taking a couple of minutes to talk to Major Stocking? He'd heard I was interested in some acreage the railroad owns and stopped me to inquire about it. Actually, I really think he was more interested in finding out about the ranchers' meetings, and when the men plan to start shipping. The major tried not to look it, but he's nervous. If all the cattlemen stick together, the railroad can't afford to jack up shipping rates at the slightest whim."

"Then I can't imagine why you're here with me when you could be with him." Leaning forward, she snatched the reins and yanked.

Its head bowed from the sudden pull, the horse halted.

"What *is* the matter with you? Don't you know it's you I want to be with tonight?"

"A busy man like you? And, pray tell, how do I explain away your telling those men that I'm your fiancée? I'll have more trouble stomping out that spicy tidbit than I would a grass fire."

To her astonishment, he grinned, a grin so big and bodacious his straight white teeth actually reflected the light coming from the building across the street. "How would you like to have breakfast at my hotel before we leave in the morning?" he asked, absurdly casual as he retrieved the reins and started the buggy moving again.

Charlotte threw up her hands. "You're impossible."

"Eggs," he said. "Eggs and a big, thick steak. It would be nice if you had something else to chew on besides me."

# ᗏᕮ 17 ᕮᗏ

In the glaring light of day, Charlotte knew she'd have
to apologize to Atlas. She'd been outrageously rude.
Rude and intolerant. Men did talk to one another at social
events. She doubted if there had been a single man at the
reception who hadn't left his lady unattended for a few
minutes.

With her carpetbag in hand, she started down the
boardinghouse stairs. It was a good ten minutes before
seven, but she didn't want to add tardiness to her list of
transgressions.

Stepping out onto the porch to wait, she was doubly
glad the pinstriped shirtwaist she'd brought for the ride
home covered her from the top of her neck to well past
her wrists. And, she thought relievedly, the bodice
bloused ever so discreetly over her bosom. Apologizing
for the things she'd said last night would be difficult
enough without providing any reminders of her daringly
cut gown.

Placing the carpetbag beside one of the straight-
backed chairs linging the porch, she sat down with stiff
propriety, then glanced down the street. Atlas, too, might

be early. But she saw only one lone horseman riding in the opposite direction.

She wanted to get it over with, yet dreaded his contempt . . . a contempt that would've surely emerged once he'd had time to mull over her dreadful behavior. Anxiously, she checked her brushed-cotton gloves for smudges, then raised her fingers to the sides of her straw beehive bonnet, making sure it sat precisely atop her head. Prim, proper, *and* polite. That's what she would be at breakfast and on the ride home today. Polite and nothing more.

She heard the unmistakable roll of wheels.

A second later, her borrowed horse turned the corner, then the buggy, with Atlas driving and his sorrel stallion tied behind.

Like a coiled spring, she shot to her feet, reached for her carpetbag, then changed her mind. She shouldn't act anxious to see him.

But then she shouldn't act coy, either.

Picking up the bag, she lifted her chin and strolled at her ladylike best down the brick walk to the street. After all, he, too, was early.

"Morning," Atlas called with a cheery smile as he stopped the buggy beside her and leaped down. He took her satchel and tossed it behind the seat, then turned back for her before she had a chance to say anything.

Once they were both aboard and heading for his hotel, her courage began to fizzle. "I—uh—" She took a fortifying breath and forced herself to look at him.

He stared back with his own uncertain expression, his lips parted.

"I don't know what to say." Her hands started to

tremble. She clenched them together. "I had no right to speak to you so rudely last night. You'd been nothing but the perfect gentleman all evening, and—"

"No." He covered her knotted fists with his free hand. "It's all my fault. I knew you were still skittish around men. *And in that dress.* Leaving you there alone was like staking out a calf in wolf country."

Feeling her cheeks flush with embarrassment, she looked down to see his much larger hand completely engulfing hers. Swiftly, she glanced away. "I *will* be adding several rows of lace to that neckline."

"Must you? You and that dress were absolutely stunning."

"Too stunning."

"Well," he said, giving her hands a squeeze before releasing them, "you don't have to worry about eyes popping this morning. You've managed to hide everything but your face. But, like it or not, my beauty, you're still a head-turner." He tossed her a sidelong grin. "Probably always were and always will be. So buck up; it's just your lot in life."

His grin was infectious, but she toned hers down with a raised brow. "You do have a glib tongue, Atlas Daltry. Is it something you studied in Chicago, along with your other pursuits?"

"Quick-witted, too. I doubt if anyone has ever accused you of being slow or boring." With a teasing wink, he returned his attention to his driving.

Boring? No, never boring. But bored? Merciful heavens, yes. So bored she thought she'd shrivel up and die from it when she lived with Cecil. Cecil who talked, ate, and breathed nothing but money and how much he could squirrel away. There was never any for today. He always needed more, always more, for that proverbial rainy day that never came.

She sighed. At least she now had that money in the bank in Abilene so she'd never have to worry about any *real* rainy days, such as last winter when it had been too stormy to travel.

Without her realizing it, Atlas had stopped and now stood beside the buggy, his arms outstretched to help her down. Charming Atlas, witty Atlas. Atlas with a princely face and body that would only improve with age. *He was the devil's own temptation.*

She'd had no trouble keeping men at bay for two years. Somehow she would this one, too. But, Lord, he was an eyeful.


Later that morning, as they followed the railroad tracks east, Charlotte's resolve gained strength. Not only had she managed to keep the conversation at breakfast light, but due to her curiosity to know more about his family's labors, *and* after her sworn promise never to repeat a word to a living soul, he started talking.

In great detail he told the stories of his brothers and sisters—how big, hulking Lee ended up being a schoolmarm for a year, how Persy was sent to New York to get over being shy and came home with a worldly saloonkeeper. Then there was C. J., who was tricked into using his talents with the ladies to turn a wallflower into the love of his life. And beautiful but vain Venus. She was sent to assist a blind man, who could see nothing but her soul. Allie and Hal, best buddies who were blind, too, until with a little help from Grandmother, they learned there was more between them than their love of horses.

Reaching the crossing into town, Atlas fell silent as he slowly guided the horse and rig over the iron rails . . . stopped talking long enough for Charlotte to realize what a determined matchmaker his grandmother was. And no doubt this latest of the matron's oh-so-innocent labors was intended to match her with Atlas.

Not that she didn't appreciate the fact that Mrs. Daltry valued her enough to want her to be a part of their family. But nonetheless the old gal had made a whopper of a mistake this time—his grandmother didn't know the first thing about her. To think when Mrs. Daltry had introduced them, all she could talk about was what an industrious young man her grandson was, what ambitious business plans he had. If she'd only known that that was the last thing Charlotte would want to hear.

Once the wheels were safely on the Clyde side of the tracks, Atlas turned to her. "Before I get you delivered, I'd better ask if you'll be available next Saturday evening after you're through selling in Paradise."

"You want to meet again? So soon?"

"I thought we agreed to complete our deal as soon as possible."

It sounded as if he wanted to get rid of her, and quickly. She felt the sting of rejection.

But hadn't she just been telling herself she wouldn't let things get serious between them? "The tongues of Paradise Plains will start wagging for sure."

Atlas halted the horse. "I would think anyone as independent as you wouldn't put much stock in a little talk."

"There's talk, and then there's *talk*. That kind I can't afford, for more reasons that you can guess."

"Charlotte, I would never intentionally compromise your good name. You know that. How about if you and Opal come out to the ranch next Saturday afternoon to look at a new team you're supposedly thinking of buying?"

"Oh, have you found a good pair?"

"No, but I will before Saturday if that's what it takes to get you there. Now that you've heard all about my brothers and sisters, I'd like to show you what my parents have been up to all these years. Those two are a story in themselves. Mother's always adding flower beds, and Pa's always building something. Between the two of them, it's quite the sprawling place."

Charlotte couldn't help grinning. "I've heard tell."

His grin matched hers. "I'll bet. I suppose you know folks around town have dubbed it Mount Olympus."

She tried to compose her features, to no avail. "I've heard it mentioned once or twice."

"And I'm sure they've also told you what neighborly folks we are. So nobody's going to be a bit surprised if we ask you to stay for supper."

His reasoning was flawless. Taking it one step further, she knew he couldn't let her ride back to town by herself, not across five miles of open prairie after sundown. Opal would surely fall asleep before they were halfway, then the two of them would be all alone in the vast darkness . . . hearing nothing but the rustle of sweet grass . . . and their yearning sighs. Very dangerous. Very dangerous, indeed.

Clyde, though smaller than Paradise Plains, boasted

two places of worship along with its stores and post office. Passing the first clapboard church just as it was letting out, Charlotte waved to various friends and customers.

"Is that the church you attend every other Sunday?"

"Actually," she said with a chuckle, "I switch off. One week I go there and the next time through I attend the one down the road. Don't want to offend anyone."

He looked happily surprised. "Why, Charlotte Clairmore, whether you want to admit it or not, you have very good business sense."

"That's not why I do it," she said, slanting him a scathing glance.

Her expression didn't seem to faze him. He placed a hand on her knee—*of all places*. "I never meant to suggest that you were insincere." He gave her leg a light squeeze before releasing it.

Charlotte couldn't decide whether to pretend he hadn't touched one of her lower limbs or to reprimand him for his bold behavior. Once she knew Mrs. Newsom hadn't noticed, she opted to let it slide. He hadn't seemed motivated by lechery. But his behavior was probably her own fault. She'd already allowed him too many liberties.

Her mind skipped to another day when he'd so tenderly washed the blood and tears from her face . . . and held her within the safety of his encircling arm. An act she would always cherish. Nonetheless, he'd come to think her hands, in particular, were his for the taking. And now her legs! What next?

A naughty thrill chased through her. *Naughty.*

"There's your wagon." Atlas clucked the lagging mare

into a smarter walk and headed toward Charlotte's outfit, parked beside Parson Daggett's house.

As he pulled the buggy to a stop before it, Opal spilled out of the minister's picket gate. "Mama! Atlas!" She scrambled into the rig and onto Charlotte's lap, giving her a long, fierce hug. "I missed you so much."

Her own thoughts had been so full of Atlas, she'd almost forgotten her precious jewel. Feeling a bit guilty, Charlotte returned her child's embrace with equal fervor.

"That's a mighty fine hug you're giving your ma." Atlas had hopped down and now stood beside the buggy. "But if you'll unwind yourself long enough for—"

The imp let out a squeal and leaped from Charlotte to Atlas, like a tree squirrel flying from limb to limb.

Atlas grunted upon impact; then, chuckling, he rumpled Opal's unruly mop.

Clinging to Atlas's neck, Opal swung back to Charlotte, her eyes wide. "Guess what happened while you was gone?"

"Were gone," Charlotte corrected as she warmed to the sight of Opal cuddled in Atlas's arms.

"Goliath didn't mean to do it. The train whistle scared him. So it was really the train's fault."

"What did he do, Opal?" Charlotte couldn't imagine the gentle horse getting out of hand.

"He jumped back and stepped on poor ol' Whistle's foot. And, Mama, you shoulda heard what came outta his mouth. Wash-the-mouth-out-with-soap words, for sure."

"Where is he, pumpkin?" Atlas asked. From the twitching at the corners of his mouth, one would think getting stepped on by a hulking horse was a laughing matter.

"In the parson's house. He heard Whistle a-cussin' and come charging out. He was fit to be tied at first—this being the Sabbath, and all. But once we got Whistle's boot off and saw his squished foot, they was nicer to him then."

Squashed? Charlotte exchanged a worried look with Atlas.

He set Opal on the ground and lifted Charlotte out of the buggy. Then, with Opal running ahead, Atlas accompanied her to the door.

Opal burst through without knocking. "Whistle? Mama's back. Mama and Atlas." She dashed from the entry hall into the parlor. "Everything's going to be all right now. Atlas is here. My guardian angel's here."

# ⚙ 18 ⚙

For someone who was supposed to be so lighthearted and gay, Charlotte sure could be difficult. And foolhardy. All yesterday afternoon and this morning she'd argued against his accompanying her. The woman truly was beyond understanding. Never had Atlas seen anyone so ridiculously concerned about her reputation. Recklessly concerned.

Now that she knew it was useless to argue, she was ignoring him. Or pretending to, anyway. Perched up on her wagon as they headed northwest toward the Clear Fork of the Brazos, she'd put on one of those big, floppy sunbonnets women wore for gardening. But it hadn't totally hidden the glances she slanted his way.

And vindictive? Not only had she refused to let him ride on the wagon with her and Opal, but he noticed that whenever the road narrowed, she wouldn't steer to one side to make room for him and his sorrel. He'd eaten her dust more than once before he learned to spur Red Jack ahead of her outfit.

But accompany Charlotte he would.

Whether she admitted it or not, she was still as jumpy as a frog in a frying pan.

Even if she weren't, she couldn't have persuaded him to let her ride out alone. Not after the incident. And not after her eyes had told him she wanted him as much as he wanted her—even if she stubbornly refused to admit it.

As they neared the river, the dips in the rolling meadows were clogged with cottonwoods. He appreciated the stretches of shade, but the trees blocked his view of the winding road, and since the blasted woman was too obstinate to share their destination with him, he couldn't scout ahead. In her frame of mind, she'd probably take off up some obscure cow path just to spite him.

"See, Atlas?" Opal called from the wagon seat. She held up the kitten, which now wore his bandanna around its scrawny neck. "Ain't she pretty?"

Atlas expected Charlotte to correct Opal's grammar.

She didn't. She kept right on staring at the road ahead, her nose stuck up so high that if it rained she'd drown.

He guided Red Jack alongside the tot. "Yep. Gypsy looks like a regular cowhand. Put a rope in her paw, and before you know it, she'll be out lassoing those wild range steers."

Opal scrunched her face in a disbelieving frown. "No, she won't. She's too—"

Without warning, Charlotte cut the team across his path.

Red Jack reared.

Atlas nearly lost his seat, then his hat, but managed to keep both as Charlotte steered her outfit into a thick-posted entrance and onto wagon tracks cut into the prairie grass.

She looked dead ahead, but for the first time today he caught her smiling—the ornery wench.

Determined not to let her rile him, Atlas glanced up to the cross beam before he passed through. On it was carved the Lazy R brand. The Richards ranch—a big outfit that ran almost as many head of cattle as the Daltrys *and* a lot more head of females. Atlas couldn't help smiling now himself. John Richards not only had his mother and his mother-in-law living with him, but his wife had never given him anything but girls. Nine, the last Atlas heard. Three or four were married off, but there was still a passel at home.

"This is not a laughing matter." Charlotte's voice rang with indignation as her narrow-eyed glare bore into him.

"What?" he asked innocently, while keeping a safe distance.

"You know very well. I can't have you with me. Too many folks are talking already. I can't afford—" She broke off abruptly, her darting eyes mirroring her agitation. Her gaze steadied into a steely glare. She pinned him with it. "*It's not good for business.*"

"Did you hear that, Opal? Your mama just said a bad word." Amusement rang in his voice as he grinned up at Charlotte. "She just said *business*."

"Ooh, you're impossible." She swept her fiery gaze to Opal. "He is *not* with us. Do you understand? *He is not with us.*"

The Richards women came pouring out their back door before Charlotte had brought her team to a halt in their barnyard. One good thing about the jingle of a multitude of harness bells was that no one mistook

Charlotte's coming for any other wagon. Today she was particularly glad for this. She was so angry, there was no telling what might come out of her mouth had she announced her arrival.

To others, she knew it would appear as if the arrogant bullhead had taken responsibility for her. And of course when they asked themselves why, there'd be no end to the gossip. All he seemed to care about was keeping her unharmed until he won that blasted prize; but if he *truly* cared about her, he would've heeded her wishes, her countless pleas.

Lord knew, Edgar had spies watching her every move. This would be all he needed.

"Howdy, Miss Charlotte." The cheery cries came from all sides as ranch hands also poured out of the barns and work sheds.

She forced a smile and waved gaily. "Howdy!" Out of the corner of her eye she saw Atlas dismount, looking as if he planned to make himself right at home. She opened the half door above Opal's seat, and they climbed into their living quarters. On the way through to the back, she gathered up a couple dozen peacock feathers and the order sheet for peachicks, then went out to her customers.

And blast her rebellious eyes, they immediately searched out Atlas again. Mr. Bullhead was exactly where she would've expected . . . off to the side, talking to Mr. Richards. And she'd take odds it wasn't about the weather. The ranch hands had also joined them . . . which made her seethe all the more. Now he was even distracting her customers with his infernal business talk.

"Hey, Charlotte," cried one of the younger girls, "how

come you're not wearing your gypsy skirt and all your fancy beads?"

"Oh, don't be such a dummy, Kate," one of the older ones crowed. "Can't you see Charlotte has a beau to impress today?"

"He's not my beau," Charlotte grated through clenched teeth.

"Oh, really?" Milly, the oldest, tore off her apron. "He's one of those handsome Daltry boys from Paradise Plains." Tossing the apron onto a fence rail, she smoothed the hair alongside her shiny black bun, and for the first time Charlotte noticed what a striking young woman she was becoming. The girl turned toward Atlas.

Charlotte felt a stab of jealousy.

"Milly, wait!" Opal cried. She shoved the kitten at Charlotte, then held out her arms to the Richards girl.

Milly didn't look thrilled by the delay as she helped the tyke off the wagon platform.

As Opal's feet hit the ground, she took off at a dead run for Atlas, leaving Milly to trail behind. When Opal reached him, he picked her up, gave her a hug and a peck on the cheek, then resumed talking.

Opal didn't seem to mind his preoccupation as she smiled over his shoulder at Milly.

In spite of herself, Charlotte grinned. The imp had no intention of letting the girl get between her and her guardian angel.

But how must it look to the others? Charlotte's smile vanished.

"Would appear Dora's right," Grandma Richards said. "You can't stop looking at your fella long enough to remember what's in your hand."

Charlotte glanced down and saw she was clutching the kitten, the order sheet, and a bundle of peacock feathers to her chest. Setting the kitten on her shoulder, she looked back at the woman whose mind, she hoped, wasn't as narrow as her long nose. "Mr. Daltry is not my fellow. He's not even with me."

Everyone looked skeptical, particularly the two grandmothers.

"All right," Charlotte added uncomfortably. "He may be with me, but *I'm* not with him." She held out the plumes. "Did you ever see a prettier feather?"

"Now, just how can he be with you if you're not with him?" asked the second grandmother, her sagging cheeks crinkling in a teasing grin.

They weren't going to let it be.

"He's decided I need protection, and nothing I've said about how improper it looks has made the slightest dent in his thick skull."

The younger Mrs. Richards sighed. "My John's just like that. Once he gets something in his head, there's just no reasoning with him."

"Speaking of John," Charlotte said, thankful for a change of topic, "I have his violin."

"You have?" The younger matron's dark eyes shone. "He'll be so pleased."

"I'll get it." She handed Mrs. Richards the bundle of feathers and escaped inside.

When she returned with the musical instrument she'd taken to Abilene to have repaired, all was finally as it should be . . . the women were admiring the plumes, and one of the girls wanted to know if Charlotte had any of those fancy bone buttons left—buttons that had been the surprise item a couple of months ago.

As Charlotte was taking Mrs. Richards's money for their purchases, one of the girls shouted from the side of the wagon. "Ma, come here and look! A Jersey cow!"

Her mother rushed around to the slate board that hung on the side, then called up to Charlotte, "Is it for sale, or does someone want a cow? There's a name here, but it's smudged."

She couldn't recall off hand. She walked around and took a look. "Oh, yes, that's Spencer Long's name. I believe he has one for sale."

"John!" Mrs. Richards called. "Spencer Long has a Jersey cow for sale."

Her husband, a weathered and wiry man, strode over with Atlas, and the others followed along. Milly, her hips in full swing, walked beside Atlas, but he didn't seem to notice. His half-cocked smirk was directed at Charlotte.

When Mrs. Richards's husband reached her, she cautioned, "*Maybe* there's one. Charlotte's not sure if the cow's for sale, or one that's wanted. But do go right away, just in case. You know how much I need a better milk cow."

He got that put-upon look. "But, Dee, it's a good twenty miles to the Long place, and you don't even know if he's— What's that in your hand?" He pointed to the violin case.

While Mrs. Richards opened it and showed him the repaired instrument, Charlotte peeked from beneath her bonnet at Atlas.

Off to the side, he was studying the slate, but he must have felt her eyes on him. He glanced her way.

She quickly averted her own gaze.

In the meantime, Mr. Richards had pulled out the violin. He placed it beneath his chin and ran the bow across the strings a few times, then smiled. "Just like new." He pulled his wife into an embrace. "Thanks, sweetie. This is a wonderful surprise." Then, stepping back, he held her at arm's length. "You want that cow? Well, by gum, I'll go get it for you right now."

Folks might laugh about him running nothing but a herd of females, but from the look in his eyes at that moment, no one could say he wasn't a man in love with his wife and his life. It was a look that gave others hope, showing that some folks really did get married and live happily ever after.

"Well," Charlotte said, "guess I'd better get on down the road."

Mrs. Richards whirled around, her cheeks all aglow. "Wait just a second. Milly, you and Kate go fetch that basket of tomatoes by the back door."

Milly gave an exasperated sigh, but did as she was told.

"Because of the drought, we had to carry water to our tomatoes this year," Mrs. Richards said. "Thought they wouldn't do much good at all. But instead we've got tomatoes coming out our ears. So I want you to take some to town with you. Maybe you can make yourself a few pennies off of them."

"Thank you, Mrs. Richards. That's mighty nice of you."

"Pshaw. If we get that cow, next time you're through, I'll have a butter pie waiting that'll melt in your mouth."

The girls returned with a bushel basket brimming with the plump red vegetable.

Putting Opal down, Atlas took it from them as if it were his place to do so.

"I told you, you're not with me," Charlotte snapped, reaching for the basket.

"Whether I am or not does not forfeit my obligations as a gentleman." He sidestepped her and hoisted the basket up on the wagon bench.

Incensed, but not wanting to cause a scene, she swung back to find three very amused women. "It's late," she said, ignoring their irritating expressions. "I'd better get going." She turned around to climb aboard.

Strong hands clamped around her waist.

*That* she didn't have to put up with. She wrenched around . . . and found Mr. Richards behind her.

She felt really dumb.

To make matters worse, Atlas stood off to the side, grinning like a jackass.

"I—uh, thanks again for the tomatoes," she mumbled to Mr. Richards, then meekly allowed him to assist her.

"Mama," Opal called up from the ground. "Can I ride with Atlas? He says I have to ask you first."

Every eye turned toward her, waiting for her answer, and Atlas's gaze of feigned innocence was the most exasperating of all. "Sweetheart, I'm sure by the end of the day Mr. Daltry won't be going in the same direction we are."

"Oh, Mama." Opal planted her little fists on her hips. "You know he's our guardian angel. So of course he is."

Charlotte threw up her hands. "Do as you please." Threading the reins through her fingers, she snapped them, and the yellow-plumed draft horses jerked the wagon into a creaky start.

She hadn't traveled more than a few yards when she heard gales of laughter spilling after her.

Nobody understood.

But then, how could they? They knew nothing of her plight.

## ⋘ 19 ⋙

Atlas galloped into foliage near the river with Opal seated in front of him. Chasing another fool rabbit, they were almost immediately out of sight, but Charlotte had no trouble keeping track. Every few seconds, Opal, the little traitor, shrieked her delight.

Charlotte felt like doing some shrieking of her own. There was no way anyone would think Atlas was simply their protector. He never once passed by without beckoning her with those eyes. And it took every vestige of her willpower not to respond to them.

If she couldn't make Atlas go home, Edgar would finally have the ammunition he'd been waiting for.

Atlas and Opal came riding out of the brush, Atlas laughing and she like some wild child of the woods. Her long, curly hair bounced about her with each prance of the horse. Her cheeks glowed with excitement. Atlas's arms surrounding her made the picture even more dear.

*No*! Charlotte railed silently. She couldn't allow herself to succumb to those thoughts anymore. She had to be strong. Too much was at stake.

Atlas reined the sorrel next to the wagon. He was still chuckling as he looked at her.

The promise in his eyes sorely tested her resolve.

"The Dedman ranch settlement is just around the bend," he said. "Opal mentioned we'd be spending the night there."

"Not you. Go home, or I'll have a word with your grandmother. *About your labor.*"

The joy faded from his eyes. "We all must do what we must."

"Mama. It's not nice to be mean to Atlas."

He kissed the top of Opal's head. "It's all right. Your mama doesn't want to be mean. She just thinks she has to." He lifted her up and handed her to Charlotte. "I've scouted the road to town. It's safe. So I'm going to ride on ahead. I have some business to take care of."

He galloped away, leaving Charlotte to eat his dust as well as any kind thoughts she'd ever had about him.

*Now that he has business to take care of, our knight in shining armor has decided the fair damsel can fend for herself.*

"Hold still, Opal, or I'll never get your dress buttoned." Sitting on the bottom bunk, Charlotte held the wiggle worm between her legs.

"Don't see why I had to change just to go to supper."

"You smelled like a horse."

"You think Atlas will know the food's at the cookhouse? It don't have no sign pointing to it."

She gave her lovesick child a quick hug, then resumed fastening the tiny seed buttons. "Don't worry. When it comes to food, men are real good at sniffing it out."

Charlotte, herself, however, was beginning to wonder about him. When she'd driven into the settlement earlier, she hadn't seen him at the general store or the smithy's, the only two enterprises other than the ranch. His sorrel wasn't tethered in front of the main house, either. It appeared he'd taken her threat of exposing him to his grandmother seriously and actually gone home.

A wave of disappointment wafted through her. Where was that steadfast knight he'd pretended to be? A true knight might even have saved her from Edgar.

"There," she said as she finished fashioning a sash bow on Opal's gingham dress. "All done." She set her child aside and stood up.

A loud bang reverberated off the opposite wall of the wagon. Then more sharp bangs.

Charlotte rushed out to the platform and looked around to the side.

Atlas! Hammer in hand, he was nailing something to her wagon. "Howdy," he said from out of the corner of his mouth. The rest held nails. "You needed two." He resumed pounding.

Two? Not worrying about being ladylike, Charlotte slid off the back, belly-down.

Opal tried to do the same.

Charlotte plucked the dangling child off, then strode around the corner.

"Hi, Atlas," Opal cried. "We was getting worried."

"*Were*," Charlotte corrected, more sharply than she intended.

Pulling the nails from his mouth, Atlas smiled lazily. "I'm real pleased to hear that."

She refused to be baited. Ignoring him, she looked to see what he was hammering to the side.

A new slate, with a red frame to match her wagon trim

and the words FOR SALE boldly printed across the top in bright yellow. It looked so much nicer than her chipped piece of blackboard.

Atlas moved to the old one, pried it off, and nailed up a second framed slate at the other end. This one said WANTED. He turned to Charlotte.

She bit back a snide remark about him and his lists, saying instead, "Thank you. That was very thoughtful."

He was obviously pleased by her approval of his afternoon's accomplishment. "I think you'll find having two lists more efficient. And the bright colors will make them more noticeable. Draw more folks to your wagon." His tone was so serious, one would've thought he'd *invented* advertising with color.

She smiled in spite of herself. "Yes, I know. Just like my surprises do."

"Did you paint it yourself?" Opal asked. "I'm a good painter. I could've helped."

"Maybe next time, pumpkin," he said without a whole lot of conviction.

Outside the cookhouse, a ranch hand clanged a rod around the inside of an angle iron.

"Supper!" Opal cried and reached for Atlas.

"No!" Charlotte took her from him. "You wait here until Opal and I are inside. So far nobody here knows you're with us. I'd like to keep it that way." She started across an open field toward the dinging hall, practically dragging her reluctant child.

"But, Mama!"

"No buts. We are not here with Atlas. If anyone asks you, you say, *No, he didn't come with us.* Do you understand?"

Opal frowned up at her defiantly.

Charlotte halted. "I mean it, young lady."

Pressing her lips together, she kicked the dirt before following along. The child had the makings of a real rebel.

When Charlotte stepped through the screen door of the raw lumber building, the usual bunch were already seated. Close to a dozen ranch hands, Matt Woods, the manager, and Widow Broom, the washerwoman, sat at the long table.

Seeing Charlotte and Opal, the men scrambled to their feet with lighthearted greetings. And, as usual, Widow Broom, a taciturn woman of middle years, scarcely bothered to glance up.

This evening's fare was plain but plentiful: beans, fried potatoes, beefsteak, cornbread, and slices of those tomatoes Charlotte had sent the cook when she first arrived. Once everyone was settled, the big serving bowls started flying around the table, only to come to a screeching halt whenever they reached Opal. She dillydallied over every one, waiting for the men to coax her into taking a spoonful of this or that. The squirt had almost as big a flirtation going with these rough-looking cobs as she did with Atlas.

Remembering Atlas, Charlotte tensed, wondering when he'd come banging through the screen door.

"Thought Whistle McSween had hired on with you," one of the older hands said from across the table.

"Goliath squished his foot," Opal piped, rising up on her knees. "But he didn't mean to, did he, Mama?"

Charlotte offered her child a reassuring smile. "No, pet—"

Boot taps echoed across the porch.

Her heart lurched.

The screen door creaked open and slammed shut.

Everyone else looked toward the entrance.

But not Charlotte. She wasn't about to let anyone think she even knew him.

Opal, the upstart, waved. "Ever'body, this is Atlas. He's the fastest runner in Callahan County. I got his blue ribbon to prove it. Ain't that right, Atlas?"

"Yeah, reckon so," he drawled.

Charlotte heard amusement just below the surface. Sensing doom, she nervously shoveled in a mouthful of beans.

A chair scraped across the floor, and she knew Atlas was seating himself on the other side of the table, but, thank goodness, several places down.

"Oh, I almost forgot," Opal added, holding up her spoon as if it were a flag. "We did *not* come here with Atlas. No, sir, we didn't come here with him."

Charlotte shot a glance at Atlas.

He'd pulled out a kerchief and pretended to cough into it, but she knew he was just hiding his hee-hawing.

She looked back at her plate again, trying to ignore other snickers from up and down the table.

"Well, now, Miss Opal. I can see that's a pure fact." The snaggled-toothed wrangler directly across from her grinned so big, he displayed every gap. "Considerin' your ma's looking so prim and proper, she'd make a school-marm, for sure. And your Atlas here, why . . ." The man paused, eyeing him. "Why, you're Bub Daltry, ain't you? Thought you was up north going to some fancy school."

"I've been back awhile."

"I can see that." The old coot's tone suggested much more. He gave Atlas a bawdy wink.

Charlotte gasped.

Atlas's own expression hardened . . . darkened . . . and his knuckles turned white as he gripped the table edge. He looked coiled to spring. "Folks have been having trouble with some roving saddle tramps," he ground out menacingly. "Down in Taylor County. They've been molesting ladies on the road. So to be on the safe side, Whistle McSween hired on to ride shotgun for Mrs. Clairmore until the situation has been handled."

"But Goliath squished Whistle's foot," Opal repeated brightly. "But it weren't Goliath's fault."

"*Wasn't*," Charlotte and Atlas corrected in unison.

"Wasn't Goliath's fault." Opal smiled blithely as Charlotte's face grew hotter.

Atlas settled back in his chair, no longer the gallant defender, as low chuckles came from all sides, *including his*. Her only consolation was Widow Broom.

The stout woman ate with gusto, seemingly oblivious to Charlotte's discomfort.

"And you see . . ." Opal continued, leaning forward as if something very important would follow.

Charlotte had a most intense urge to gag the child.

". . . Atlas is my guardian angel. And you know how it is with guardian angels. Whenever I need him, he comes."

All pretense at decorum collapsed. The men guffawed, stomped the floorboards, and slapped the table till the whole room shook. Even Mrs. Broom's face cracked with a brief smile.

Atlas was not amused.

Glancing over at him, Charlotte saw his face turning as red as the washerwoman's hands.

Good! He deserved a taste of what he'd caused her to suffer today.

Opal, thank heavens, sank back on her heels and picked up her cornbread. Wide-eyed, she seemed confused by all the men's flopping around, making braying fools of themselves.

As their laughter finally diminished to bursts of snickering, Opal, too, tittered, though it was obvious she had no idea why.

At that, Atlas erupted into his own belly laugh, sputtering something about schoolmarms and guardian angels.

The uproar started all over again.

What was the use? This was all too ridiculous to be taken seriously. Charlotte let loose with a whoop, and laughed until tears streamed down her cheeks.

Sometime later, when the last chuckle had subsided and the last tear had been wiped away, Matt Woods, the lantern-jawed foreman, called down the table. "Daltry, you heard anything from that New York brother-in-law of yours? The one what went back East to deal with them greedy slaughterhouse bastards?" He shot a sheepish glance at Charlotte. "Sorry, ma'am, the word just sorta slipped out."

Without waiting for her to reply, Atlas regained Woods's attention. "Just the one message over the telegraph wire." Picking up his fork, he grinned. "It said, *Looks like I have them doggies on the run.*"

"I'll drink to that." Woods lifted his coffee cup high.

The others did the same, even little Opal. Only the laundress at the end ignored their toast . . . the washer-woman and Charlotte, who couldn't avoid noticing that same spark of excitement in Atlas's eyes that surfaced whenever a subject shifted to business. Now, nothing else, *no one else*, mattered any longer.

She lost her appetite.

Atlas came away from the bunkhouse poker game with a little extra change jingling in his pockets. There were times when being a methodical thinker paid off.

But not always.

Looking across the field to Charlotte's wagon silhouetted against the starry sky, he sighed and headed for their camp more confused than ever. After she'd started laughing, any logical person would've assumed she'd finally understood that no one was judging her. She should've relaxed and enjoyed the meal and company.

But, no. She'd taken Opal and left quite abruptly, her supper scarcely touched.

No, there was more to it than that. She *had* relaxed. The disapproving wall didn't go up until the talk had turned to the cattle deal the ranchers were hoping to put together. Why any kind of business talk should offend her was beyond him . . . but particularly a deal that would extend a lifeline to western Texas.

Unless . . .

He slowed to a stop and stared at the wagon. Had her husband been grossly neglectful all in the name of business? She'd never once mentioned him. . . . Or maybe there never was a husband, just a lover. One who'd been afraid his business would suffer if he admitted he was Opal's father.

Had she taken Opal and run away in disgrace?

Atlas suddenly realized he was letting his imagination take over. But the fact remained, he knew virtually nothing of Charlotte's past.

He'd told her just about everything there was to tell about his family, yet she hadn't volunteered one single fact. Not from where she'd come, or *from whom*. And the wagon. How had she come to possess a bandwagon?

*And Edgar*. Who in blazes was this Edgar she'd accused him of working for that day at the train station?

Maybe she wasn't the widow she claimed to be, but a runaway wife.

That possibility was the least palatable. But whatever the truth was, it frightened her terribly, kept her from him.

His chest tightened with his own fear of losing her.

Tomorrow, first thing, they were going to have a very serious talk.

Reaching the wagon, he picked his way through the dark to where his saddle straddled a nearby corral fence, and retrieved his bedroll. Spreading it beside one of the big wheels, he couldn't believe how his dream just two mornings ago had fizzled so quickly. That dream of a kiss he'd wanted so much.

Lying down, he stretched out and propped his head on his arms and let Charlotte's face fill the emptiness. Those lips were meant to be kissed. Even Grams had known that.

Abruptly Atlas sat up. *And Grams probably knew a*

*whole lot more.* Grams never would've named Charlotte as his labor if she weren't sure Charlotte was free.

*That's right*! He almost shouted it out loud. Edgar was probably just some miserly old uncle who was trying to keep tabs on her.

Just like he was. Grinning, Atlas settled back. Charlotte simply needed to learn to relax. Tomorrow morning he'd assure her that no one was condemning her for having him along. And once he got her to take an honest look at her fears, maybe the two of them could get on with more important things . . . like that kiss.

Above him, the wagon creaked. Charlotte was probably rolling over, stretching her nimble arms, those long, slender legs . . . arching her back . . . her ripe breasts thrusting upward, begging to be taken.

As the picture spilled across his brain, fires of hunger ripped through his body. They streaked down to his manhood with such force he almost cried out. His desire for her was becoming unbearable.

And to think a couple of days ago he'd fooled himself into believing all he wanted from her was one little kiss.

## ❧ 20 ❧

The next morning, Atlas, a man with a purpose, had the coffee water started over the campfire by the crack of dawn and was sitting on a split-log bench with his first cup when Charlotte stepped outside.

She wore her gypsy skirt—a good sign.

He sprang up to help her down from the wagon.

"Good morning," she murmured with the barest glance as she reached for his shoulders with hands filled with a towel and a bar of soap.

"Morning," he returned, trying to keep his mind off of where his own hands were as he swung her to the ground.

Without another glance, she whirled away and headed for the river at the back of the meadow.

But he wasn't discouraged. By the end of this day, if he hadn't vanquished her fear, he'd at least know what he was fighting.

Surveying their location, he noticed that they were quite secluded despite the fact that they were in the middle of a settlement of thirty or forty people. A barn stood on one side of the campfire, the meadow stretched to an empty horizon on the other, and the tree-lined river lay behind them. Blocking them from the street was

Charlotte's wagon. She wouldn't be able to use prying eyes as an excuse when he questioned her.

Waiting for her, he tried to concentrate on his steaming coffee rather than the path she'd taken. He didn't want to appear too anxious, scare her off before he got his answers. But at every bird's chirp or shuffle of a horse, he couldn't help glancing up.

When it seemed as if she'd been gone forever, she emerged from a veil of weeping willow limbs. She came toward him in a kaleidoscope of color, her many-tiered skirt having a life of its own as it swam around her hips and ankles. A bright scarf held back her hair, while strands of crystal beads sparkled in the morning light.

Rising to pour her a cup of coffee, he had the hardest time keeping his eyes off what lay just beneath those beads.

She reached him, her face all dewy and smelling of lilac soap. Moisture spiked her lashes.

He desperately wanted to kiss them dry. Instead, he handed her the tin cup and motioned for her to sit.

Her gaze lingered on him, caressing his face, his mouth . . . then, abruptly, she glanced off and sat down.

He joined her on the bench, but not too close. He didn't want to make her nervous, and besides, *he* needed to be able to think clearly. "Charlotte," he began as her flowery fragrance tortured him, "I know you think I'm being bullheaded."

She turned to face him. "You could say that." She agreed too readily, yet a smile played across her lips.

Those lush lips.

It took a second to remember what he wanted to say,

how he wanted to start. "And you think I'm butting in where I don't belong. But I can't help worrying about you any more than you can help worrying about Opal. The rest of the folks in the countryside feel pretty much the same as I do. After you left last night, everyone at the table told me how glad they were that I'm with you. Even that surly-looking woman at the end. You know, the one who just sat there sour as old Scrooge."

This time she really did treat him to a flash of a smile. "Isn't Widow Broom a delight?"

Encouraged, he continued. "Well, Widow Broom picked up her knife and wagged it at me—I think she meant it as a threat, but I'm not sure. Anyway, she said, 'High time that gal got herself a man.'"

Charlotte cracked into laughter. She instantly smothered the sound with her hand and looked toward the wagon where Opal slept. "So," she whispered, amusement still dancing in her eyes. "The woman *can* speak. The foreman said she could, but I had my doubts."

"So you see, you can stop your infernal fretting. Folks don't think any less of you for having an escort. And now, if you don't mind, there's one more thing we need to talk about. It's that look you get anytime we men start talking business. The more I've studied on the why of it, the more I realize how little I know about you. Who you are. Where you came from. Where did you get that wagon? And, why, Charlotte, are you so secretive?"

Her expression didn't take on the cornered look he'd expected—she grinned. "I was always told a lady needs a little mystery to keep the gentlemen interested."

"Trust me, in your case it isn't necessary."

Her smile wavered. "Well, I'm afraid you'll find I'm really quite ordinary."

"I doubt that."

"I was born just across the border in Shreveport, Louisiana. My parents were older when they had me. From what Papa said, my mother never regained her health afterward. She died when I was five. By that time my brothers were all grown and gone, leaving my father with just me and his drugstore. And, from what Papa said, when this snake oil salesman came to town in a fancy wagon and got himself shot for cheating, Papa bought the wagon at auction. Said it was time we saw the country. Folks around Shreveport thought he'd lost his mind, but he sold the drugstore anyway, and we went on the road, hawking his all-purpose remedy—one he'd been perfecting for years."

"Are you saying your father was the Professor Puffinwick that's on the bottle? That your name was Charlotte Puffinwick?"

"It does have a way of puckering the lips, doesn't it?" She burst into another glowing smile. "Now you know why I had to develop such a keen sense of humor."

Atlas had an overwhelming urge to sip from that smile. He took a swallow of coffee instead.

She did, too, then lowered her metal cup. "Hmm, where did I leave off? Oh, yes, I spent my growing-up years with Papa, taking his remedy to folks here in Texas. We had a lot of good times, met a lot of wonderful people."

"But schooling. He must've sent you to school."

"Papa was a college graduate, just like you. He taught me himself." Glancing up at the wagon, she chuckled. "I have a feeling I'm going to have to hog-tie Opal to give her lessons. She's such a busy little thing."

"Yeah, full of mischief." But now, tucked in her bed, he pictured the tyke curled around her kitten and sleeping like a cherub.

"When Papa passed on, God rest his soul, I married Cecil Clairmore, and now I have my beautiful baby," Charlotte said, standing up. "Then when my husband died, I took to the road again, and we've been selling Papa's powders ever since. And that's pretty much it."

*That was not it.* Atlas caught her hand. "Please. Sit down."

"I—" Her gaze flitted away.

"Please." He tugged, and she dropped to the log bench again. "Your Mr. Clairmore, how did he die?"

"The doctor called it galloping consumption. He was sick about two months, then he was gone."

"I'm sorry. That must've been very hard on you. Was he a rancher?"

"No."

He waited several seconds for her to volunteer more. But she didn't.

"What was his trade?"

She stared straight at him, then released a pent-up breath. "Cecil was a mortician. He took care of Papa when he died. That's how we met. We'd just arrived in Austin, and I didn't know a soul. I felt so lost, and Cecil took pity on me." She paused, looked away. "I'm sorry to say I regretted marrying him almost immediately. We lived above the funeral parlor. Do you have any idea what it's like to go to bed with dead bodies laid out just below you? To smell formaldehyde day and night?"

"No. But I'm sure it wasn't pleasant. Why didn't you live elsewhere?"

Charlotte laughed, a harsh, bitter laugh. "Cecil was a very frugal man. He said it would be a frivolous waste, that I'd get used to living there. I never did. And believe me, none of the church ladies were inclined to come up for tea, either." She set aside her coffee cup. "It was a very lonely time. Now, I'd better go see about Opal."

"Not yet." He reached out and took her face into his hands. "Sweetheart, not all men are like that. I'm not like that."

Though she didn't resist his touch, she cast her eyes away. "I think men who have slaughterhouses to build, the whole of Texas to save, might be more like that than they know."

"Look at me." He caressed her cheeks with his thumbs until she raised her lashes and he saw the depth of her pain. "My sweet gypsy, you're so wrong. Don't you know it's as natural for a Texan to talk about cattle as it is for you women to discuss babies and recipes and the latest fashions? It's the way of it. A woman tends her family, and her man gives her a safe and comfortable place to do it, or he's no man at all. His first duty is to his wife and his children. To care for them with love and compassion. Do you understand what I'm saying?"

Tears turned her eyes into shimmering green pools. With a watery smile, she nodded, slowly, hesitantly.

He slipped a hand behind her head and drew her close to taste a salty prism rolling down her cheek.

A soft moan escaped, and she shuddered as her fingers, trembling, moved up to his face.

*She wasn't rebuffing him.* He was so incredibly grateful, he took her fingers, kissed each and every tip, then the top of her nose.

She stopped breathing for a moment.

So did he.

He kissed her temple and felt the rapid rhythm of her pulse—a stacatto that matched his own, telling him everything he needed to know. Pulling her into his arms, he found her lips. Soft, supple, sweet lips.

She sighed, and he wove his fingers through her hair and deepened the kiss.

Firm breasts melted against his chest, and she wrapped her arms around his neck.

An instant later, she broke free. Leaping to her feet, she ran for the wagon.

Stunned, he reached for her. Too late.

"Mornin', Daltry."

Atlas swung around.

Woods, the foreman, rode across the field, leading a string of horses toward the river. The man's grin left no doubt as to what he'd seen.

Hours later, Charlotte still couldn't believe what she'd done. He simply had to look at her and she was ready to fall into his arms. She stared down the road at Atlas.

He rode across the plain with Opal, his hat fallen to the back of his neck. The sun gleamed off his hair, burnishing it to the gold of the gods. And a god he must be, for he'd taken her will. Bewitched her with overpowering urges she couldn't begin to understand.

With Cecil, she had hardly been able to hide her revulsion when he'd so much as put a hand on her shoulder. She shuddered at the remembrance. Those had been the hardest momerts of her life. But usually she'd managed to submit. To do her duty.

But with Atlas, she yearned—no, ached—to be touched . . . to feel . . . *what*?

What on earth had come over her? She'd heard of women becoming addicted to laudanum—but to a man's touch?

Charlotte smoothed her fingers over her lips. Even after a whole day, they tingled with the memory . . . the pressure of where his mouth had moved recklessly across them, across her face. Her heart pounded again at the thought of how deliciously light-headed she'd felt, how exhilarated. And hot. As if she would melt right into him.

She glanced at Opal's bouncy curls, which now rested against his chest. Thank heavens for the presence of her child.

She never thought she'd use the excuse of Opal's innocent ears to shield herself from someone, but throughout this entire day, going from ranch to farm to village, she had. She'd had to use something, anything. She certainly couldn't trust her own betraying mind, and especially not her body.

And now, Grayson's horse ranch was in sight. In a couple of minutes they'd reach tonight's layover, and she'd again have to try to give a plausible explanation for Atlas's presence . . . Atlas who was now being more stubborn than ever.

But more vital, she had to make sure he didn't catch her alone.

Even if she didn't already have Edgar to worry about, she must never succumb to Atlas's good looks again, his clever words, the mesmerizing effect of his touch. For underneath he was surely the same scheming dictator as Cecil. The fact that he'd cheated on his labor was proof of that.

Never again would she be owned by a man. Told what to do, when to get up, where to sit, what to say, to think. Never again.

Her gaze swept past a fenced horse pasture to the main house. She'd simply fight fire with fire. Men weren't the only ones who could manipulate a situation. Mrs. Grayson had been dying to teach her to crochet. Tonight would be the perfect time for her first lesson . . . right after Charlotte suggested that Atlas tell Cal Grayson all about his dream of a meatpacking house.

She smiled bitterly. That ought to do it.

And it did.

Charlotte managed to stay clear of Atlas all evening and escaped to her wagon with Opal soon after the rancher's curiosity was sufficiently whetted.

Despite the fact that the temperature had scarcely dropped since sunset, after she fanned Opal to sleep, Charlotte closed and bolted both doors. As harried and frustrated as Atlas had looked all through supper, she didn't trust him to be the perfect gentleman he professed to be.

Changing quickly into her oldest, thinnest summer shift, she blew out the lantern. She then flung open the top hatch in the hope of catching a breeze and lay down on top of the sheets, as restless as a caged cat.

Stars studded the square patch of sky overhead, and she counted every last one of them . . . anything to take her mind off every tingling inch of her flesh, this tingling that had spread from her devastatingly kissed lips this morning to every part of her body.

And Atlas's hungry looks over the supper table certainly hadn't helped.

Lord, it was hot. Even her night braid lying across her shoulder seemed to suffocate her.

Swiping it aside, she brushed across a breast. A shock streaked from it to her heart, then raged down to her womb. A person would think she'd just rubbed her feet on a carpet.

She massaged the electrified nipple, and found it had turned to a hard nub.

The other one also begged for her touch. And so did her womanhood. It, too, had come alive with a gnawing hunger of its own. It craved something. Atlas. Charlotte squeezed her legs together as tightly as she could, but even that didn't quench her craving.

Flinging herself onto her feet, she stretched her arms up through the hatch to wash herself in cooler air. Anything—

The wagon lurched. Someone was climbing aboard.

She glanced both ways, even though she knew the doors were barred.

"Charlotte, we need to talk," Atlas's loud whisper came from the direction of the back door.

She moved to it. "Go away; Opal's asleep."

"Come outside, then."

"No."

"Then I guess we'll just have to wake her."

"No."

"If you don't come out," he said in a much louder voice, "I'll wake the whole danged countryside."

"If you do, Mr. Grayson will come out with his shotgun."

"Yes, and tomorrow *Mrs.* Grayson will be telling her missionary society all about it."

The bully was right, damn him. "Okay. But just for one minute."

Moving to the drawer below her closet, she felt around for her silk wrapper. As she threw it on, the wagon bounced, and she knew he'd jumped off. Knew he'd be standing below, waiting, unwilling to give up.

Tying the sash in a bow, she lifted the bar from the door. Steeling herself to ignore her wildly yearning body, she stepped out into the velvety darkness.

# ❦ 21 ❧

To a soft tinkling of shelved bottles, the door slowly opened.

Atlas held his breath. He knew he was forcing her out by threatening her reputation, but he couldn't help himself. They couldn't share a kiss that had so profoundly proven the depth of their feelings just to have her shun him from that moment on.

She slipped out the door, and as she turned to close it, the faint starlight illuminated her braid and the large blossoms on her kimono. Lilac-scented tresses and peonies . . . When she turned back to move across the platform toward him, the flowers near the hem fluttered, and he caught the flash of ankle. A bare foot.

His heart swelled, crowding his lungs. He inhaled deeply as he stretched out his arms to her.

Her face was no more than a mysterious silhouette as she gracefully bent her legs and folded down to place her hands on his shoulders.

They were hot, searing through his shirt. A tremor ran through them. It touched his soul, yet branded him with a new jolt of desire.

His own hands, which circled her waist, were no less heated as they reveled in her silk-wrapped softness.

She moaned, and he felt the rapid expansion of her ribs . . . her feathery breaths . . . his own manhood throbbing.

Lowering her from the platform, he took an inordinate amount of time, delaying the moment he would have to release her. He paused when her stardusted gaze came level with his . . . those same eyes he'd kissed this morning, one then the other. Holding her there, he was caught in their spell. They drew him closer . . . begged him. His breath caught. His mouth was hers, on hers. Brushing it, tasting . . . taking.

To his utter joy, he discovered her arms were now around his neck, her hands in his hair, down his back. His own were cupping her bottom, holding her tight against his burgeoning need.

Moving, moaning, she came alive in his hands. Her lips parted, and he thrust his tongue into her warm, moist sweetness. She started, but for only the merest second before welcoming his entreaty.

He held his breath as her own tongue moved tentatively to touch his, then learned to dance with his in this mating ritual older than time. As their tongues made love more boldly, he discovered he was moving her across his manhood in the same rhythmic undulation.

Her breath caught, and unbelievably she wrapped her legs around him, pressing closer. Then, with a low moan, she broke free from his mouth and dropped her head on his shoulder, panting as if she'd come from the bottom of the ocean.

He moved his hands along her thighs . . . thighs only

partially covered with fabric, as he tasted her throat, her ear . . .

The screen door of the ranch house slammed.

Charlotte gasped and dropped her feet to the ground.

But it would've been impossible for Atlas to release her. He pulled her against him, held her fast as he listened to the crunch of footsteps receding toward the outhouse.

Charlotte placed her palm against his chest. "We can't—"

Any further protest he smothered in a kiss. He couldn't let her flee from him this time. Not after they'd come this far. He careened his mouth across hers, seeking a return of their passion, demanding it.

Gradually he felt her body surrender. Then she began to make her own unspoken requests. Her nipples, which had become hard little pebbles, rubbed back and forth across his chest, sending him into a hungry frenzy—a frenzy that could not be denied.

With his mouth holding hers captive, he scooped her up and carried her away from the wagon, away from the house, to the far side of the barn where fodder for the stock was piled several feet deep. Then he lowered her onto the haystack and spread himself over her . . . every quivering, hungering inch of her.

She knew she was supposed to stop him, supposed to cry out . . . do something. But the ripple of muscles across his shoulders, the strength in his back as he bent to her throat, the thought of his yet-unleashed power, sent shivers of excitement through her. She kissed the side of his neck, breathed in the intoxication of his musky male scent mixed with a hint of bay rum.

His own mouth followed the trail his hand blazed. It dipped into the scooped neck of her thin shift and took possession of a breast.

She gasped at the intense sensation.

He groaned, and his hips moved against hers, reminding her of the bulging manhood trapped inside his jeans. His tongue traced her collarbone. His thumb tantalized her nipple, teased until she could think of nothing else. Lowering his mouth to it, his tongue circled her crest, then took it, suckled, drawing so deeply from it that a delicious thrill surged all the way up from her womb.

Her own hands fell away, helpless to do anything as wave after wave of rapture washed over her.

So overcome was she with this untold ecstasy, she was scarcely aware that he'd rolled to her side.

His mouth moved to treat her other breast to his shattering magic, as a hand untied her kimono and reached beneath her skimpy shift.

Not until he ran his hand between her legs did she again react, and with a response that astounded her as profoundly as any of the wondrous things he'd done to her. She willingly—no, gladly—parted her legs, opening the way to that secret part of her that had been hungering for his touch.

Lifting his mouth from her breast, he pushed her summer gown up to expose all of her to his caressing ministrations.

She again forgot to breathe.

"My God, Charlotte, you're so soft, so smooth. So perfect. I never knew I could want anyone, love anyone, this much. I—" His mouth fell upon hers in a ravaging kiss.

He said he loved her. Her own hands were reborn. They roved his back, his chest. Yet she needed to get closer, to get inside his shirt. She tore at his buttons. Bared his chest.

His own fingers ran along the tender skin of her thigh, caressing, exploring, and she fell still again, waiting . . . hoping.

His hand covered her velvety mound. A finger teased at the entrance of her inner secret.

She found herself arching against it, begging.

His tongue thrust deeply into her mouth, and as it did, he drove his finger into her.

She cried out and arched against him, urged him deeper. Spiriting her tongue into his mouth, she grabbed his arm, felt the power in its tensed muscles. Rode with it as he drove into her, then retreated and plunged again. She was on fire, melting hot and wet.

Suddenly he jerked away from her. "I can't."

Her eyes flew open. Her heart stopped. "*What?*"

"I can't wait," he groaned, and began ripping at his belt buckle.

Her heart started beating again. "Let me help." Frantically she tore at his belt.

Once she'd unbuckled it, she fought with him over the fasteners until enough were undone, and she felt the immenseness of his erection as it broke free.

In wonder, she encased its huge, bone-hard length with her hand.

He sucked in a breath and shoved his jeans down to his ankles, then lowered himself between her legs. "I'm sorry. I can't wait." His rasping breath burned against her ear as he pressed the tip of his manhood to her yearning sheath.

Opening herself, she wrapped her legs around him as he slowly slid his hugeness into her, stretching every inch of her walls until she could ask for nothing more, knew nothing more.

Eventually he came to the end of himself, or her, she knew not which. It didn't matter. He was feeding that intense craving that had been building since she'd first laid eyes on him. She tightened the grip of her legs. She never wanted him to leave her.

"I love you," he whispered just as his mouth captured hers, and though she tried desperately to keep him deeply buried, he slowly began to abandon her. Then just before he removed himself altogether, just as his tip teased the edges of her need, he thrust again, this time hard and swift. He drove so deeply, she was surprised he didn't rip her apart. But instead of pain, she felt pleasure beyond pleasure.

He pierced her again. And again with growing power.

She met every thrust fully, eagerly. And all the while she knew that somewhere, far away from this consuming rapture, their mouths, too, were making love. And their hands. His were all over her face, hers urging his thighs to take her more powerfully, more deeply, more completely.

She clamored for more, always more, until he filled her so full, so deep, she burst. Exploded into a million tingling stars. The Fourth of July and New Year's Eve. The brilliance, the excitement, spilled through her in a shower of awe.

A second explosion, his, sent her spiraling into ecstasy once more.

He shuddered again and again.

She clung tightly lest they lose each other in their fall back to earth.

But it was a gentle fall, eased by the tender kisses he rained across her face, her neck, her shoulders, and by his whispered words of love.

Brushing his lips across her lashes, he abruptly jerked up his head. "You're crying."

She ran fingers over her eyes and felt their wetness. "I didn't realize."

"I hurt you. I should've been more careful, but I couldn't—"

"Shh." She pressed her fingers to his lips. "You were perfect. Everything. More. I never knew it could be so—so thrilling, so . . . I can't find the words to describe it. It was like being shot into the heavens and exploding into a sky full of stars. But more. More." Suddenly embarrassed, she buried her face in the hollow of his neck. "You must think I'm loony."

He kissed the top of her head. "If you're loony, so am I."

Smiling, she nuzzled his throat. "I always thought this was something a woman had to endure, her duty. But you were so . . . I'll never forget tonight. Never. Not as long as I live."

"Neither will I, my sweet, sweet Charlotte." Then before she could stop him, he removed his spent manhood and rolled to her side.

She sighed in disappointment, and he gathered her close, pressing her bare breasts to him, and for the first time she felt the prickles of his chest hair, felt the comfort of his pad of muscles layered just beneath. She smoothed her hands across his sweat-dampened shoulders, picking off bits of straw, exploring, memorizing the texture of his skin, its firmness, the shape of an arm, a hand, his fingers. She could feel his eyes on her, but it was too dark to see more than the faintest reflection. But if she had been able to, she knew they would be filled with love because his other hand, which was taking its own leisurely measure of her, told her so.

It slid up her leg and over her hip, dipping to her waist, then traveled across the softness of her belly and up to the swell of a breast. Then, as if in worship, he bent and kissed one tip, then the other.

Slowly, deliciously, her blood began to heat again, and her own hand found itself traveling down his body to that part of him that had given such indescribable pleasure. When she touched it, she heard him moan *his* pleasure.

It began to grow again in her hand.

He nibbled her breast.

She stroked his shaft.

It grew larger still.

She rubbed it against her leg, her belly.

His fingers covered hers, and together they parted her legs and rubbed his manhood between them, filling her with new cravings, less hurried ones. She moved herself against his hand, and his shaft kicked within her own palm.

His breathing quickened to match her own shallow breaths as he began to thrust his shaft back and forth through her encircling palm. Then, unwrapping his fingers from around hers, he penetrated her with two of them, throwing her whole being once again into a vortex of passion. A cry escaped her throat.

A dog barked. It yipped again and again, each yelp sounding louder, closer than the last.

"The Graysons' dog!" Charlotte pushed away from Atlas and sat up as the shepherd raced around the barn.

"King!" Sliding off the haystack, she called as loudly as she dared. "It's me—Charlotte."

The dog, thank heavens, stopped barking and trotted up to her, sniffing, but not before she'd managed to pull her nightshift down over her hips again.

Atlas reached through the shadows for her. "Come back. He won't make any more noise."

"I have to go. He may have awakened Opal. Or Mr. Grayson might come out to see what all the ruckus was about." She closed her kimono around her and retied the sash.

"I'm going to miss you. Desperately. But," he added as she heard him lie back on the crunchy straw, "I am unbelievably happy to say I haven't proven to be nearly the gentleman I thought I was." He began chuckling. "Next time, I promise, we'll have a feather mattress and sheets. Maybe I'll even take the time to remove my boots."

Her heart lurched painfully. "Oh, Atlas, I'm sorry, but there won't be a next time. There can't be." Before he could respond, she fled. Her only solace was that it was too dark to see his face. If he looked anything like she felt, the sight would be too painful to bear.

# ⨍ 22 ⨍

"Atlas?"

Coming out of a deep sleep, he vaguely heard a child's high, thin voice, then felt a nudging at his shoulder. He rolled over and found little Opal staring wide-eyed, her hair spilling across her cheeks, tickling his nose. Blowing the lock away, he smiled at the little sweetheart and pulled her down onto his pallet for a hug. "You're sure up with the birds this morning."

"Watch out!" She pushed away and sat back on her knees. "You'll squish Gypsy."

Seeing the kitten tangled up in the hair at her neck, he reached out and scratched the tiny thing behind its ears.

It started to purr.

"Gypsy doesn't seem to mind traveling on the road, after all, does she?"

Opal pulled her needle-clawed pet down to her lap. "It's the cat box Mama don't like."

At the mention of Charlotte, myriad images of last night's lovemaking swarmed over him, through him, enveloping him in an intoxicating glow. Immediately he sought her. He scanned the campsite and the corral beyond where the horses were penned, but didn't see her. "Where's your mama?"

She shrugged. "When I woke up, she was already gone."

Atlas sat up and checked the ranch clearing again. The sun had risen some time ago, but Charlotte had yet to start the campfire. Had she slept as heavily as he after their lovemaking and just recently gone to take care of her morning needs?

Or was she avoiding him? After her parting words last night, she surely knew another very serious talk was inevitable. He shook his head. The woman could be such a trial. He'd sweep away one obstacle, and she'd place another in his path.

Opal giggled, and he found the kitten was licking her neck.

He ruffled the child's hair, then pulled on his boots and rose. "Come on, let's go get cleaned up." Brushing dust and leftover bits of straw from his plain gray shirt—straw that he wished he could keep forever—he noticed the need for a clean change. When they reached Abilene today, he'd buy himself a new set of work clothes. It would be three more days before they reached Paradise Plains.

He picked up Opal and tossed her onto the wagon platform. "Scoot inside and get us a bar of soap and a couple of towels."

While he waited for her to return, he raked his fingers through his mussed hair.

More sprigs of hay fell out.

Pulling out his comb, he removed the last of the evidence. Considering how concerned Charlotte was about her good name, he didn't want either of the Graysons wondering why he'd been rolling in the hay.

He noticed he was smiling. Last night would be just the beginning. Making love to someone you loved . . . nothing on earth could possibly compare. Nothing.

"Whatcha grinnin' at, Atlas?" Returning with the soap and towels, Opal had caught him.

"Oh, just the beautiful day." He tossed her onto his shoulders and started for the stream behind the corrals. "The blue sky, the birds singing."

He thought they'd run into Charlotte at the water's edge, but they didn't, and when they returned to the wagon, she wasn't there, either.

His elusive gypsy was avoiding him. He looked toward the small batten-board ranch house shaded by a porch stretched across the front. Most likely she was inside, hiding out.

"Come on, pumpkin. Let's get you dressed, then we'll go find your mama." He lifted her onto the wagon, then hoisted himself up. "Find your brush. I think I'd better try my hand at taming that Moses bush growing out of your head."

Inside the cramped quarters, Atlas buttoned Opal into a bright pink blouse and helped her with one of her gypsy skirts, then was quite proud of himself for managing what he considered a passable braid. After tying it with a turquoise ribbon from a collection hanging on a large nail beside the mirror, he patted her on the bottom. "Let's scoot on out of here and find that mother of yours."

Opal plucked her kitten off the counter. "Mama's probably inside with Mrs. Grayson. Mrs. Grayson never had no young'uns of her own, so she likes to pretend we're hers. She always fixes us breakfast."

"Why didn't you say so before?"

"We had to get dressed first."

Shaking his head, he led the way out and leaped off the wagon. He supposed her answer contained some bit of logic . . . about as much as her mother's did sometimes.

Just as he swung Opal and her kitten to the ground, the rancher's wife slammed out of the screen door. "Come on in. Your breakfast will be ready in two shakes. I just put your eggs on to fry."

The instant Atlas stepped inside the big square kitchen, he saw Charlotte at the sink, washing dishes. Her expression was so intent, one would think the task took every ounce of concentration.

Opal ran to her, arms outstretched.

Her mother pulled her into a hug.

"Good morning, Miss Charlotte," he said, but she didn't even come close to looking up at him before turning back to her chore.

But he didn't miss the flaming red flush on her cheeks, a stark contrast to the yellow-and-white checked apron she wore over her peasant blouse.

He'd had the most wonderful night of his life, and all she could be was embarrassed. Fine, he'd honor her feelings for now. But once they were out on the road again, she wouldn't put him off the way she had yesterday.

"Sit down, sit down, son." Rail-thin Mrs. Grayson brought a plate heaped with ham, biscuits, and eggs. "Don't want Janie Daltry thinkin' we didn't take good care of you. How is she, anyways? Is she still experimenting with her irises?"

"Yes, ma'am," he said, tearing his eyes from Charlotte. For the moment.

They'd ridden no more than a few yards from the Grayson ranch house when Atlas reined Red Jack alongside Charlotte's wagon. "About last night," he began.

A hand flew out to ward off his words. "Surely," she murmured, looking somewhere past his shoulder, "you're not going to expound upon certain events in front of a little pitcher. One with very big handles . . . and an even *bigger* spout."

"I will if the big pitcher refuses to find an empty shelf to sit on with the water jug. They need to compare their contents."

"What are you talking about?" Opal, sitting beside Charlotte, looked from him to her mother. "We don't have no pitchers. Pitchers break too easy."

"You're absolutely right." Charlotte looked directly at Atlas for the first time this morning—and quite pointedly. "Little pitchers are very delicate. They must be handled with care."

Atlas had the strongest urge to leap aboard and take her in his arms, demand she stop all this foolishness. They needed to discuss last night. *And they would, or his name wasn't Atlas Daltry.* "Now, jugs, they're very hard to break. And even harder to lose. A good jug will last a lifetime. Throwing one away would be very foolish. Especially when it's glued to the table. And," he added with what he hoped was a maddening smile, "that table is nailed to the floor. With spikes."

"Very well," she ground out. She looked down at Opal. "Sweetheart, when we get to Abilene, would you like to go play with your friend Blessing for a little while?"

Opal lifted the kitten from her lap and held it up. "Can I take Gypsy? Can I?"

"Yes, you *may*," Charlotte corrected, then glanced back at Atlas. "This afternoon. But don't think the pitcher will ever let the jug pour anything into it again." Her gaze faltered and flitted away as the deepest color swept up from her neck to cover her entire face. It was the most spectacular blush he'd ever seen.

Any other time he might have teased her, but right now too much was at stake. He'd just won uninterrupted time alone with her and would do nothing to jeopardize it.

Several hours and a number of stops later, Atlas was immensely relieved to be passing the first warehouses lining the tracks into Abilene. With Opal sitting in front of him, he reined Red Jack to a stop and waited for the white draft horses to pass, their plumes fluttering, their harness bells tinkling. He then guided his sorrel alongside the colorful wagon.

Charlotte had that cornered-cat look, but he didn't care. She loved him. Even if she hadn't actually said the words.

"Where does Opal's friend live?" he asked, wanting to expedite her departure. His whole body sprang to life at just the thought that any minute now he and Charlotte would be alone again.

She stared straight ahead. "Several blocks past the train station. First we'll stop off and pick up this week's order."

She'd be able to stall only so long. He shoved back his hat. "Whatever you want."

Within moments, they arrived at the Texas and Pacific's pastel green hotel and depot. As Charlotte pulled alongside the loading dock, Atlas dismounted with Opal, then strode over to the wagon.

"The train hasn't even arrived yet." He was becoming more frustrated. One delay after another. If he could just get her alone, settle her down with a little kiss, they could work this out. He reached up for her.

She seemed reluctant to place her hands on his shoulders.

Proof that he was right.

She stalled. "What time is it?"

He pulled out his watch. "Ten till two."

"It's as late as we are. It'll be here any minute." Finally she came down into his arms . . . and gasped. Faintly, perhaps, but a gasp nonetheless.

Pretending not to notice, Atlas was left with no doubt. She *would* be his again tonight.

"Mr. Daltry?" A man's voice called from behind.

Reluctantly Atlas released Charlotte and turned to see the ticket agent. The little man stood at the entrance to the hotel, peering over a pair of spectacles.

"Yes. That's me."

"Thought so. I have a message for you." He then disappeared inside.

Atlas turned back to Charlotte. "Probably Pa, bawling me out for leaving that line of fence half-finished."

"I do hope he received the telegraph wire you sent him."

"Oh, sure, or he wouldn't have known where to track me down."

Opal snugged her hand into his. "Can I come?"

Grinning, he swung her up into his arms. "Wouldn't think of going without you."

Luckily the message contained no reprimand, simply his mother's request that he purchase ten yards of Spanish lace for her.

As he turned away from the ticket counter, Opal pointed at the entrance to the hotel dining room. "They have the best lemonade in there. They put ice in it and everything. Mama sure would love to have some. Maybe then she wouldn't talk so mean to you."

"Do you think she'll like it as much as she did the kitten?" he teased.

Displaying those darling dimples, she raised her brows innocently. "More. Much more."

"Then I guess we'll have to get her a glass." He stuffed the telegram into his pocket and started for the dining room. "You know, I think I'd like some, too. How about you?"

She glanced away as if it mattered little to her. "If you're going to, I guess I could."

After placing an order for the lemonade and an assortment of tea cakes, Atlas strode out to fetch Charlotte with Opal still perched on his arm. He scanned the length of loading dock but didn't find his gypsy lady among those waiting for the train.

"There she is," Opal said, and nodded in the opposite direction.

She stood next to her bandwagon with two men dressed in suits and city hats.

One, a gaunt fellow, pointed a long, bony finger inches from Charlotte's face. A threatening gesture. The hawk-like expression on his skeletal features added to Atlas's alarm.

He set Opal down. "Go into the dining room and wait. We'll be there in a minute." Giving her a light shove in that direction, he wheeled and strode toward the stairs, keeping a close eye on the men.

As he reached the top step, the two left. The skeletal one, in particular, stalked away with jerky strides, as if he were enraged.

Atlas swung his attention back to Charlotte.

Her expression was stark, stiff.

Not bothering with the stairs, he vaulted off the side of the dock. "What is it? Did they threaten you?"

Her gaze swept past him to the departing men. Then, in a blur of color, she whirled and fled to the wagon.

In her wake, a piece of paper floated to the ground. It looked like some kind of a legal document.

Atlas picked it up. Quickly perusing it, he discovered it was a subpoena ordering her to appear before a judge the following Tuesday, to answer specific charges of her unfitness as a mother. The complaint had been filed by an Edgar J. Clairmore, uncle of the minor child in question, Opal Marlene Clairmore.

*Edgar!*

Atlas stared from the paper to the wagon into which Charlotte had disappeared.

"What's the matter?" came Opal's cry.

Looking down, he found her beside him. "I told you to wait in the dining room."

"Somethin's wrong." She ran for the wagon. "Mama! What's wrong?"

Snagging Opal, Atlas swung her away and set her up on the dock. "Wait there," he commanded sternly. "I'll check on your mother."

When he opened the back door, he found Charlotte kneeling before the lower bunk, counting bills and coins she'd dumped onto it. He held out the document. "What is this? What grounds could your brother-in-law possibly have?"

Startled, she glanced up, then resumed counting greenbacks into piles.

"Charlotte, does he have grounds to take Opal from you?"

"More now than ever," she said without slowing. "I knew I was being watched. That he was just waiting for one little slip-up. He sure didn't waste any time, now, did he? Thirteen days. Thirteen lousy days from the time Whistle started driving for me. And just now, that stinking spy of his said you weren't Whistle. *That you were another of my men.* That pretty well cinched it for *dear old Edgar.*"

Atlas grabbed her arms, turned her to face him. "It'll be all right. We'll testify on your behalf. Explain that you're really a very moral person, and that you merely needed protection."

"Are you crazy? After last night that would be perjury. And even if they didn't guess, Edgar would then accuse me of placing my daughter in danger. He told me before I left Austin that he'd get the proof he needed to *save Opal from my insanity.*" She wrenched away and pulled a small metal chest from beneath the bunk, then dumped the contents onto the bed. More money and a bankbook.

"Charlotte, sit down and let's talk this out."

"I don't have time."

"The court hearing's not set for six days—surely you can give me five minutes."

She came to her feet. "Look, Atlas, you're a very nice man. A wonderful man." Her expression softened for the briefest instant before she started stuffing the bills and coins into her pockets. "If things had been different, who knows?"

"Mama! What's the matter?" Opal stood in the doorway, her eyes saucers of fright.

Charlotte flashed her an unconvincing smile. "There's nothing to worry about, sweetheart. Remember when we talked about going to California? Well, guess what? We're leaving for there on the train today."

"California?" Opal's voice was almost inaudible. She looked from her mother to Atlas.

He was no less stunned.

Charlotte brushed past him and stopped before Opal, taking the child's face in her hands. "I have to go arrange for the wagon and horses to be loaded, so would you be a big girl and watch for the train?"

"For God's sake, Charlotte." Atlas finally found his voice. "Don't run off like this. You haven't even spoken to a lawyer."

She rose to her feet and took Opal's hand. "Edgar wouldn't be here if he wasn't sure he'd win. He's been biding his time, just waiting for the right moment. You see, his wife can't have children. They've coveted my daughter from the day she was born." She started for the door.

Opal broke free, ran to Atlas, and clutched at his pant legs. "Somethin's bad wrong. Fix it. Fix it!"

Her cry tore at his heart. He picked her up and looked back to Charlotte.

But she was gone.

After taking a moment to help Opal down, Atlas

discovered that by the time he caught up with her, Charlotte was already negotiating with the freight agent.

"The train should arrive any minute," the pockmark-faced agent said. "When it does, it'll pull out one hour later. But don't you worry, we'll get your wagon and animals safely loaded."

"Thanks, Bert. I'm going to the bank now. I'll pay you when I come back." Turning away, she came face-to-face with Atlas and Opal.

"You're acting out of panic. You need to—"

Sweeping past him, she hurried into the hotel.

He followed on her heels. "What about us?"

His words had no effect as she rushed toward the passenger ticket counter.

"How can you act as if last night never happened?"

She halted and spun around. "Will you please keep your voice down?"

"What difference does it make if you're leaving?"

"I told you from the start, we could never be. Surely now you understand why." She turned back to the ticket agent. "Good day, Mr. Feinstine. One adult and one child to California, please."

"You're going to California, Miss Charlotte?" The agent removed his glasses. "For how long?"

"I'm not sure exactly. How much?"

"Where in California?"

"I don't know. How about San Diego? That's the closest city, isn't it?"

"Yes." He looked none too pleased as he pulled a packet of tickets from a drawer and started stamping them. "That will be sixty-four dollars and eighty cents."

She pulled wads of bills from her pockets.

Opal, in Atlas's arms, leaned close to his ear. "Do something," she whispered.

The child's plea propelled him into action. He grabbed Charlotte's wrist. "You have over an hour. Plenty of time to come with me to a lawyer's office."

Pulling away, she gathered up a raft of tickets and stuffed them into a pocket. "I don't have time, so you might as well give up. I'm going to the bank now. The fate of my child is at stake."

Atlas forcibly placed her hand in the crook of his arm. "Fine. To the bank, *then* to a lawyer."

On the three-block walk, Charlotte set a fast pace, scarcely acknowledging the greetings of other shoppers they passed on the boardwalks. The whistle of the arriving train blew, and she charged ahead with even more determination.

Passing the newspaper office, Atlas noticed a sign in a second-floor window. DAVID K. GROSSET, ATTORNEY AT LAW—a convenient stop on their way back.

They walked into the marble-floored bank. No customers waited in line at the teller's cage. A lucky thing! Most likely Charlotte would've shoved them aside.

Rushing up, she asked for two hundred fifty dollars in cash. Then, to Atlas's amazement, she had the bank teller make out a bank draft for the remainder. *Over thirty-eight hundred dollars*! By no means was she the pauper he'd imagined, eking out a meager existence.

"Mama," Opal asked as they left the bank, "do you have enough to buy Atlas a ticket, too?" She sounded as frantic as Atlas felt.

Avoiding his eyes, Charlotte reached across him and touched her little one's cheek. "Sweetheart. Atlas can't leave here. He has far too much to do. He has the whole of Texas to save."

He refused to be baited. "Up those stairs at the side of the building is a law office." He steered her in that direction.

She balked. "I don't have time."

"You do." He pulled her along.

"Five minutes. And not a second more. I won't miss that train. This may be my only chance. I'm sure Edgar believes I could never manage to leave within an hour, since he knows I would never go without my wagon. But you can bet he'll have the Saturday train watched."

Reaching the top of the stairs, the strong smell of printer's ink permeated the air as they walked into a dark hallway. Several doors lined either side. The second one on the right had the lawyer's name painted on it. Atlas knocked, praying that Mr. Grosset would be available.

"Come in," came a booming voice from the other side.

Stepping in behind Charlotte, Atlas noted that bookshelves lined one wall, while on the other side stood filing cabinets and a large mahogany desk.

Behind it stood a portly man with a neatly trimmed goatee. He was shrugging into the frock coat of his brown pinstripe suit. "Have a seat," he offered. "What can I do for you?"

As Atlas handed the attorney the subpoena, Charlotte muttered, "This is a waste of precious time."

Atlas smiled an apology to the lawyer and took one of the two seats in front of the desk. Sitting Opal on his lap, he watched the face of the man scanning the summons.

Showing no apparent interest, Charlotte moved to the window and looked toward the train station.

Mr. Grosset looked up from the paper, his expression skeptical. He stared at Opal a moment, then Charlotte. From his growing disdain, it was obvious their gypsylike attire made a poor impression. He looked back at Atlas. "Legal advice is not free of charge."

"No problem." Atlas's own disdain for the lawyer was mounting. "You'll get your money. Up front, if necessary." He shifted his weight and reached into his pocket.

Atlas's apparent ability to pay must have impressed the man. He waved a hand. "We'll discuss my retainer in a moment." He eyed Opal again. "I assume this is the child in question."

"Yes." Atlas smoothed his hands over the flyaway strands of the hair he'd braided that morning. "And Charlotte is an excellent mother *and* a very moral person. I'm sure I could get scores of people to testify on her behalf."

"Yeah," Opal added brightly. "Ever'body loves Mama."

"I see." The attorney settled back in his leather chair and laced his fingers together over his protruding belly. "Nonetheless, charges are being levied against her. I can't imagine this brother-in-law filing suit unless he had grounds."

Atlas glanced at Charlotte, hoping she would join them, but she didn't even seem to be listening as she stared out the window. He returned his attention to Grosset. "His grounds have no real basis. Mrs. Clairmore is an independent businesswoman with an unblemished reputation. She travels a circuit with her daughter, selling medicine powders and other assorted items. She's—"

"Yes. Now I recognize her. She's the woman with the bandwagon."

"That's us," Opal proudly declared.

"The problem," Atlas continued, "that led to Edgar Clairmore's suit started a couple of weeks ago when it became unsafe for a lady to travel the road alone because of some no-account drifters. She hired an older man to ride shotgun for her. Mr. Clairmore is now using this emergency situation to imply immoral conduct on his sister-in-law's part."

Grosset glanced up at Charlotte again—who might as well not have been in the room. "Speaking of parts," he said, "exactly what is your relationship to the lady?"

"I've been accompanying her since Sunday when Whistle McSween injured his foot."

"Goliath squished it," Opal popped in. "But he didn't mean to."

Grosset held up his hand, halting any further explanation. "If I might play devil's advocate for a moment, sir, where exactly have you been spending your nights? Mr.—I don't believe I caught your name."

Before Grosset's last words were out, Atlas sprang to his feet. If the man didn't watch his mouth, a fist would be in it. He stood Opal on the chair and edged closer. "My name is Daltry. Atlas Daltry of the Circle D, the biggest spread between here and Fort Worth. And as for where I spent my nights, I slept outside the wagon *by myself.*"

"Can you provide witnesses who will testify to that?"

"You mean someone who stayed up all night, every night, to watch me? Of course not. That's—"

"Well, that's exactly what it would take." Grosset folded the subpoena and handed it back to Atlas. "Two unchaperoned young people spending days and nights within close proximity . . ." He clucked his tongue. "No matter how much of a gentleman you may profess to be, the judge will see it as a compromising situation."

Opal grabbed Atlas's hand. "What is he saying? What do the big words mean?"

He picked her up and held her close. No one was taking her from him. Or Charlotte. "What if we were to marry?"

Spreading his hands, the lawyer smiled. "Now that's a horse of a different color. If she were to marry into the influential Daltry family before next Tuesday, this brother-in-law wouldn't stand a chance. At least, not in a Taylor County court."

"Does that mean everything's okay again?" Opal asked.

Atlas patted her back. "It will be as soon as we're married."

*"Married."* Opal threw her arms around his neck, nearly choking him, then flipped around and yelled, "We don't have to go away, Mama! Atlas fixed everything. He's gonna marry us!"

Charlotte whirled from the window. *What did you say?"*

Atlas met her halfway. "Marry me, and you'll never have to worry about your brother-in-law again."

The shock on her face melted into the tenderest expression. Reaching up, she touched his lips. "You are a sweet, sweet man. But I married once because I had nowhere to turn. And it was a—" She glanced at Opal. "I'm sorry, but I can't be owned again."

"I don't want to own you. I simply want to love you. Every day for the rest of our lives."

"That's what you say now, but I know different. You would insist I give up my business, the traveling, my friends."

She was right! Atlas stood speechless. He felt her slipping through his fingers. He tightened his grip on her daughter. "What about Opal? You said yourself she would be difficult to teach on the road, and she'll be five next month. She needs to start school this fall. In one place."

That stopped her. She looked from him to Opal and back again. Then abruptly she ripped Opal out of his arms. "If you'll excuse me, we have a train to catch."

## ❧ 24 ❧

Charlotte was leaving him!

Atlas reached the door right behind her and stopped her from opening it with his hand.

She glared up at him.

He had to think fast. Say the right thing. "I understand your dreams are as important to you as mine are to me. So summers we could follow yours, winters mine."

If anything, her expression hardened. "You say that now in the heat of the moment. But later, once I married you, you'd decide it was much too impractical, much too difficult. Just like following the rules of your grandmother's labor."

Was she right? Or did he really mean what he'd said?

*He did.* He had no doubt. Sharing a life with her was more important than anything else. "This is completely different."

Tilting her head up to him, she didn't look at all convinced. "Is it?"

He was losing ground. "I hated being manipulated by her. But you're right; I should have handled it much more honestly. I'll speak to her the next chance I get."

"Then perhaps some good has come out of this after

all." Smiling sadly, she moved his hand aside and opened the door. "Good-bye, Mr. Daltry."

This couldn't be the end. He caught her arm. "Charlotte, I know that when I first came to you my motives were questionable. But if you could just look past our dubious beginning and listen to your heart. *Please*. I didn't say I'd go with you summers lightly. Truly, I could never be happy if you weren't."

"Me, too!" Opal cried, sounding as desperate as he.

Atlas pressed his advantage. "And aside from the fact that I'm hopelessly in love with you, my proposal really is quite practical. Most cattle aren't sent to the slaughter-house until fall, after they've fattened up on summer grass."

Charlotte looked at him so intently, he felt her reaching into his soul.

Would she believe what she saw? What she felt?

"You'd actually be willing to go on the road with me, selling trinkets?"

"Absolutely." Feeling more confident, he took her arm and started down the hall. "You should've guessed by now that I'm not that easy to get rid of. If you still insist on going to California, I'll be on that train with you."

She stared at him openmouthed. Then a smile began to tickle the corners. "For a list-maker, you sure are making some rash decisions. Proposing to a woman you've known less than two months. Offering to run away with her to the Wild West. Leaving all of Texas to fend for itself."

"*Mama*," Opal scolded. "You know we love him. Say yes. Say we'll marry him."

"Yeah, Mama," Atlas mimicked. He took her hand. "If you do, I'll buy you that feather mattress I promised."

This time, her smile didn't stop until it reached her eyes. Stepping closer, she whispered, "I kind of like straw myself."

Charlotte lifted the hem of her green satin gown and stepped onto the bench just inside the half door. Bending low, she then climbed out onto the driver's seat, trying not to muss the elaborate chignon she'd fashioned.

Atlas, driving the team, turned to help her through, then forgot to take her arm. Instead, he stared open-mouthed . . . at her chest.

She looked down at the blasted low neckline. Her bosom bulged, threatening to pop out. Slapping a hand over it, she stepped down to the floorboard and took her seat. She really wished she'd remembered to buy some lace to fill it in. "A gentleman wouldn't stare," she said, arching a brow.

Chuckling wickedly, he pulled her close. "I thought we decided during these last three utterly carnal nights that I'm no gentleman where you're concerned." He shot a wary glance to the open half door, then leaned down and rained a trail of nuzzling kisses across the bare swells and in the deep valley between.

Shivers of anticipation shot to every extremity, every hollow, that had learned so quickly to crave his touch. Nonetheless, she shoved him away. "Opal could peek out any second."

Groaning, he straightened and took a breath, then pulled his pocket watch from the plaid waistcoat of the charcoal dress suit he'd worn to the Tucker wedding a week ago . . . a lifetime ago. He flipped open the top. "Hours and hours yet before bedtime. It's only one forty-three."

Charlotte's heart leaped with panic. "Only seventeen more minutes before two. Are you sure the pastor received our telegraph wire? That he'll actually be there waiting?" She clutched at his arm. "And your family? Tell me again—exactly what did you say in the wire you sent them?"

"Exactly?" He wrapped an arm around her again and grinned. "Now who's becoming the stickler for detail? It said, CHARLOTTE'S BROTHER-IN-LAW TRYING TO TAKE OPAL. STOP. AM MARRYING CHARLOTTE 2 PM SATURDAY OUR CHURCH. STOP. PLEASE COME. STOP. BRING BOUQUET."

Icy fingers raced up her spine. Her insides fluttered. She couldn't imagine his family accepting such a sudden wedding. "The butterflies in my stomach just took flight again."

"Butterflies in your stomach!" Opal popped her head through the half door, looking like a bouquet herself in pink floral polished cotton. "How'd they get there?"

Charlotte swung around. "The same way Atlas's feet sprouted wings."

"Oh, yeah. I loved those wings. In my dream they took us way up in the clouds. And we rolled and rolled and rolled. Didn't we, Atlas?"

"You bet, pumpkin face."

Opal looked as if she'd been tumbling around on some clouds, all right. The wide pink ribbon holding aloft the front half of her curls had turned cockeyed. "I finished fixing your hair not two minutes ago. However do you manage?" Stretching around, Charlotte retied the bow.

"Look, Mama," Opal squealed, nearly shattering her mother's ears. "Paradise Plains. See the church steeple sticking out of the trees? I better find Gypsy. She'd hate to miss the wedding."

As Opal dropped out of sight, Charlotte called after her, "Be careful. Don't get dirty." Turning back, she spotted the big barn at the Horse Hotel, and realized how very close the town loomed. As they passed a rangy pecan tree, the back of Lucky's Saloon came into view, and she could easily count the windows.

Her hands began to sweat inside her black lace gloves. *Black.*

It simply wasn't appropriate for a wedding. "Atlas. Are you sure you want me to wear this outfit? This low-cut dress? Your family will take one look at me and try to talk you out of it. I look like a—"

"Hush," he said, pressing her head to his shoulder. "They love you no matter what you wear. The whole bunch of them. It's me they're not sure of. In fact, you may not be so sure either after I tell you something. Remember that big speech I made the other day about honesty? About always telling you the truth?" He removed his arm from around her. "There's something I haven't told you."

His tone had grown solemn. Charlotte moved far enough away to see his face fully. The smooth golden tan, his strong yet refined features . . . which couldn't hide the worry in his gray eyes.

The blood drained from her face.

"Grams told me if I couldn't get you to accompany me to the outings, she would give my prize to you. I withheld that information from you. It was wrong of me, and I'm so very sorry. If you'll forgive me, I promise never to keep anything from you again."

"That's it? That's your confession?" With profound relief, she brushed a strand of hair from his forehead. He was going to be the dearest, most considerate husband. "I probably would've done the same in your place."

"You're sure?"

Smiling with all her heart, she nodded.

He caught her hand to his lips and kissed the center of her palm, then lifted his shimmering gray pools to meet her own gaze. "I thought you'd be upset."

"Will saying I love you even more now reassure you?"

His lips moved toward hers. "I couldn't think of anything I'd rather hear."

The front wheel dropped into a hole, forcing his attention back to the road.

Her gaze followed, and fear gripped her again. Another minute and they'd be turning onto Main Street. How could his family possibly want their educated young gentleman to marry a loudmouthed gypsy? Then she remembered something else equally damning. "Are you going to tell your grandmother about my part in your plot to win the prize?"

"I had planned to tell her everything. I want to wipe the slate clean before I marry you and have nothing hanging over us. Besides, you're all the prize I could ever want."

"The packing house was such a worthy cause, though. But still, your grandmother will be disappointed. And possibly very angry. With both of us."

"Tell you what, sweet one. I want your wedding day to be filled with nothing but happiness. I'll wait a couple of weeks before I tell her. Okay?" He pressed his lips to her temple.

Again this very special man was putting her first. "I know I'm being a coward, but I'd appreciate that."

A twig fell from an oak they passed under.

She brushed it from the sleeve of his charcoal coat. "But I just hate to think that because of me you'll lose your dream."

"Sweetheart, don't worry. I'll get backing somewhere else. Remember, I can fix anything. Ask Opal."

Driving past Lucky's, Charlotte noticed more than the usual number of horses tied at the hitching rail. "Are the ranchers having another meeting today?"

"Could be. They're very serious about this alliance." He reined the team onto Main Street . . . and it looked like the Fourth of July all over again.

Hundreds of people clogged the street, all dressed in their summer best, their outfits topped off with straw floaters and spectacular bonnets. When the crowd spied Atlas and Charlotte, a low rumble of voices grew into a cheer so loud, the very buildings lining the street reverberated.

"Hip-hip hooray! Hip-hip hooray!"

The horses shied.

Atlas tightened his grip on the reins.

Charlotte tightened hers on his arm. "What's happening?" she shouted over the roar.

Turning to her, he sported the grandest smile. "I think they've come to our wedding."

Speechless, she looked from face to familiar face. There stood the gaggle of Richards women, and the McCutcheons from Buffalo Gap. The Priddys and the

Newsoms from Clyde. The Carpenters, the Spoolers, Mrs. Bennet, the Tittles . . . folks from all over, waving or clapping, and shouting, "Congratulations!"

Charlotte swiped the tears from her eyes and turned to see more exuberant faces on the other side. She started waving to the Graysons, the Spears, the Youngs, the Kimbles. The Gillespies. And more, many, many more . . . Her wonderful friends had all somehow found out about her special day and had come to share it with her.

The tears couldn't be stopped now, and the remaining scores of friends they passed on the way to the church became nothing but a happy blur.

"Would you look at that!" Atlas pressed a cloth into Charlotte's hands. "Wipe your eyes and see what's taking shape beside the church."

She did and spotted something huge, bright, and colorful billowing like a giant sail. Then it swelled in size and began to slowly rise up among the trees.

A balloon. A giant balloon.

But, even more remarkable, standing on the steps of the church stood Atlas's family. Every last one of them. Even Venus and Persy had returned with their husbands and children.

They'd managed to return in just three days. Would the wonders of the modern world never cease?

And Atlas's mother held the biggest, most gorgeous bushel of flowers she'd ever seen.

Choked with emotion, Charlotte could do nothing but blow them kisses. Especially Grandmother Daltry. If it hadn't been for her meddlesome matchmaking . . .

A basket attached to the huge balloon lifted off the

ground. It floated as far as its line would allow, then began to revolve slowly. Words written in bold letters across the balloon's face came into view: DALTRY'S MEATPACKING PLANT.

Atlas leaned close to her ear. "That'll be coming off," he yelled above the din, "after I confess."

"What about those droughts and blizzards?" she shouted back. "Let's name our next daughter after your grand-mother first, then tell her the truth."

"Our next daughter?" Atlas pulled hard on the reins and brought the team to a halt several yards short of the church. Uncaring that he'd stopped in the middle of the street, he set the brake and pulled her into his arms. His gaze consumed her in a fiery promise. "You are the joy of my life." His mouth fell upon hers, and he kissed her long and hard and with staggering passion.

Somewhere outside his embrace, Charlotte vaguely heard more rowdy cheering, but she couldn't bring herself to pull away. She melted against his chest, deepening the kiss.

A tiny hand clutched her arm. "Oh, Mama, look! A big balloon!" Opal had returned to the opening.

Reluctantly Charlotte tore herself away.

When she did, Atlas pulled their little darling through the opening and sat her on his lap. "Isn't it a beauty?"

Her eyes, sparkly bright, were glued to the magnificent balloon. "It's the most beautifulest thing I ever saw."

At that moment Atlas's family descended upon the wagon.

Allie reached them first, holding a white gown of lustrous satin, covered with pearls and lace.

C.J. followed with his daughter, Thalia, riding his shoulders.

Then came all the rest.

Minerva called out. "Welcome to the family, dear Charlotte, and you, too, my sweet Opal."

Odie then stepped to the front. "Yes, Charlotte, welcome. And son . . . ?" He placed a hand, big and powerful, on Atlas's knee. "I owe you an apology. All the other ranchers think having our own slaughterhouse is the way to go. So, as you've probably already read on the wedding present from your grandmother, we're all going into business with you."

Atlas looked from the balloon to his grandmother. "It's not her prize to me?"

Grandmother Daltry reared back her head and laughed. "Course not. You don't get that until your twenty-first birthday."

He winked at the dear old gal. "And maybe not even then."

His mother, looking as elegantly blond as ever, stepped between Mr. Daltry and Atlas's grandmother. "We're so pleased, Charlotte. You've done what we've always hoped for—you've brought us home a son who's no longer afraid to think with his heart."

"And see with it, too," Atlas returned. "I want to thank you, Mother, for all the years of beauty you've given us with your flowers." He blew his mother a kiss, then took the huge bundle of long-stemmed blooms and laid them in Charlotte's arms.

As she breathed in the heady aroma, Opal cried, "Look! The balloon has a *big* basket. Big enough to ride in!" She grabbed hold of Charlotte's neck and pulled her close, then wrapped her other arm around Atlas's. "Now we really can go up to the clouds. Just me and Mama and kitty . . . and our new daddy."

Atlas looked from Opal to Charlotte, his eyes mirroring more love than the whole state of Texas. He rose to his feet and drew them up with him. "Then what are we waiting for? Come along, my sweet gypsies. This Atlas has been holding up those dang clouds long enough. It's time we go play in them."

Dear Reader,

I truly hope you were entertained by *The Perfect Gentleman*. If you have any comments or questions, I would love to hear from you about this novel or any of my others.

Sincerely,

Elaine Crawford
66-365 West 5th Street
Desert Hot Springs, CA 92240

P.S. Your self-addressed stamped envelope would be greatly appreciated.

# Our Town

## ...where love is always right around the corner!

### All Books Available in July 1996

__Take Heart by Lisa Higdon
0-515-11898-2/$5.50

*In Wilder, Wyoming...a penniless socialite learns a lesson in frontier life—and love.*

__Harbor Lights by Linda Kreisel
0-515-11899-0/$5.50

*On Maryland's Silchester Island...the perfect summer holiday sparks a perfect summer fling.*

__Humble Pie by Deborah Lawrence
0-515-11900-8/$5.50

*In Moose Gulch, Montana...a waitress with a secret meets a stranger with a heart.*

*If you enjoyed this book,
take advantage
of this special offer.
Subscribe now and get a*

# FREE
## Historical
## Romance

*No Obligation (a $4.50 value)*

Each month the editors of True Value select the four *very best* novels from America's leading publishers of romantic fiction. Preview them in your home *Free* for 10 days. With the first four books you receive, we'll send you a FREE book as our introductory gift. No Obligation!

If for any reason you decide not to keep them, just return them and owe nothing. If you like them as much as we think you will, you'll pay just $4.00 each and save at *least* $.50 each off the cover price. (Your savings are *guaranteed* to be at least $2.00 each month.) There is NO postage and handling – or other hidden charges. There are no minimum number of books to buy and you may cancel at any time.

### Send in the Coupon Below

To get your FREE historical romance fill out the coupon below and mail it today. As soon as we receive it we'll send you your FREE Book along with your first month's selections.

---